THE HAWK OF
EGYPT

JOAN CONQUEST

1st WORLD
LIBRARY
Literary Society

The Hawk of Egypt

Joan Conquest

© 1st World Library, 2007
PO Box 2211
Fairfield, IA 52556
www.1stworldlibrary.com
First Edition

LCCN: 2007901813

Softcover ISBN: 978-1-4218-4284-4
Hardcover ISBN: 978-1-4218-4186-1
eBook ISBN: 978-1-4218-4382-7

Purchase *"The Hawk of Egypt"*
as a traditional bound book at:
www.1stWorldLibrary.com/purchase.asp?ISBN=978-1-4218-4284-4

1st World Library is a literary, educational organization
dedicated to:

- Creating a free internet library of downloadable ebooks

- Hosting writing competitions and offering book
publishing scholarships.

Interested in more 1st World Library books?
contact: literacy@1stworldlibrary.com
Check us out at: www.1stworldlibrary.com

1st World Library Literary Society

Giving Back to the World

"If you want to work on the core problem, it's early school literacy."

- James Barksdale, former CEO of Netscape

"No skill is more crucial to the future of a child, or to a democratic and prosperous society, than literacy."

- Los Angeles Times

Literacy... means far more than learning how to read and write... The aim is to transmit... knowledge and promote social participation."

- UNESCO

"Literacy is not a luxury, it is a right and a responsibility. If our world is to meet the challenges of the twenty-first century we must harness the energy and creativity of all our citizens."

- President Bill Clinton

"Parents should be encouraged to read to their children, and teachers should be equipped with all available techniques for teaching literacy, so the varying needs and capacities of individual kids can be taken into account."

- Hugh Mackay

"IN LOVE AND GRATITUDE
TO
THE DEAREST OF WOMEN
'MIVES'
MY MOTHER"

Author's Note: All names in this book are fictitious.

CHAPTER I

". . . allahu akbar—la ilaha—illa 'llah!"

Across the golden glory of the sky floated the insistent call of
the *muezzin* just as Damaris, followed closely by Wellington,
her bulldog, turned out of the narrow street into the Khan el-
Khalili. Shrill and sweet, from far and near it came, calling the
faithful to prayer, impelling merchants to leave their wares,
buyers their purchases, gossips their chatter, and to turn in the
direction of Mecca and offer their praise to Allah, who is God.

As the entire male population of the native quarter knelt, the
girl drew back beneath an awning of many colours which
shaded silken goods from the rays of the sun, whilst curious
eyes peeped down upon her from behind the shelter of the
masharabeyeh, the harem lattice of finely-carved wood. Yards of
silk of every hue lay tumbled inside and outside the *dukkan* or
shop in the silk-market; silken scarves, plain and embroidered,
hung from strings; silk shawls were spread upon Persian
carpets; a veritable riot of colour against the yellow-white
plaster of the shop walls, above which flamed the sky, a cloak

of blue, embroidered in rose and gold and amethyst.

The native women behind the shelter of the wood lattice or the *yashmak* or the all-enveloping *barku*, talked softly together as they watched the beautiful girl who serenely and quite unveiled walked amongst men with an animal of surpassing hideousness at her heels.

She stood with her head uncovered—it is permissible at sunset—and with her face lifted, as she listened to the call to prayer, so that a sun-ray silting in through the silks blazed down upon the positively red curls which rioted all over her head and were of a tone sharper than henna, yet many times removed from the shades of red known as carrots or ginger.

Her skin was *matte*, her mouth crimson, and curved, the teeth perfect, and her heavily-lashed eyes of so deep a purple as to appear black. She was slim and supple, unencumbered by anything more confining than a suspender-belt, a fortnight off her eighteenth birthday and entirely lovable in looks, ways and temperament in the eyes of all mankind, which includes women.

The prayer over, and the men again about the business of the hour, she enquired her way of the vendor of silks who, having quickly replaced his shoes, had as hastily returned to his shop, his heart rejoicing at the prospect of perhaps one or two hours' more bargaining—for where is to be found the Oriental who knows the value of time?

Loving animals, Damaris wanted to find that corner near the silk-market where can be purchased anything from a camel to a hunting cheetah, a greyhound to a falcon.

It is not wise for European women to saunter about the old Arabian quarter unaccompanied, especially if they have been blessed by the gods in the ways of looks. Damaris Hethencourt most certainly ought not to have been there, but you must perforce follow the path Fate has marked out for you, whether it leads through country lanes, or Piccadilly, or the Arab quarter of Cairo.

The vendor of silks salaamed deeply before her beauty and the graciousness of her manner, for she smiled when she talked and spoke the prettiest broken Arabic in the world.

So, putting the huge two-year-old bulldog, which one day was to claim the proud title of champion, on the leash, she wended her way through the narrow streets in which two camels may scarce squeeze past each other and where the *masharabeyeh* of the harems almost meet overhead.

Water-carriers, camels, sweetmeat-sellers; lowly women in black gown and *yashmak*; coffee-sellers; donkeys which continually bray and dogs which unceasingly bark; cracking of whips; shrill cries of "*Dahrik ya sitt* or *musyu*," ("Thy back, lady, or sir"); shouts of *U'a u'a*; clashing of bronze ware; snarls of anger; laughter; song; dust and colour, all the ingredients which go to the entrancement of the bazaar.

And the odours?

Scent and perfume, aroma and odour; cedars of Lebanon and *harem* musk; tang of the sandy sea, fume of the street; the trail of smoke and onions; the milk of goats; the reek of humanity; the breath of kine. Make a bundle of that, and tie it with the silken lashes of women's eyes; secure it with the steel of a needle-pointed knife—and leave it at that.

There is *no* describing the smell of the East.

The sale of really good animals—the other kind you can buy by lifting a finger in the streets—takes place twice a month in a small square near the Suk-en Nahlesin; but as the way to it leads through many dirty and twisting lanes, few Europeans ever get so far.

The stock is tethered to iron rings in the ground, the vendors squat near by, but at a safe distance from teeth, claws or hoofs; the purchasers stand still farther off; there sometimes occurs a free fight, when the length of the chain that tethers the jaguar next the hunting cheetah is too long by a foot or so; and the noise is always deafening.

Abdul, falconer of Shammar—which district is to be found on the holy road to Mecca—being of that locality specialises in the *shahin*, which is a species of hawk; visits the market by appointment only, and, being independent and a specialist, does not always keep that appointment.

Damaris turned suddenly into the market and hurriedly looked round for shelter, which she found in an arched doorway leading to the usual court of the native house.

Zulannah the courtesan peered down upon her from between the silken curtains of her balcony, and clapped her hands twice so that her woman-slaves ran quickly to watch and whisper about this white woman who stood unattended in the open market. They giggled in the insufferable Eastern way, and pointed across the Square, where the whole of the male population surged about two men. But Zulannah, the recognised beauty of the North of Egypt, shrugged her dimpled shoulders as she stuffed over-large portions of sweetmeats between her dazzling teeth and stretched herself upon a divan to watch the scene over the way.

Abdul, falconer of Shammar, bearded and middle-aged, stood with a *shahin* of Jaraza upon his fist and a hooded eyess—which means a young hawk or nestling taken from the nest—of the same species upon a padded and spiked perch beside him, whilst hooded or with seeled eyes, upon perch or bough, were other yellow or dark-eyed birds of prey; short-winged hawks, a bearded vulture, a hobby, a passage Saker.

But it was not upon Abdul or his stock that the girl's eyes rested, nor, peradventure, the eyes behind the silken curtains.

The central figure of the glowing picture was that of Hugh Carden Ali, the eldest and best-beloved son of Hahmed the Sheikh el-Umbar and Jill, his beautiful, English and one and only wife; the son conceived in a surpassing love and born upon the desert sands.

"An Englishman," said Damaris softly as she withdrew yet further into the sheltering doorway and unleashed the dog; and still further back, when the man suddenly turned and looked across the Square as though in search of someone. "No! a native," she added, as she noticed the crimson *tarbusch*. "And yet . . ."

She was by no means the first to wonder as to the nationality of the man.

In riding-kit, with boots from Peter Yapp, he looked, except for the headcovering, exactly like an Englishman.

Certainly the shape of the face was slightly more oval than is common to the sons of a northern race, but nothing really out of the ordinary, just as the eyes were an ordinary kind of brown, with a disconcerting way of looking suddenly into your face, sweeping it in an all-comprehensive lightning glance and looking indifferently away.

The nose was good and quite straight; the hair thick, brown and controllable; the mouth covering the perfect teeth was deceptive, or maybe it was the strength of the jaw which belied the gentleness, just as the slimness of the six-foot of body, trained to a hair from babyhood, gave no clue to the steel muscles underlying a skin as white as and a good deal whiter than that of some Europeans.

He moved with the quickness and quietness of those accustomed to the far horizon as a background; he was slow in speech; and dead-slow in anger until aroused by opposition.

For the physically weak-born, he had the gentle sympathy of

the very strong; for the physically undeveloped and the morally weak he had no use whatever—*none*. In the West, his reserve with men had been labelled taciturnity or swollen-headeduess, which did not fit the case at all; whilst, in spite of his perfect manner towards them, his indifference to woman *en masse* or in the individual was supreme and sincere.

He was the direct descendant of the founder of Nineveh where horses were concerned, and his stables in the Oasis of Khargegh would have been one of the sights of Egypt, had he permitted sightseers.

Educated at Harrow, where he had excelled in sport and captained the Eleven at Lord's for two succeeding years; respected by the upper Forms and worshipped by the lower, he had developed the English side of his dual nationality until masters and schoolfellows had come to look upon him as one of themselves.

From Harrow he had gone to Brazenose; then had quite suddenly thrown up the 'Varsity and returned to Egypt.

Love?

Not at all, for was not his indifference to woman supreme and sincere?

Just the inevitable ending of a very commonplace, sordid little story which had taught the youth one of life's bitterest lessons.

One of a multitude of guests at Hurdley Castle, he had met a woman, beautiful but predatory, whose looks were taking on an autumnal tint, and whose banking account had shrivelled under the frost of extravagance.

His utter indifference to her wiles and her beauty had culminated in a degrading scene of anger on her part, when, forgetting her breeding, her birth and her nationality, she had first of all twitted him and then openly laughed at his mixed parentage.

He had stood without uttering a word, white to the lips during her tirade.

"Do you think that any white woman would marry you—a *half-caste*?" had cried the woman, whose bills were coming in in shoals.

"Yes, many," he had quietly answered as he bent to pick up her torn, handkerchief. "Am I not a rich man?"

He had returned to Egypt upon a visit to the Flat Oasis where dwelt his parents, who, though noting the indescribable hurt in the eyes of their firstborn, yet asked no question, for in Egypt a youth is his own master and ofttimes married at the age of fourteen; how much more, therefore, is he a man at over twenty years?

He had visited his own house in the Oasis of Khargegh, with the purpose of putting his stables in order and his falconers through a stiff catechism, and had finally set out to see something of the world.

Not in a desire to cover his hurt, for he was as stoical as any high-bred Arab; and, Mohammedan from belief as well as early training, did not kick against what he looked upon as the commands of Allah.

As for women—well! The sweet, docile woman of his father's race interested him not at all, so that he refused to listen to any hint anent the desirability of his taking a wife and establishing the succession of the House 'an Mahabbha, which is the eldest branch of the House el-Umbar; and racial distinction barred him from the virile, lovely women of his mother's race.

He had his horses, his hawks, his hunting cheetahs, his dogs; one great treasure which he prized and one little conceit.

The treasure had been found in the ruins of the Temple Deir-el-Bahari. An ornament of gold set with precious stones. Its shape was that of the Hawk, which had stood as the symbol of the North in the glorious days of Ancient Egypt. The wings were of emeralds tipped with rubies; gold were the claws and gold the Symbol of Life they held; the body and tail were a mass of precious stones; and the eye of some jet-black stone, unknown to the present century.

As an ornament it was of great value; as an antiquity found in the Shrine of Anubis, the God of Death, its value could not even be guessed at; and how it had come into the possession of Hugh Garden Ali will never be known, though of a truth, unlimited wealth works wonders.

And upon his horses' saddle-cloths, his falcons' hoods, his hounds' coats, and the fine linen and satins of his Eastern raiment he had the emblem worked in thread or silk or jewels, or painted in soft colours.

It was just a pretty conceit, but in conjunction with one-half of his lineage and his love for his birds, it had earned him the title of "The Hawk of Egypt."

And such was the man as he stood in the market-place, having followed the path which Fate had marked out for him through the twisting lanes of the bazaar.

CHAPTER II

"Dog, ounce, bear and bull, Wolf, lion, horse."

DU BARTAS

Damaris should not have been strolling by herself in the native quarter.

If you are drab or flat of chest or soul or face, you can saunter your fill in any bazaar without adventure befalling you; if, however, nature should have endowed you with the colouring of a desert sunset, if, in short, you *can* add a splash of colour to anything so colourful as a native bazaar, then 'twere wise to do your sauntering under the wing of a vigilant chaperon, so that the curiosity and interest resultant on your splash may reach you obliquely and "as through a glass, darkly."

But there was no one to worry the girl at this hour before sunset, so that little by little and quite unconsciously she moved forward until she stood outside the doorway.

She stood, outlined against a background of blazing colours, which served in no way to dim her beauty. Through the yellow-white arch of the doorway showed a stretch of turquoise-blue sky across which, upon a string, swung golden onions and scarlet peppercorns, whilst underneath ruminated a fine, superbly indifferent dromedary.

For a moment Hugh Carden Ali, jogged by Fate, looked straight across at the beautiful picture, staying his talk with Abdul, who, with the courtesy of the East, did not turn his head as he stroked the breast and head of the *shahin* on his fist.

But Damaris, with envy rampant in her heart, had no eyes for mere man; she wanted to walk across and get near the coal-black stallion from Unayza, a district famous for its breed of large, heavy-built horses. He stood impatiently, with an occasional plunk of a hoof on the sandy stones, or nuzzled his master's sleeve, or pulled at it with his teeth, whilst two shaggy dogs of Billi lay stretched out awaiting the signal to be up and going, perhaps, in a sprint across the desert after the *hosseny* or red rascal of a fox which had been trapped and caged for the sole purpose of hunting.

Ride out with the caged *hosseny* on a thoroughbred camel or thoroughbred horse, take with you a couple of greyhounds and a dog or so from Billi, get right off the tourist track and let the red rascal out, and see if you don't have some fun before breakfast.

Only get off the tourist track, else you will have all the bazaar camels and ponies loping along behind you.

The only wild beast this afternoon for sale was a jaguar, black as ink, smooth as satin, short, heavy, with half-closed green eyes fixed steadfastly upon a plump white pigeon foolishly strutting just out of reach of the steel-pointed claws.

"Take her upon thy fist, O Master," said Abdul of Shammar, as he lengthened the jesses, the short, narrow straps of leather or woven silk or cotton with which to hold the hawk. "See, she is well reclaimed, being tame and gentle and altogether amiable. When thrown, she is as a bullet from a rifle, binding her quarry in high air even as a man holds his woman to his heart upon the roof-top under the stars. She is full summed"— and he ran his slender fingers through the new feathers, full and soft after moulting; "she is keen as the winter wind—behold the worn and blunted nails; she will not give up, my master, yet will she come to the lure as quickly, as joyfully as a maid to her lover."

Hugh Carden Ali, the greatest authority after Abdul on the *shahin*, took the bird upon his fist, looked at the sunken, piercing eyes which were partially seeled; ran his hand over the narrow body, short tail and black back, and a finger over the large beak and deep mouth; held up the ugly face to the light, examined the flight-feathers and, moving his hand quickly up and down, caused the bird to flutter its wings—and so give him a chance of measuring the distance of the wings from the body. Finding her altogether lovely, he nodded and handed her back to the delighted falconer of Shammar, just as with a decisive pat the jaguar landed, its huge paw upon the strutting pigeon, which had forgotten to keep its distance.

For a moment the attention of the spectators, who were mostly squatting on their heels, was diverted from the master and the falconer. They laughed, they moved, whilst some in the back row stood up to see the fun, leaving for one second an open space through which Damaris could see the fluttering white bird.

"Ah!" she cried, heartbroken at the sight; then, "Fetch!" she commanded the dog, pointing across the square.

Now, the dog, who had dispensed with his spiked collar on account of the heat, had no more idea than the man in the moon what he had to fetch for his beloved mistress; but, restless from prolonged inactivity and the smell of strange beasts, he hurled himself in the direction pointed; and his speed, once he got going, was as surprising as that of the elephant or rhinoceros and other clumsy-looking animals, and in very truth, his appearance was just as terrifying.

He crashed head-foremost into the back row of spectators, which, as one man, yelled and fled; tore along the path made clear for him, and sensing an enemy in the growling jaguar, was at its throat like a thrown spear; missing it by an inch as the black beast flung itself back to the full length of the steel chain which fastened it to an iron ring in the ground.

Damaris in her turn rushed, across the square, passing the astounded spectators, who salaamed as she ran. And as she ran she shouted:

"Let the animal loose," she cried. "Give it a chance; let it loose."

But Hugh Carden Ali, not in the least understanding the sudden onslaught, but with every sporting instinct uppermost, had already leant down in the seething, growling mass of fur and hate, and loosened the chain; whilst, with screams of fear and delight, the crowd raced for the adjacent houses, from the upper windows of which they could hang in safety to watch the fight.

Disgusting?

Quite so! But have you ever heard of bull-fighting or pigeon-shooting in civilised, humane Europe?

There followed a frightful scene, during which Abdul, having picked up the pigeon, hastily flung his birds far behind the growling, spitting, raging couple, whilst the stallion, rearing in terror, nearly jerked his master, who had the bridle slipped over his arm, off his feet.

The two dogs of Billi and the two greyhounds leapt and barked and snapped at the belligerents until Wellington, taking an off-chance, suddenly turned and bit one of them clean through the shoulder; whereupon it yelped and howled and fled, whilst shouts of "*Ma sha-Allah*" and much clapping came from the upper windows.

Damaris ran straight towards the man, who, slipping the bridle, put both arms round her to draw her to safety; then, suddenly realising the beauty, the youth and the pure whiteness of her, as suddenly let her go.

"Shall I separate them?" he asked simply.

"No! Not even if you could. Once my dog's blood is up, nothing but death will satisfy him."

She stood quite still, as white as a sheet, with both hands on his arm, whilst the great dog hurled himself at the spitting brute, only to meet the teeth and claws which drew blood at every attempt, until the ground was crimson where they fought.

And then, with tears streaming down her cheeks, Damaris looked up into the man's face; then buried her face on his shoulder.

And the seed of love which is in the heart of every human burst through, the clogging mould of custom and convention and, taking root, put forth shoots and sprang in one moment into the great tree of love of which the fruits, being those of purity, honour and sacrifice, are golden.

Yet he did not touch her, having learned his lesson; instead, he raised his right hand above his head.

"Allah!" he said, in praise of that which had come unto him, "Allah, there is no God but Thee," just as, with a sudden swish, a flock of startled pigeons flashing like jewels in the setting sun new low down across his head, bringing an end to the battle.

For one half-second the jaguar's green eyes shifted, and the dog was at its throat. There was a mighty, convulsive effort of the hind-legs which ripped the bulldog's sides, a click, a shiver, and the black brute fell dead, as the dog, a mass of blood, foam and pride, hurled himself onto the skirt of his beloved mistress, whilst the enraptured spectators, yelling with excitement, rushed out into the square with shouts of "*Ma sha-Allah*," which means, "Well done, well done!"

"Keep quite still," said Hugh Carden Ali, gently, as Damaris made an effort to turn; then, speaking quickly to the beaming, salaaming spectators, who had had the time of their lives gambling on the chances of either animal, ordered them to remove the dead beast and to strew the place with sand. And "*Irja Sooltan*," he called to the stallion, which, terrified at the sounds and sight and smell of battle, had bolted up a side street, where he stood fretting and fidgeting himself into a fine sweat, until he heard the clear call which could always bring him back to the man he loved. He stood for one second, then flung up his heels to the devastation of a stall of earthenware, and raced back to the square at a most unseemly pace, causing the spectators once more to fly in all directions with cries of "U'a u'a," which means, "Look out, look out!"

He pushed his soft nose with determination against the woman who stood so close to his master, so that she looked up, and then smiled and stretched out her arms.

"You beauty!" she cried. "Oh, you *beauty*!"

"You ride?"

Damaris, thinking of the hack, the only thing with the shape of a horse she had been able to get so far, and upon the back of which she loathed to be seen, made a grimace.

"I go out on horseback," she said. "I have not ridden since I left home."

The man's reply, whatever it might have been, was interrupted by Abdul, who, all smiles, stood before them, with the white pigeon in the left hand and the *shahin* upon his right fist.

The native had no intention of causing the white woman pain; in fact, wishing to find favour in the eyes of the nobles, he only wanted to give them a chance of witnessing a little of, to him, the finest sport in the world.

"Look, lady!" he cried.

He tossed the pigeon high into the air, allowed her a little distance, then threw the hawk.

"No! Oh, no! don't!" cried Damaris, as the hawk rose, "stooped" and missed the pigeon by a hair's-breadth as it "put in", which means that it flew straight into a small niche of a minaret for cover.

"Ah!" cried Damaris, and "*Bi-sma-llah*!" ejaculated Abdul, as he threw the lure of a dead plover and called his hawk with the luring Eastern call. "Coo-coo," he called; "coo-coo," to which the hawk responded as a well-trained *shahin* should.

Hugh Carden Ali stood with his hand on the stallion's mane, looking up at the sky, in which shone a great star.

"The hawk of Egypt failed," he said to himself. "Flown at a white bird, it failed. The House of Allah, who is God, gave sanctuary to the little white bird. Praise be to Allah who is God."

He looked down at the girl, who was kneeling, consoling the dog, who, reft 'tween pride and pain, showed a lamentable countenance. Suddenly she looked up and rose, and stood silently.

"Come," he said simply, while he longed to pick her up and ride with her to his home in the Oasis. "I will take you to your hotel."

"My car is waiting for me in the Sikket el-Gedideh," she replied.

* * * * *

Later, a vision of loveliness, she walked down the dining-room behind the Duchess of Longacres, whilst continuous lamentations were wafted through the spring-doors from the spot where sat a dog with sticking-plaster across his nose and middle girt with a cummerbund of pink boracic lint.

Beside the girl's place lay a huge bunch of crimson roses tied with golden tassels; there was no card, name nor message.

She asked no question, neither did her godmother.

To what purpose should they? The one *knew*; the other firmly believed in allowing the young to work out the salvation of their own souls; which did not, however, mean that she would not keep a sharp look-out in the future over the troubled sea of Life.

"I knew something would happen," thought the wise old lady, as she passed a biscuit up to the parrot on her shoulder.

"*Kathir Khairak*," it said delightedly.

It merely means "thank you," but had taken weeks of teaching and repeating to master.

CHAPTER III

"Lor! but women's rum cattle to deal with, the
first man found that to his cost;
And I reckon it's just through a woman, that the
last man on earth'll be lost."

G. R. SIMS

Damaris was the only daughter of Squire Hethencourt. Her
mother was an Italian from the Udino, where the hair of the
women is genuine Titian-red and the eyes are blue; which
perhaps accounted for her colouring and some part of her
temperament.

Her type of beauty was certainly remarkable—given, it must
be confessed, to a certain amount of fluctuation—and she
danced divinely, which gift must not be counted as a parlour-
trick; she was slow in her movements and quiet in her manner
until she talked of horses or anybody she loved; then her great
eyes would flash and her laugh ring out, also she would
gesticulate as her mother had been wont to do, until the
climate, maybe, of a northern country had served to repress the
spontaneity of her Latin mannerisms.

She was simple and unsophisticated and would have made a
splendid little chum, if only one out of every three men who
met her had not been consumed with a desire to annex her for
life by means of a gold ring.

"Dads," she exclaimed, two months before the beginning of this story, having enticed him to her bedroom one night and offered him cream chocolates as he eat at the foot of her bed, facing her. "Dads, what am I to do? Guy Danvers says he is coming to see you to-morrow, and I—I am sure it will only turn out to be—well—you, know."

"But, Golliwog dear, I'm the one to be pitied. This makes the—how many is it?"

"I don't know, Dads, and it isn't the number; it's the awful *habit* they've got into—and I don't understand anything and I don't encourage them, do I? Do lend me a hankie—this chocolate has burst—and what am I to do?"

"Turn a deaf ear, or a cold shoulder, or put a brave face on, until—" said Dads, retrieving his handkerchief.

"Until what?"

"Until the right man comes along, darling, as he surely will."

The girl's lids suddenly dropped until the lashes lay like a fringe upon the white cheek over which very slowly but very surely crept the faintest of rose-colours.

"Hum!" said Dads to himself, as he made great use of the hankie.

"Do smoke, dearest!"

"No, thank you, pet; I couldn't here."

The man who worshipped his wife and adored his little daughter looked round the white and somewhat austere room, and ran his eye over the bookstand at his elbow.

Books on horses, a treatise on bulldogs, the New Testament, essays in French and in German, the History of Egypt in

Arabic, Budge's "Book of the Dead," and "King Solomon's Mines."

"But what am I do *meanwhile*, Dads?" and the girl threw out her hands imploringly.

"Be cold, deaf or brave, Golliwog, as I have suggested."

"But I've been all that, and it's quite useless. Do you think it would help if I let my hair grow and did it up in a tight knob?"

"I think it would help a lot if you shaved your head entirely, kiddie." And the man leant forward and ran his hand through the red curls.

Once upon a time Damaris had read the advertisement of a certain powder guaranteed to darken hair of any colour, and life having been one long torment owing to her violent colouring, she had, greatly daring, acquired a packet; had followed the directions by mixing the powder with water and covering her head with the muddy result, and, "to make assurance doubly sure," had sat with her clay pate for an hour instead of ten minutes near a fire; had cracked the clay, washed her head, and found her hair grass-green.

She had chopped the verdant masses off without a thought, and had ever after refused to allow it to grow to hairpin length, and to her father only had granted the privilege of calling her by the pet name of Golliwog.

"Would you like to travel a bit, pet?" And the man smiled, though his heart was heavy at the thought of the blank which his Golliwog's departure would leave in the home and the daily round.

"Travel! Travel! Oh! darling—to Egypt?

"Why Egypt? Why not France or—or Italy?"

"Because I've *got* to go to Egypt sometime or another, Dads. I've got to see the desert and the mosques and the whites and blues and oranges and camels. It's *in* me *here*," and she thumped her nightgown above her heart. "I shall never be happy until I have seen them all. Oh! Dads, I wonder if you can understand; it—it sounds so—so silly—"

"Tell me," and the man moved over to the head of the bed and took his daughter gently in his arms.

"I'm so out of the picture, somehow, here, dearest," said the child, striving as best she could to describe what was really only the passing of the border-line between girl and womanhood. "This terrible colouring of mine, for one thing. Why, amongst other girls, I am like a Raemaeker stuffed into a Heath Robinson folio, like a palette daubed with oils hung amongst a lot of water-colours. I want to find my own nail and hang for one hour by myself, if it's on a barn-door or the wall of a mosque—as long as I am by myself."

"Good Lord!" said the man inwardly, as he patted his daughter's arm; then, aloud. "As it happens, Golliwog darling, I had a letter from *Marraine* yesterday, asking me to let you go out to her in Cairo for the winter and see as much as possible of the ordinary sights. We'll talk it over with Mother to-morrow."

"Oh, Dads—how wonderful! And can't you and Mother come? And oh! *can* I take Wellington?"

"I think so, dear, if he hasn't hydrophobia," and the man bent to pat the head of the great dog which had crept from under the bed at the sound of his name.

And later Dads stood at his window, smoking two last pipes, whilst a glimpse into the future was allowed him.

"Can it be—can it possibly be," he said, puffing clouds of smoke into the creeper, to the annoyance of many insects, "Big

Ben Kelham?—and the estates run alongside. Wonder if Teresa has noticed anything. And—by Jove!—of course!—he's at Heliopolis, getting over his hunting accident. I wonder—"

And Damaris sat at her window, with her arms round the dog, who longed inordinately for his mat.

"The desert," she whispered. "The pyramids—the bazaar— life—adventure. How *wonderful*!" There came a long, long pause, and then she added, as she turned towards a coloured picture of the Sphinx upon the wall, "And who cares if the nail is a tin-tack or a screw?"

As it happened, it was destined to be the jewel-hilted, double-edged, unsheathed dagger of love.

And Fate, having mislaid her glasses, worked her shuttle at hazard in and out of that picture of intricate pattern called Life, and having tangled and knotted together the crimson thread of passion, the golden thread of youth and the honest brown of a deep, undemonstrative love, she left the disentanglement of the muddle in the hands of Olivia, Duchess of Longacres.

Her Grace was over eighty.

Of a line of yeomen ancestors ranging back down the centuries to the William Carew who had fought for Harold, she had been, about sixty-five years ago, the belle of Devon. Against the warnings of her heart and to the delight of her friends and family, she had married the Duke of Longacres, whose roving eye had been arrested by her beauty at a meet of the Devon and Somerset, and his equally roving heart temporarily captured by the indifference of her demeanour towards his autocratic self.

She had lost him, to all intents and purposes, two years after the marriage, but blinding her eyes and stuffing her ears, had held high her beautiful head and high her honour, filling her empty heart with the love of her son and the esteem of her legion of real friends; showing the bravest of beautiful faces to the world, until a happy widowhood had set her free.

Some years of absolute happiness of the simplest kind had followed; the marriage of her son and birth of her grandson, who had cost his mother her life. Then the following year had come the Boer War, and the heroic tragedy of Spion Kop, which left her childless; after that, many years of utter devotion, to her grandson, who adored her; then the Great War and the Battle of the Falkland Islands, which left her absolutely bereft, with the care of the boy's greatest treasure, even the grey parrot, Quarter-Deck, Dekko for short.

Methuselah of birds, it was possessed of an uncanny gift of human speech and understanding, and had been promoted through generation to generation, from sailing-vessel *via* Merchant Service to British Navy.

As time and tragedy worked hard together to silver her hair and line her face, so did a veritable imp of mischief, bred of her desolation, seem to possess the old darling. She cared not a brass farthing for the opinion of her neighbours, so that after the death of the great Queen, who had been her staunchest friend, she had instructed Maria Hobson, her maid and also staunchest friend, to revive the faded roses of her cheeks with the aid of cosmetics. Things had gone from bad to worse in that respect, until her pretty snow-white hair had been covered by a flagrant golden perruque and the dear old face with a mask of pink and white enamel. Her eyes were blue, and keen as a hawk's, undimmed by the tears shed in secret during her tumultuous and tragic life; her teeth, each one in a perfect and pearly state of preservation, were her own, for which asset she was never given the benefit of the doubt; her tongue was vitriolic; her heart of pure gold, and she owned a right hand which said nothing to the left of the spaces between its fingers through which, daily ran deeds of kindness and streams of love towards the unfortunate ones of the earth.

Joan Conquest

Her dress was invariably of grey taffeta or brocade, bunched at the back and trailing on the ground; there were ruffles, of priceless lace at the elbow-sleeves and V-shaped neck; a plain straw poke-bonnet served for all outdoor functions, and an ebony stick, called "the wand" by the denizens of the slums, who adored her, completed her picturesque toilette.

The majority feared this *grande dame*, a minority, if they had had the chance, would have fawned upon her in public and laughed at or caricatured her in private; those who really knew her, and they lived principally east of London town, would willingly have laid themselves down and allowed her ridiculously small feet, invariably shod in crimson, buckled, outrageously high-heeled shoes, to trample upon their prostrate bodies, if it would have given her pleasure so to do.

She adored young things, and had an enormous family of godsons and goddaughters, out of which crowd Ben Kelham and Damaris Hethencourt were supreme favourites, and about whom she had been weaving plots when she had written her letter of invitation to the Squire.

She smoked Three Castles, which she kept in a jewelled Louis XV snuff-box, and had a perfect tartar of a maid, who simply worshipped her.

Of a truth, a long description of a very old and very wise old woman, of whom the great Queen had once remarked to her Consort:

"I wish I were not a queen, so that *I* might curtsey to Olivia."

And in this wise old woman's jewel-covered hands Fate placed the twisted threads of passion, youth and love, and a wiser selection she could not have made.

A bronchitic cough had taken her to Cairo just as a sooted-up lung, left behind by the pneumonia which had followed the hunting accident had taken Ben Kelham to Heliopolis, and for recuperation of body or mind there is nothing to equal an Egyptian winter, even in a tourist-ridden centre.

Ben Kelham, Big Ben for short, on account of his six-feet-two, was heir to Sir Andrew Kelham, Bart., whose estate joined the lands of Squire Hethencourt, whom he looked upon as his greatest friend, and vice versa. Educated at Harrow, Ben Kelham and Hugh Carden Ali had been known on the Hill as David and Jonathan; so that the crimson, golden and brown threads were more than uncommonly twisted.

Ben was heavy in build and slow in every way, but he was still more sure than slow, and had never been known to give up when once he had set his mind to the accomplishment of a task, and although he had stood in absolute awe of beautiful Damaris since the day she had lengthened her skirts, yet had he determined to make her his wife, even if it meant following in Jacob's footsteps to the tune of waiting many years.

He had confided his determination to his godmother, who had immediately taken the case in hand, and proceeded to throw bucketsful of cold water upon his suggestion of being on the quay or doorstep to welcome the girl to Egypt.

"My dear man," replied the tactful old lady as she rasped a match on the sole of a crimson shoe and lit a fragrant Three Castles, "do remember that everything will be new to the child; she will be one vast ejaculation for at least a month. Let her get over that, let her realise that you are close at hand, but not the least bit anxious to be under her feet, and you'll see. Remember, she is very young, just like a bit of dough which must be stuffed with the currants and raisins of knowledge and then well-baked in the oven of experience before it can be handed across Life's counter to anyone. Further, take care not to blunder into any little trap she may set you out of pique."

"But, dearest, I always *do* blunder when I'm out of the saddle."

"Well, even if you do, for goodness' sake keep your mouth

shut. Be the strong, silent man; women love 'em. We revel in being clubbed and pulled into the cave by the hair; we may squeal a bit for the sake of appearances, but we cook the breakfast nest morning without a murmur! But just ask us to honour the cave by placing our foot over the threshold, and as sure as anything, you'll find yourself making the early cup of tea."

CHAPTER IV

"Wide open and unguarded stand our gates,
Named by the four winds, North, South, East and West;
Portals that lead to an enchanted land. . ."

T. B. ALDRICH

Damaris duly arrived in Egypt, accompanied by Wellington—who had shown no sign of incipient hydrophobia—and Jane Coop, her maid.

It were best to describe them both now, and so get it all over.

Whilst waiting one exeat upon Waterloo station, the girl had annexed unto herself a holy terror in the shape of a brindle bull-pup.

The hilarious quadruped had twined its leash about one leg of its master—who was an alien from Wapping—and the spout of a zinc watering-can which a porter had left upon the platform; for which joke it had received a vile cuff on its wrinkled physiognomy from the alien master.

Like some avenging goddess, Damaris, the ladylike, almost finished product of Onslow House, sprang straight at the man, smote him with the flat of the hand upon the face, and pounced upon the yelping pup.

"Take your leg out of the dog's chain, you idiot!" she cried, her eyes blazing, her perfect teeth flashing in a positive snarl. "Be quick; don't be so clumsy. How dare you hit a dog. He *hit* him," she announced to the interested, sympathetic crowd. "Hit him on his lovely face.

"You gif that dog back to me, missie,—he's mine."

"He's mine. I've got him, and my mother is one of the heads of the Society that protects children."

"That's got nothing to do wif dogs."

"This is a puppy, so it's a child," had come the decisive reply. "And I'll buy him, though I needn't really, if I refer it to the Society."

"I'll take ten poun' for 'im."

The child fished for her purse, which, contained half-a-crown and her ticket, and flung it with a supreme gesture of contempt at the man's feet; then, squeezing up the dog in her arms, tore a simple gold bracelet off her left arm and flung it after the purse.

"Worv two poun' at the mos'."

Then, from out of a first-class carriage of the train waiting to start for Southampton slowly descended Olivia, Duchess of Longacres.

The girl and the alien had their backs turned to her, but the crowd had seen; had looked; started to laugh, and then had become silent, so great was the dignity of the old lady.

Clad in a voluminous grey taffeta gown, from under which peeped little crimson shoes; covered with a huge loose ermine wrap, with the black poke-bonnet on top of the outrageous golden perruque and the grey parrot bobbing up and down excitedly upon her shoulder, she stood silently taking in the scene.

There was the light of battle in the famous hawk's-eyes as she listened to the girl defending the pup, and her splendid teeth shone in a grin of enjoyment as she suddenly rattled her ebony stick upon the alien's ankle-bones, those most tender bits of anatomical scaffolding.

There was a yell of pain as the alien backed hastily into the arms of a lusty youth who had continuously besought Damaris, to allow him "ter put it acrorst ther blighter's h'ugly mug," and a cry of delight as Damaris ran to the old lady's side and, squeezing the pup in one arm, made the sweetest little reverence in the pretty continental way before she excitedly wrung her god-mother's hand.

"*Marraine*, he hit the puppy, and I've bought him for ten pounds; at least, Dad will send a cheque tonight. I've given him half-a-crown and my bracelet on account."

"Call Hobson," said her grace to the bird, who, obeying, had shrilly piped, "Tumble up, men, tumble up," until Hobson the maid suddenly surged, from the second-class and ploughed her way through the delighted crowd.

"Give the purse and bracelet to my maid, you—"

"Swab," supplemented the parrot.

"—at once," finished her grace, just as, with a cry of "Here's Dad!" Damaris ran to meet her father, who, having got hung up in the traffic, had failed to meet the train. He listened patiently, with dancing eyes, to the story, smiled across at the duchess, gave the man a pound-note and a jolly good talking to, and acquired a bull pup with the Rodney Stone strain, which they promptly christened Wellington, as it had won at Waterloo.

Wellington forthwith developed an inordinate jealousy of Jane Coop.

Jane Coop was maid, adviser and buffer to the girl whom she loved more than anyone on earth.

Born on the Squire's lands, she had developed a positive genius for mothering delicate lambs and calves and sickly chicks, so that when a crisis had arrived almost immediately after the birth of Damaris, the Squire had bundled the highly-certificated nurse into a motor and sent her packing back to London, and called upon Jane Coop to rise to the occasion.

She had risen.

Bonny and plump, she had taken the weakly little bit of humanity, also the situation, into her strong, capable hands; treated the mother and babe just as she would have treated a couple of delicate lambs, and pulled them both through.

From that day forth she had dominated the house, tyrannised over the Squire and his lady, defied each and every governess who had shown signs of undue strictness, and found her reward for her devotion in the love of the child who teased her to death and—in the long run—obeyed her.

She had shown herself a positive sheep-dog on board the boat. She had rounded up her white lamb and yapped upon the heels of those who dared approach with too great familiarity; had bristled and shown her teeth upon every possible occasion, until those who would fain have led the girl into new and verdant pastures had fled at the sheep-dog's approach, leaving them both to enjoy the novelty of everything, each after her own kind.

Damaris revelled in it all: the seagulls; the lighthouses; the ships that passed in the day and night; and the tail-end of a storm they hit up in the Bay, whilst Jane Coop invented new verses to the Litany as she tried, in her cabin, to solve the problem of two into one, and Wellington, somewhere under the water-line, daily gave a fine imitation of hell-bound to a circle of admiring seamen.

To his last hour at sea Captain X will forever retain the memory of what it cost him in strength of will to maintain his dignity, when, standing straight and exceedingly beautiful, with one hand full of lists, the huge bulldog at her feet, with a black bow under his left ear, and an assembly of the greatest sufferers before her, Damaris, two days before arriving at Port Said, solemnly read out the items and the shop price of each article chewed, damaged or totally destroyed during the voyage by the dog.

"Shoes, boots, pants, edges of trousers; two pipes, one pouch, six packets of gaspers; one entire tray of crockery; one air-cushion dropped in fright by stewardess; one coil of rope, one life-buoy, one tin can dented, one man's ankles slightly bruised; one bare patch to ship's cat's back. . . ." And so on and so forth; whilst murmurs arose from the sufferers, who chorused that "they didn't want no compensation, only too pleased to part with their bits, as long . . ." etc., etc.

"I do not think the fault was all on one side, Miss Hethencourt," summed up the Captain, speaking in guttural consonant and flattened vowel from suppressed emotion. "The—er—the plaintiff must have approached the dog as he was chained and—"

"A bulldog," broke in Damaris, "is a magnet to the best in every human being. They simply could not help themselves; they were drawn within reach of his teeth; they—"

"I cannot quite—" interrupted the captain. "Yes?"

Chips, the carpenter, showed signs of bursting with information withheld.

"Beggin' your pardon for interruption, sir, but what; the lady says is true; we just couldn't keep away. I saw the Chink—beg pardon, sir, I mean Ling-a-Ling the laundryman, burning joss-sticks in front of 'im,"—pointing of stub finger towards shameless dog—"one night when the dawg was asleep. Jus'

Joan Conquest

worship, please, sir, on all parts. And Mrs. Pudge what didn't oughter 'ave been down in our quarters, dropped the air cushion, sir, 'cause she missed in stays—"

"I cannot," interrupted the captain—then choked at a mental vision of Mrs. Pudge, who scorned such frivolous inventions as whalebone to support the figure—then trumpeted behind his handkerchief, ending in that combined half-snort, half-giggle which is so disastrous to dignity and complexion, "I cannot allow the—the—er—form of the Company's stewardesses to be so discussed."

"Beggin' yer pardon, sir," fiercely rejoined Chips—who was getting a bit of his own back on Mrs. Pudge—"I'm using the nautical expression, sir; she failed to get about when that there dawg"—pointing of stub thumb at heedless dog—"growled 'cause she has water in the knee. I'm usin' a an—anatomical expression now, sir—her knee—this, sir"—slapping of knee with horny hand of toil—"The ship's knees, miss," addressing Damaris, whose straight brows had almost met in puzzlement, "is a chock on the forepart of the lowermast on which the 'eel—heel, miss, of the topmast rests. Yuss, sir. Her knee may 'ave water in it; but no one couldn't say the same of her *grog*."

To prevent death from combustion, the speechless captain here intimated by signs that the culprit should stand up. And the brindle of Rodney Stone strain stood, whilst the men's eyes glistened as they fidgeted upon their feet from very joy in the spectacle.

His skull was massive and perfectly-shaped, the under-jaw square and strong, thrust up and beyond the upper; the teeth were perfect, even, large and also strong; the nose was black and large, well back between the eyes, which were set low down and wide apart, but well in front and round, with a deep "stop" between them; the honestest outward sign of his gallant loving heart. The ears were rose; not in colour, of course, but of rose-leaf shape, set high and small and fine; the face was closely-wrinkled, the "chop" well down, and the loose skin in abundant folds about his throat and neck.

The chest was wide and deep and prominent; the shoulders were tremendously muscular; the body was short, with a Roach back, fine in the rear; the forelegs, short and strong, with the developed calves which give them the appearance of being bowed, whereas the bones are really straight; the feet turned out a bit, with toes split up and arched; the tail set low and straight down and anything but a glad tail. His heart was of the finest, honest, loving, courageous, capable of hurling its owner to instant battle or death, in defence of the one loved, at other times rendering him, in its gentleness, an almost ludicrous spectacle of adoration. Of such was Wellington, and if the description is somewhat detailed and technical it is because he happens a good deal into the book.

The duchess had been put into the train for Port Said by Ben Kelham, who, inwardly kicking at her sage advice, looked as despondent as a camel who considers its strength unequal to its burden.

"Cheer up, lad," she cried as the train moved off. "Cheer up; something is sure to happen before long."

Which was a perfectly safe prophecy to make where Damaris was concerned.

Arrived at Port Said, she put off in a boat with her maid and her parrot, and found her godchild, who did not expect her, on deck, entranced with all she saw.

Yes! of course Port Said is a sink of iniquity and a place of odours and a fold for native wolves in sheep's clothing; also a centre for antiquities made in Birmingham, or by the vendor himself in the hot weather; and a market for things which should not be sold, much less bought.

In fact, in one short sentence, it is a deal of cosmopolitan wrong-doing.

All the same, you need not buy and you need not listen nor look, and if it is the first bit of the Orient you have meet with for the first time in your life, well! it is the East, and jolly exciting and interesting, too.

Damaris rushed at the old lady, and having curtsied to her, gathered her up in her strong arms and hugged her tightly, just as Captain X, who during one trip had had the duchess as passenger and therefore loved her, came along.

As they turned in the direction of the dining-saloon, the girl looked over her shoulder at the two maids, and smiled.

With a great love of their respective mistresses as their sole bond in common they stood, otherwise divided, staring at each other.

"Pleased to meet you again," volunteered country-bred Jane, offering a plump hand.

"Hoping you are in good health," responded Maria Hobson, making a corner in strawberry-leaves as she just touched the finger-tips.

"Wellington, you have met Dekko, I think," laughed the girl.

"Woomph!" grunted the dog disdainfully, as he cocked an eye at the bird, which ruffled its feathers, spread its red tail and looked down sideways and spitefully for a long moment.

"My Gawd!" it suddenly shrieked. "My Gawd!"

And it swung about and rubbed its soft grey pate against its mistress's outrageous golden perruque, then hurled itself onto the captain's shoulder.

CHAPTER V

"Oh, yet we trust that somehow good
Will be the final goal of ill."

TENNYSON

After the fight in the bazaar, the ducal party stayed for another fortnight in Cairo, during which time Damaris saw as much of the place and its surroundings as she could in fourteen days and a few hours out of each of the fourteen nights; whilst her godmother played bridge or poker, paid and received visits, took her to dances and parties, and busied her fingers in the tangled threads Fate had tossed into her lap.

It was an understood thing that the girl should be ready to conduct the old aristocrat to the dining-room at the dinner-hour and give her the evening; other than that her time was her own, though, owing to her innate courtesy and her love for her godmother, she never once absented herself without having obtained permission.

"You are a positive tonic, child, in these perplexing days," remarked her grace, when the girl had concluded the recital of the fight in the bazaar. "Only, do remember to come straight to me if ever you get into a real scrape."

And that night, the old lady, who had lost heavily at poker, fairly snapped at Maria Hobson, who, tucking her up in bed, remarked, greatly daring, upon the amount of liberty allowed the child.

"Don't be foolish, my good woman," she said, "and do for goodness' sake mind your business of looking after me. Although my god-daughter may bluff a bit for the fun of the game, and get let down a bit for her own good, yet I shouldn't advise anyone to get seeing her too often. Fate dealt her a royal straight flush in hearts, and better that you can't—no! not even if you hold a full house of intrigue and bad intent t'other end of Life's table."

"Humff!" replied the maid heavily through her nose, not having understood one word of her mistress's admonition.

Each day at breakfast and at dinner a bunch, big or little, of simple or hothouse flowers lay beside the girl's plate, without name or message.

Now, the finding of flowers upon your table does not, in Egypt, necessarily imply that the donor thereof is a son of the desert; the maitre d'hotel has been known to do it out of deference to your rank or purse; and only once had Jane Coop had the mixed pleasure of meeting the deaf-mute Nubian who daily left the posies at the hotel.

Refreshed from her siesta, she had descended to the hall *via* the stairs instead of the lift, and bumped into the ebony-hued slave as he bent to lay a sheaf of flowers upon the matting outside her mistress's door.

He had straightened himself and salaamed almost to the ground—which had delighted Jane Coop—and had offered the bunch to her.

"Oh, no, my man!" she had said, bridling, "you don't come over me that way. Just you take that trash back to where it came from. My young lady ain't that kind," and had shaken her fist in his face and flounced downstairs to lay a complaint.

What with the militant maids, the parrot and the dog, the ducal party was continually breaking out in some direction or another, but the maitre d'hotel, who simply worshipped the old lady, merely smiled and poured the oil of soothing words upon the troubled waters.

The girl had quite casually recounted the fight in the bazaar, and the wise old woman had made no comment; but, all the same, next day she indifferently asked a few questions of Lady Thistleton, who had a big heart, narrow mind, an ever-wagging tongue and two daughters.

"Oh, that's the son of the Arab and the English girl. You must remember the fuse there was in England over the runaway marriage—what was her name?—how she could, you know—"

"Ah! yes. You must be talking of Jill Carden. I knew her very well. Naughty girl, she refused the invitation I sent them asking them to come to England and stay with me, and gave up writing to me after a while. Does she live in Cairo?"

It seemed that Jill, the wife of the Sheikh el-Umbar, lived in the Flat Oasis t'other side of the Canal, in Arabia proper, but, according to current gossip, was at the moment upon a visit to her son at the House 'an Mahabbha, which had been built for the elder branch of the House el-Umbar on a verdant patch watered by the springs, from the limestone hills which stretch on the desert side of the Oasis of Khargegh.

"He's not in Cairo, then?"

"No; he left to-day," replied the gossip. "You see, his mother is expected any time at his home, if she isn't already there. My maid will chatter so, there's absolutely no stopping her. Funnily enough, I arrived at the station as he was leaving in a special train. Such a handsome man, educated in England, millionaire too. Of course it's a case of a touch of the tarbrush—such a pity, too!"

Joan Conquest

The duchess suddenly shivered.

"Little Jill!" she said gently. "Little Jill! I must go and see her if she will let me. Ah! General, what about a hand at ecarte before dinner?"—and she rose with a stormy rustling of her softly-scented silks, leaving the gossip wondering in what way she had put her foot in it.

That night, as she lay like a little brown mouse under the mosquito-net, watching the stars through the open window, the old lady suddenly decided to bestir herself.

"It's too risky! She's too beautiful, too young and unsophisticated," she murmured as she lit a cigarette under the curtains, which is strictly against the rules. "I'd bet my last *piastre* that Jill Carden's son's all right, but, all the same, one has to reckon with the glamour of the East. Love's all very well in a cool climate, but it's the dickens out here. Must get her anchored in safe waters. What d'you think, Dekko old friend? What course shall I set? Shall we go home, or to Heliopolis?"

The bird scrambled awkwardly on to the dressing-table.

"Well, old man, how about it?"

"Steer a straight course for hell, old dear," came the muffled reply, as the bird twisted its head under its wing, then untucked it to murmur sleepily: "T'hell!"

So she made up her mind to move on the very day after the girl's birthday, which fell in a fortnights time. She would, indeed, have left at once if it had not been that she had issued invitations on a gigantic scale for a fancy-dress ball in honour of the anniversary.

Inwardly Damaris rebelled at the suggestion of moving on to Heliopolis; outwardly she acquiesced without enthusiasm.

"But if it will do that nasty little cough good, dearest, why wait for the ball?"

"Do you want to go, Maris?"

"The desert will be so near," evaded the girl. "Half-an-hour's ride at the most, so—so Ben Kelham told me, and there you see the desert, miles upon miles of it stretching right away like the sea."

The hawk-eyes flashed across the girl's face, taking in the forced indifference of the expression and the light which gleamed far down in the eyes.

"I had a letter from Ben this morning. His lung has been troubling him; that is why he hasn't been over."

"Did you—has it—is it—?" rather lamely replied the girl.

He had written Damaris a perfunctory note of welcome to the Land of the Pharaohs; then, a week later, had come over to dine. He had ached to take his beautiful little chum up in his arms and shake her for her haughtiness and by sheer strength of arms and will force her to say "yes" to the question which it took him all his strength not to ask.

Since childhood he had been her slave, her door-mat, and the butt of her various moods, feeling infinitely well rewarded by a careless smile or word; so that he found it difficult, in fact well-nigh impossible, to act up to her grace's plans and suddenly transpose himself into the strong, silent man.

The girl, spoilt and accustomed to slavish devotion and used to his worship, felt incensed, then hurt, and finally perplexed, and, to hide it all, retired therewith into a shell of icy reserve.

He had adored her openly, and now, seemingly, looked upon her as just one of the crowd of women in the hotel; she had taken his adoration for granted and as a right, to waken one morning to find the gem she had tossed in amongst the rubbish of her little experiences, gone!

Is there a greater mistake in the world than that of looking upon love as an ordinary possession, instead of as a rare jewel?

They were both very young, so that they suffered the agonies of doubt and uncertainty, whilst the worldly-wise old dame smiled up her sleeve.

From the hour of the early cup of tea until breakfast-time on the morning of the ball, which was also the girl's birthday morning, tarbusched, impudent young monkeys of messenger boys, bearing gifts and flowers, arrived in a stream at the hotel.

Flowers in pots and vases and bunches lay everywhere in the suite; shawls of many colours, silken veils, slippers, albums of views of Egypt, rare antiques (made mostly in Birmingham), one mummied cat (genuine), scarabs (suspicious), and one live gazelle littered the place.

Ben Kelham had bought her a finger-napkin ring of dull gold; through it he had forced some flowers, and sent it along.

She held it tight in her hand for a moment, then deliberately and ostentatiously laid it amongst the clutter on the table, whilst her grace peeped from behind the newspaper which she was reading in bed.

Arrived at the table in the breakfast-room, the girl suddenly flushed pink and then went quite white.

Right in the centre, flanked on one side by the glass dish of glowing fruit and the other by a cut-glass jar of Keiller's marmalade, stood a cage tied at the top with silver ribbon and containing two cooing doves.

The doves were just ordinary ones, but their prison was no ordinary cage. Fair-sized and square, it was made of fine white bars of ivory. The underside was also ivory, square and unblemished, and would have made an ideal hairpin-tray; it stood upon ebony feet inlaid with infinitesimal precious stones.

"It has but just arrived, Miss Hethencourt," said the maitre d'hotel, who had been fluttering around upon the tiptoe of a most unusual curiosity. "There is no name, no message."

"Please send it to my room," she replied indifferently, whilst, for some unaccountable reason, her heart throbbed as she responded to the birthday greetings which came from every corner of the room.

Joan Conquest

CHAPTER VI

"A mother is a mother still,
The holiest thing alive."

COLERIDGE

"May the blessing of Allah who is God be upon thee, O woman!"

The sonorous words, of the benediction rang through the room as Hugh Carden Ali stood with the silken curtain drawn back in one hand and the right raised in blessing upon his mother, who stood with arms outstretched in the centre of the room.

Then he knelt to receive the benison of the woman he loved, smiled when he felt the small hands upon his head and, leaping to his feet, swung her up into his arms, covering her face with kisses.

"You beautiful darling!" he said, as he crushed her up, to the derangement of her perfumed silks and satins and many jewels. "It's just heavenly coming back to you, you dear, under-standing mother."

The woman's heart leapt to battle, for in the last words, in the way her beloved son looked down upon her in the tone of his voice, she knew that, somewhere out in the world, he had received a hurt. She knew so little of him, had only had him for such a little, little while under the influence of her love and in the shelter of her heart, and she loved him, her firstborn, with a love beyond words. Thinking to do the best for him, and making the biggest mistake of all, beating down her beloved husband's opposition, she had sent the boy to England, and in the subsequent eight years had only seen him twice.

"He is of the East, Woman of my Heart! Behold, I have studied him," had said the Sheikh, all those years ago. "Let him be, else evil may befall him."

But Jill, his beautiful wife, had insisted, and his love for her being beyond telling, the great Arab had submitted to her wish.

For so it had been written.

And what can be the outcome of the tragic mixing of blood? Nothing but pain.

"Come to the roof and talk, Mother, under the stars."

So up the marble staircase, with his arm about her waist, to the roof they went, where the silken awnings lay folded and the scented white flowers hung asleep.

They stood under the canopy of purple night studded with flashing, silvery points, as the soft winds carried to them the notes of a guitar softly thrummed in the shade of the palms.

"It is Mary, dear," happily whispered the woman. "She came with me to welcome you." And then she clasped her hands at the blaze of anger which swept the man's face.

"Most gracious Mother, I am master of my house, and, save for your ever-esteemed, ever-desired presence, I cannot have woman set foot in it without my consent. When I have the

Joan Conquest

desire for one as wife, plaything or servant, then I will give orders."

"But, Hugh, Mary is your sister!"

"Mary is my sister, and I do not deem it wise or seemly that she should run about the country at her own wish or whim."

"But, Hugh,—"

"Dear, let me speak. I saw so much of woman in Europe that the yashmak, the barku, the seclusion and modesty of the East have become dear to me above all else. Have you forgotten, dear, the restaurants, the theatres, the parks and, Allah! the streets? The half-stripped bodies, the craving for excitement, the wine, the nights turned into day! Why, one has but to stretch the hand, for flowers to be laid therein; the feet trip at every step with the trap of woman's hair; the quarry stands waiting for the arrow; there is not even the incentive of the chase, the hot pursuit, the lust of the kill. I speak as my father's son, and in my house I will have privacy and seclusion and seemliness. Women shall be brought to me when I desire their presence." And the steeliness of the voice brought the woman up-sitting as he gave her an order cloaked in the guise of a favour begged. "And I shall be glad if you will ask my sister to keep within the women's quarters until I send for her."

"But—"

And she ripped the corner of her veil between perturbed fingers when, upon the clapping of hands, a slave ran swiftly to learn his master's pleasure, then hastened away to find the head body-woman of the guesthouse assigned to women-visitors.

After which the sweet thrumming of the guitar instantly stopped.

On more than one night they talked under the stars, sitting on satin cushions, or leaning on the marble fret-work of the balustrade looking due east to where, so many miles away, flows the blue-green Nile, as it has flowed through the centuries, all unheeding of the passing of mighty kingdoms.

And yet had the mother learned nothing of the hurt reflected in her firstborn's eyes.

"Most precious Mother," he was saying, as he stood flicking the pages of the latest illustrated paper just arrived from Cairo, but which was really a volume of the Book of Life written, printed and published by Fate. "If it pleases you to stay when I am gone, will you do so just as long as you find happiness in my dwelling?"

"You are going, Hugh,—so soon—for long?"

"There has come a report of lion in the Nubian Desert, as far north as Deir el-Bahari. I can hardly believe it, for it is years and years since a lion has been seen even in the Khor Baraka. However, a runner from Nubia came in this morning, so there may be something in it. God grant it, for the sport and the danger would be great, killing or being killed, in the rocks and ruins of the Temple. Also I could visit my Tents of Purple and of Gold. How long shall I be gone, sweet Mother? That is known only to Allah, to whom our goings and our comings are as the drifting of the sands."

"Your tents are very beautiful, my son. The servants are waiting for your orders before pitching the—the—middle one. Without asking permission, I went to inspect them. Just before your return, just to see if everything was quite all right. One can never quite trust the servants."

Jill might have been sitting on a rectory lawn, talking about her linen-cupboard or spring-cleaning with a neighbour, instead of one of the wonders of modern Egypt. In fact, so quaint was it that the man laughed and swung her onto the balustrade.

Joan Conquest

"I'm not surprised Father worships the ground your ridiculous little feet tread on, Mater," he said, causing his mother to gasp, so English did he sound, so Oriental did he look.

"Dear!" she said gently, as she scrutinised him with a mother's eyes and touched his face and patted his cheek and pulled a bit here and there at his fine white linen coat, upon which in coarse thread was embroidered the Hawk of Old Egypt. "Dear! don't you think you would be happier if you were to marry and—settle down?"

And it was then that there came to her the full explanation of the hurt reflected in her firstborn's eyes.

"I shall never marry, dear," very gently replied the man, so fearful was he of causing pain to the woman who had borne him. "I—I—you see, I cannot."

"Cannot, Hugh? But, my dear, what is the matter? You will have to, some day, you know. You are your father's eldest son," answered the woman, who, wrapped in perfect love and happiness, had never given a thought to the far-reaching effects of her marriage with the Arabian. "Dear son, there are so many beautiful, cultured, gentle women here and at home—I mean in England—you—"

"Mother, please! Oh, Mother, you don't understand—dear heavens! you don't understand. Listen—and, how I wish my father, whom I honour, were here to comfort you. Forgive me, dear, forgive me for the pain I must cause you—"

And the woman went white to the lips under a sudden blinding flash of understanding and her proud eyes dropped to the hands clenched in her lap.

"I want to marry, Mother of mine." He spoke in the Arabian tongue, which, is so atune to love, "for behold love in the space of an hour has grown within me. The floods of love drown me, the full-blossomed trees of passion throw their shade upon the surging waters, and, behold, the shade is that of tenderness. From the midst of the flood where I am like to drown, I stretch my arms towards the rocky shore where stands, looking towards me, the desire of my soul. Behold, my eyes have seen her, and, behold, she is white, with hair like the desert at sunset, and eyes even as the pools of Lebanon. She is as a rod to be bent, and as a vase of perfume to be broken upon a night of love. And I love her—her—out of all women—a doe to be hunted at dawn, a mare to be spurred through the watches of the night—"

"Hugh!"

"I love her as my father loved you—my father, of whom I am the eldest son—son of a highborn father, son of a highborn mother—outcast—outcast!"

"For pity's sake, Hugh, stop!"

But the storm swept on, tearing the veil from the woman's eyes.

"Behold, I care not for the plucking of garden blossoms, therefore are the beautiful, docile women of the East not for me, and the thorns upon the hedge of convention defied, the barbed wires of racial distinction keep me from the hedgerow flower, born of the wind and the sky and the summer heat, which I covet.

"Among men I am nothing; I may not claim equality with the scavenger of the Western streets; or with the donkey-boys of the Eastern bazaar. Here I am served with fear and servility, being a man of riches; across the waters, I may sun myself in the smiles of women as long as I have no desire to wed." He suddenly seized the woman, holding her in a grip of iron which left great bruises on her arms. "Do you know what she called me, Mother?—that harlot of a line of noblemen—what she flung in my teeth because, seeing in her a woman of the streets hidden under the cloak of marriage, I refused to be tempted?"

There fell a terrible silence, and then a few whispered words.

"She called me a half-caste, Mother!—me—a half-caste!"

And the mother fell at her son's feet and bowed her head to the ground, and he swept her up into his arms, raining kisses upon the piteous face.

"I don't blame you, sweetheart-mother," he said in English, whilst she sobbed on his heart. "Am I not the fruit of a brave woman's great love? Could there be anything finer than that? But my father in me made my whole body clamour for the desert when I was in England; my mother in me makes my heart throb in the desert for just one hour of her cool, misty country, one hour on a hill-top in which to watch the pearl-gray dawn. Dearest, dearest, don't sob so. It is a case of two affirmatives making a negative; two great nationalities decried, derided, rendered null and void in their offspring through the dictates of those who, in religion, prate that we are all brothers. I have just got to stick it, my mother, and life is not very long. But I shall never marry." And as he spoke, Fate flicked a page of an illustrated paper, which was but the volume of the Book of Life, and perhaps only a mother's eyes would have noticed the sudden tightening of the hand upon the marble of the balustrade as the man looked down into the pictured beauty of the woman he loved.

And, having read what had been written, he knelt to receive his mother's blessing.

"To the Tents of Purple and Gold, my darling?" she asked, smiling so bravely to hide her breaking heart.

"Not just yet, dear; a bit further North first, I think."

"For long?"

"I do not know, dear. Bless me, O my mother."

She blessed him and called to him as he stood at the head of the marble stairway:

"Come back to me, my son!"

"That, O woman, is in the hands of Allah, who is God."

And he turned and left her, and she, having wept her heart out and her beautiful eyes dim, took up the illustrated paper which was a volume of the Book of Life, and turned the pages.

"Ah!" she said. "How beautiful!"

It was just a simple photograph of Damaris at a tennis tournament, and underneath the information that the most popular and beautiful visitor in Cairo would celebrate her birthday in a week's time, that in honour of the occasion her god-mother, the Duchess of Longacres, had issued invitations for a fancy-dress ball, after which social event she and her god-daughter would proceed to the Desert Palace Hotel, Heliopolis.

"I wonder," whispered Jill, "I wonder if she would come to see me. She was always such a wise old woman. I wonder if there is a way out"—and she stretched her arms out towards the desert. "Hahmed!" she called, "Beloved, I love you, and my heart is breaking,"—and she lifted her head and listened to the sound of many horses running; then bowed her head and wept.

The dawn was nigh to breaking, and yet the parade of horses was not finished; whilst the trainer, the head groom, the stud groom, the under-grooms and the rank and file of the stables tore their beards or their hair as they endeavoured to please their master, whilst they waited anxiously for the return of the man who had been hurriedly sent to fetch in the mare, Pi-Kay, who was out to grass, and as wild as a bird on the wing.

Joan Conquest

Singly, or in pairs, every priceless quadruped had been put through its paces upon the track of tan imported from England.

Three coal-black stallions, brothers to el-Sooltan, even then in Cairo, and famous throughout Egypt, tore past him like a cyclone and left him indifferent; a chestnut brood mare, whose price was above that of many rubies, trotted up at his call and snuffled a welcome in his sleeve, searched for sugar in his hand and found it, and whinnied gently when he turned away; bays, piebalds, roans, greys, trotted, galloped, jumped, whilst their master smoked endless cigarettes and the stud groom prayed fervently to Allah.

"By the patience of the Prophet," the master suddenly cried, turning on the man, "hast thou nothing else? Is there no jewel amongst my horses? Hast thou not in all my stables one of the Al Hamsa, a descendant of the mares who found favour in the eyes of Mohammed the prophet of Allah who is God? The mare Alia—has she been, perchance, as sterile as thy wits?"

And then he stopped short and stood in silence, watching the loveliest picture any human could wish to see.

Picking up her dainty feet as though she walked upon hot stones, tossing her proud little head, with big, gentle eyes, spreading nostrils and fine small ears almost touching at the tips, mane flowing, tail set high and spread, came the snow-white mare, Pi-Kay.

Allah! but the loveliness of that picture as she stood, thorough-bred, perfect, as proud as any queen, as scornful as any spoiled beauty, as confused at the sight of her master as any bride!

Ten yards away and motionless she stood from this man who seemed to take no notice of her, and then she wheeled, and flung up her heels; then stopped and looked at him along her satin flank and piqued with his indifference suddenly sped out into the desert.

Then, softly, melodiously, the man's voice called her, ringing like a bell under the lightening sky, and behold, love awoke in the mare's heart and she turned and raced back towards him, longing for his hand and the grip of his knees upon her. But with her feet upon the tan, she turned her back upon him and danced across towards the coal-black stallions, causing their grooms to hold on to them with both hands; then she came back to circle round about this man, who seemingly took no notice of her vagaries, not even when she reared just behind him, pawing the air, nor when she lashed out at a humble *sayis*, missing him by a hair; until, at last, overpowered by curiosity and love, curveting, rearing, throwing her feet and making a frightful to-do over nothing at all, she came close up—oh! very close—and whinnied gently.

With one hand clutching the silvery mane and in one bound he was across the bare back and away with her into the desert, gripping her with his knees, calling to her by every love-name he could think of.

And out there alone in the desert at the hour of prayer, he slipped from her and, turning towards Mecca, raised his hands to heaven.

"O God of the West! O Allah of the East! Give me one single hour of love!"

And the mare, Pi-Kay, wonderful in her beauty, raced from him far out into the desert, leaving him alone with his God; then stood quite still, with fine small ears pricked, waiting for the call she knew would come. And when it came ringing clear over the golden sand, she raced back to him and pushed against him, until he sprang upon her and turned her towards the East.

"*By the war-horses,*" he cried, quoting from Al-Koran, "*which run swiftly to battle, with a panting noise; and by those who strike fire by dashing their hoofs against the stones; and by those who make a sudden invasion on the enemy early in the morning and therein raise the dust, and therein pass through the midst of the adverse troops* . . . . by the Message of the Great Book and by my love will I wrest one hour from life."

And urging the mare with the whip of love to the uttermost of her wonderful speed, he thundered back across the path of sand, which was to be trodden by his feet alone, in spite of the plots which Zulannah the courtesan was even then weaving about him—to her own advancement.

CHAPTER VII

". . . . and she painted her face, and tired her head, and looked out at a window."

II KINGS

The house of the "Scarlet Enchantress," with its balconies, turrets and outer and inner courts, stood quite by itself at one corner of the Square, in a big, neglected garden. It had been built by means of untold gold and the destruction of scores of miserable, picturesque hovels, which, poor as they might be, had however meant home to many of the needy in the Arabian quarters of Cairo. It would be useless to look for that building covered in white plaster now; it was, later, looted and burned to the ground.

A beautiful wanton of fourteen summers, ambitious, relentless, with the eyes of an innocent child, the morals of a jackal and a fair supply of brain-cunning rather than intellect, Zulannah sat this night of stars in a corner of her balcony overlooking the Square, smoking endless cigarettes.

Courtesan of the highest rank, she had plied her ruthless trade for three successful years, accumulating incredible wealth in jewels and hard cash. Her ambition knew no bounds; her greed no limit; her jealousy of other women had become a by-word in the north.

Physically she was perfect; otherwise, she had not one saving grace, and her enemies were legion. She had driven hard bargains, demanding the very rings off men's fingers in exchange for kisses; shutting the door with callous finality in the face of those she had beggared; she had disowned her mother, who, stricken with ophthalmia, begged in the streets; she had no mercy for man, woman or beast, yet all had gone well until love had come to her.

Love comes to harlots and to queens as well as to us ordinary women, and they suffer every whit as much as we do, perhaps more keenly on account of the hopeless positions they fill.

It had come to Zulannah, uncontrollably, that night when, unveiled, garbed in silks and satins and hung with jewels, she brazenly graced the stage-box at a gala performance.

She looked down, and Ben Kelham, in the end seat of the first row of stalls, looked up and looked and looked, seeing nothing, being blinded with love of Damaris.

Zulannah drove back in her Rolls-Royce to the edge of the Arabian quarter, where, owing to the narrowness of the lanes called by courtesy streets, she alighted to finish what remained of the journey in a litter swung from the shoulders of four Nubian slaves, and, arrived at the great house, summoned her special bodyguard, Qatim the Ethiopian; and for acquiring information down to the smallest detail about some special individual there is, surely, no detective agency on earth to compare to one ordinary, native servant.

He loves intrigue!

So that, twenty-four hours later, Zulannah laughed shrilly when Qatim the Ethiopian repeated all he had learned of the white man and the white maid he presumably loved.

"Love!" she scoffed. "He has not met *me*!"

But in the weeks that followed no plot had succeeded, no device or subtle invitation had lured the bird to the list, so that she beat sharply upon a silver gong this night of the stars, upon which the Ethiopian came running hastily to cast himself upon the ground at the jewelled, henna'd feet.

"Get up," she said, kicking him upon the side of the head; whereupon he rose, chalking up one more mark on his own particular slate of Life, upon one side of which was written Desire and the other Revenge.

He stood six-foot-four in his loin-cloth, as black and glistening as a polished ebony statue. The enormous hands at the end of great, over-long arms almost touched his knees; the chest and shoulders and abdomen were hard as iron, rippling with muscle under the oiled skin; the feet were huge and pink of sole, and the animality of the man was intensified by a certain gleam of intelligence somewhere in the impassive negroid face.

The woman, took no notice of the magnificent physique; it neither repulsed nor attracted her—he was a slave.

"Run and give orders that no one is admitted! Hasten!"

"Mistress, a great noble waits at—"

"Desirest thou thy tongue split, thou black dog, that thou answerest Zulannah? Haste thee, and return!"

And far into the night they talked, those two, planning death or destruction, anything as long as it attained the desire of the woman who, looking into the future, took no notice of the mountain of disaster beside her in the shape of the Ethiopian who desired and hated her with all the bestial passion of his race.

Then, just as far down in the east the sky lightened, she sat suddenly upright and clapped her jewelled hands.

"Know'st thou the eunuch who guards the harem empty of women in the palace of—ah! the barbarity of the name!—E'u Car-r-den Ali? He who perchance would give one-half, nay, all of his great wealth in return for the coal-blackness of thy odorous skin. There is to be held a big entertainment within the walls of the white man's hotel, and soon. An entertainment where the whites dance foolishly in foolish raiment, disguised as that which they are not and with covered faces. What easier than for me to obtain entry as one of them under my veils and have speech with the man I love? And if he is as thou sayest, besotted with love of this white girl, then will I use the man of barbarous name as a tool to bring about that which I desire. Know'st thou the eunuch?"

"Mistress, he is my twin-brother."

"Twin of *thee*! Behold, did not thy mother die of fright, at sight of such monstrosities?"

"Nay, mistress, there are six sons younger than thy slave, each one of which could break thee in one hand."

Zulannah sprang to her feet and, seizing a short whip from a table, smote the man again and again until his face ran blood.

"Thou vile brute, darest thou so to speak! Behold, this is but a foretaste of what will befall thy black carcase before the hour is spent."

"Call thy slaves, mistress; split my tongue; whip the soles from off my feet, the flesh from my body, even to the bones, and thou shalt never meet my twin-brother, who even now prepareth the great palace for the coming of the"—he spat—"bird of different-coloured plumage."

And Zulannah, understanding that she must not overstep the limit if she desired to attain her end, flung the whip full into the stolid, indifferent face, and fled, raving obscenities, into the house.

CHAPTER VIII

*"If God in His wisdom have brought close
The day when I must die,
That day by water or fire or air
My feet shall fall in the destined snare
Wherever my road may lie."*

DANTE GABRIEL ROSETTI

"May I come in? Oh, Maris, what *do* you think? There is to be a real native fortune-teller in the Winter Garden. They've made the corner near the fountain like an Arab's tent, and he'll tell us our horoscopes in the sand, and all sorts of things."

"Not forgetting the stars, let us hope?"

"Oh, there's sure to be that."

Damaris laughed as she turned in her chair and looked at the excited little visitor in fancy-dress.

"You *do* look sweet. A Light of the Harem, for certain."

"Yes; and what do you think? There are three dozen Lights. Isn't it a shame? I thought I should be the only one. And there are two and a half dozen Sheikhs, and I don't know how many dozen Bedouins. You are—what are you? You look awfully— awfully—er—I don't quite know what."

Damaris adjusted the *selva*, the quaint silver kind of tube between the eyebrows which connects the yashmak and the *tarhah* or head-veil, took a final look in the mirror, and rose.

"I am an Egyptian woman of the humblest class."

She was all in black, as befits a member of that class. The simple bodice, cut in a yoke, of the black muslin dress fitted her like a glove; the skirt fell in wide folds from the waist and swung about her ankles encircled by big brass rings, which clashed as she moved. She wore the black yashmak and *tarhah*; upon her arms were many brass bracelets which tinkled; on one hand she wore a ring and there were flesh-coloured silken hose and sandals upon her feet. She had made a mistake and henna'd her finger-tips, which members of the humblest class have not time to do—besides, their patient hands matter so little—and her great eyes looked as black as the yashmak over which they shone.

Her beautiful face was hidden, yet was she infinitely alluring, tantilising, mysterious, under her veils.

Heavens! if only women knew how easy it is to enhance the looks by the simple method of touching up the eyes with *kohl* and covering the rest of the face!

"All of us in veils and masks will have to take them off at one."

"Yes, there'll be the rub," said Damaris, as she knelt down beside the perplexed, growling bulldog.

"Don't know Missie? Don't love her?"

"Woomph!" replied Wellington, hurling his great weight into her lap.

"How he loves you, Maris!"

"Yes, miss, he does," broke in Jane Coop. "And I firmly believe he's my mistress's guardian angel."

"After you, Janie dear," said the girl, smiling fondly up at the plump maid and tying a huge crimson bow round the neck of the long-suffering animal.

"What is he going as, Maris?"

"A gargle, miss," broke in the maid. "I think it's just fun on the part of Miss Damaris, because nothing as solid as him,"—pointing of comb to shamed dog—"could go as anything watery."

Damaris got to her feet.

"Let's go in to *Marraine*," she choked. "Gargoyle, my dear," she whispered, "is what she meant—gargoyle. Do come along!"

The girls' happy laughter rang down the corridor as they knocked at her grace's door.

She stood at her dressing-table in a beautiful dress of grey brocade. Diamonds sparkled in the laces of her corsage, on her fingers and in the buckles of her lovely shoes; a big bunch of pink carnations was tied on the top of her ebony stick; a priceless lace veil fastened over her head by a fragile wreath of diamond leaves fell almost to the hem of her dress behind. She had discarded the terrifying perruque, and her own hair, snowy-white, was puffed and curled about the little face, which was finely powdered and slightly rouged. She was a dream of beautiful old age, with Dekko just visible under a huge pink bow upon her shoulder.

"May I present a very old woman to youth?" she said simply.

"Darling," cried Damaris as she ran forward and, pushing the yashmak to one side, kissed the jewelled hand. "You are too beautiful—too beautiful! Promise me never, never, never to wear it again."

"I'm too old to get rid of bad habits, cherie," said her godmother. "And we had better go down. By the way, what is Ben coming as?"

"I really don't know," came the muffled reply from behind the yashmak, "if he comes at all."

As Cairo entire had accepted the invitation, the place was packed, but nowhere was the crowd so suffocating as round the entrance to the Winter Garden.

"Per-fect-ly wonderful," gasped a rotund Ouled Nail to a masked dancer of the same sex and size. "He told me about that terrible time when I lost so much at bridge—you remember, dear, when I had to—er—to raise money on my diamonds. How could he have seen it in my hand?"

He hadn't; he had been a guest at Hurdley Castle with her.

"What's he like?"

"Oh, I couldn't see his face, on account of the handkerchief thing, but I think he's quite common; his clothes are quite poor. I believe he is one of the waiters dressed up. I seem to recognise his voice. Have you long to wait?"

"I'm twenty-fifth down the list. Who's in now?"

"Some woman in black. There are four of them, and I can't tell t'other from which."

The hand of the woman who was twenty-fifth down the list was never told.

Damaris lifted the curtain, and walked into the corner of the Winter Garden, which had been temporarily given the appearance of an Arab's tent.

"*Salaam aley,*" she said gently, giving the word of peace.

The fortune-teller salaamed with hands to forehead, mouth and heart, in the beautiful Eastern gesture.

"*Aleykoum es-Salaam!*" he replied as gently, which is the sacrament of lips.

There was the fortune-teller's regulation small table, with a chart of the stars and a silver tray covered in sand upon it; on either side was a chair; but it was upon a cushion on the floor that Damaris seated herself, with her back against the canvas drapery of the wall, motioning the Arab to a cushion near her, whilst her eyes swept the loose cotton tunic, the *kaleelyah* or head-kerchief, which almost completely hid the face, the great white mantle and the sandals upon the naked feet.

Oh! the game of make-believe they played, those two with the jewel-hilted, razor-edged dagger of love between them.

There fell a silence.

And then the fortune-teller spoke in his own tongue, and too absorbed were they in the game of make-believe to notice that he made use of neither sand nor stars nor the lines upon her hands, which were clasped above her heart, as he read her future in her eyes.

"Two paths lie before thee, O woman, and both stretch, through the kingdom of love.

"The one to thy right hand has been marked out upon the Field of Content by feet bound in the sandals of custom and convention. There is shade upon this path, for, behold, the scorching sun of passion may not penetrate the leaves of the trees of tranquillity; the storm breaks not, neither do the biting winds of fear, nor the drenching torrents of desire, encompass those who walk thereon.

"The river, the slow, full-blossomed river of patience, flows ever beside it, on its way to the Ocean of Life in which all waters must mingle in eternity."

There fell a silence, broken by the swaying, throbbing music from the distant ball-room, causing the girl suddenly to stretch out her hands, upon which shone the ring, and the man to stretch out his, though he touched not hers at all.

"And to the left?"

"To the left, O woman whose eyes are like unto the pools of Lebanon at night, to thy left, lies the desert. The desert, where the feet are blistered by the gritting sands of passion and the eyes are blinded in desire. The vast plain where knowledge walks hand-in-hand with death; where the footprints of horror, fear, starvation, thirst, which are but the footprints of jealousy and love desired and fulfilled, mark the sands for one little second and then are gone; the desert, where there is no shade, no cool waters, no content, no peace until the wanderer lies still, with sightless eyes turned towards Eternity."

"And if a woman's feet trod upon it?"

"Then will she cut her feet upon the stones of pain; then will the scorpion of bitter experience sting her heel; then will she die with a smile upon her red mouth, for love will have come to her, maybe for a day, maybe for a second of time, but a love which will mingle her soul with the soul of her desert lover, or shatter her body, even as is broken the alabaster vase of sweet perfume. Yet is it the *love of the soul* that endureth forever, yea, even if the body of the woman passeth unto another's keeping."

The girl pulled her veil closely about her head and sat quite still, her wonderful eyes hidden by the fringe of black lashes.

And yet did she not move when he sprang to his feet, intoxicated with the mystery of her, afire with that love which is the heritage of the desert.

Then he bent and caught her by the wrists and raised her to her feet.

"Take the path at thy right hand, woman; set not a foot upon the desert sand, lest perchance a bird of prey swoop down upon thee, thou white dove."

He pulled her hands up, holding them cruelly, as in a steel vise, so that he had but to bend a finger's breadth to kiss them.

"Thy feet hesitate, woman. Why? What searchest thou?"

"Knowledge."

The man unconsciously laced his fingers in hers, crushing them until she went white to the lips.

"Knowledge is pain, woman. What know'st thou of pain? Great pain. How could'st thou endure it?"

Then he let her hands go and touched the silver tray of sand upon the table beside him.

"Behold! Love shall be offered thee within the passing of a few hours, the love of thy right hand, and thou shalt reject it. Searching for that which thou desirest thou shalt, surrounded by thy women who love thee, pass down the river even unto Thebes of the Hundred Gates. Yet shalt thou not find it in the river, nor in the temples upon the east bank of the waters, nor upon the west bank."

Drawing a square in the sand, the fortune-teller made a cross at the south-east, upon which, to see it better, the girl drew close—so close that the sweet perfume of her veils filled his nostrils.

"Then shalt thou, in thy search, go, even under the stars, to the Gate of Tomorrow, and there shalt thou find a mare descended from the mares of Mohammed, the Prophet of Allah the one and only God. White is the mare, and beautiful, yea, even is she like unto thee, thou woman of ivory; her bit is of silver, her bridle of plaited gold, her saddle-cloth encrusted with jewels. Thou wilt spring upon her, and she, knowing her way, will bring thee to the Tents of Purple and Gold."

"Ah!" whispered the girl. "The Tents of the long-dead Queen! They are the talk of Cairo, but nobody—at least, no foreigner —has seen them."

"No man but the servants, no woman but the mother of him who is the master, has even set foot within the Tents of Purple and of Gold; no one but the master has set foot in the tent which stands between them, the Tent of Death."

"And in them—if I come, what—what should I find?"

"No harm shall befall thee, no smirching of thy fair name. The master alone shall greet thee, and when thou hast found that for which thou searchest, then shalt thou return, if so thou wilt."

"And peace—rest I think I mean—is it in your Tents of Purple and Gold?"

"Peace is to be found within the Temple of Anubis, who is the god of Death, and there only."

The girl shivered and lifted her head, as from some part of the hotel there drifted the wonderful desert love-song which begins:

"My love for thee is as the sun at noon—"

Then she looked at the man whose face she had not plainly seen in the passing of the hour.

"How am I to believe you? Will you give me a sign, something, anything, so that I shall know that if I ever want to visit the wonderful tents I shall find them?"

She only spoke to gain time.

Knowing that outside the curtain there stretched the path across the Field of Content, she deliberately placed her foot upon the desert sand, and whilst common sense urged her to get out of the room, she listened to temptation and lingered, throwing safety to the four winds, opening wide her arms to danger.

"By the sign of the black stallion who awaits thee at dawn near all that remaineth upright of the City of On, shalt thou find the Tents of Purple and Gold."

"But I don't ride any more," said Damaris. "I can't find a horse, a good one, and I don't know where the City of On is."

"Thou shall know, thou ivory casket to which love is the key. And if thou see'st one afar off as thou ridest into the desert at dawn, fear not; for behold, is thy beauty spoken of, yea, even in the harem, and it were not wise for thee to ride alone."

The girl put out her hand towards the silken curtain.

"How do you know who I am?"

"By thy voice, which is as the wind of dawn."

She hesitated, divided between a desire to know more about this man and an innate courtesy which forbade her questioning.

"Search not, ask not, woman," said the fortune-teller, divining her thoughts, "for I am not worthy of thy notice. Were I to cross thy threshold, were I to lay my hand upon thee, as surely should I pollute thee. There is that within me which cries aloud, urging me to lead thy feet upon the burning desert sands; and, again, there is that within me which would fain force thee, for thy happiness, upon the path running through the Field of Content. Yet, behold, art thou all safe with me."

"Could I help you? If you were to tell me your trouble, perhaps it would be easier?"

"The moment is not yet, woman, but, being a teller of tales, even as I am a teller of fortunes, one day will I sit at thy feet and, for the passing of an hour, will tell thee the story of the Hawk of Egypt."

"You have made this hour pass so pleasantly that I should— should like to—to give you something so as—as to show you how pleased I am. But I have nothing with me, nothing."

She put out her hands and turned them down.

The man looked down at her for a moment with blazing eyes.

"Give me—as a reward—Allah—give me—" They stood quite still as the torrent surged, about them. "Give me the ring from off thy finger," he added, gently.

The girl held out her hand.

"Take it, though it seems a poor reward for all you have promised me."

"Nay, give it thou to me."

She slipped it off and held it out, showing a bruise across the back of her hand.

"Allah!" whispered the man, "that I should mark thee thus— and yet, in love—in love!"

He took the ring, of which the dull-gold setting held an emerald in the form of a scarab with heartshaped base.

The fortune-teller turned it over in the palm of his hand, then held it out.

"Nay, this I cannot take. I thought it was a ring from the bazaar to go with thy dress of fantasy. Behold, it is an amulet of the heart, of—nay, I cannot tell thus quickly of what dynasty—with words of power engraved upon it which read thus:

"'*My heart, my mother; my heart, my mother. My heart whereby I came into being.*'"

The girl listened entranced, touching the ring with finger-tips which felt as snow-flakes upon the man's hand.

"What is an amulet of the heart?"

"In the days of Ancient Egypt, when the heart had been taken from the dead body for purposes of preservation, an amulet, a scarab, sometimes heart-shaped, was placed within the body to ensure it life and movement in the new life."

They both stood looking down upon the jewel, the girl's finger-tips resting upon the man's hand.

"Keep it," she said softly. "Keep it."

"I will keep it to replace that which has gone from me. I will restore it to its shape, I will take from it the golden setting of the ring. I will wear it upon my breast." And, bending, he gently raised the yashmak in both hands and pressed his forehead to the few inches which had rested above her crimson mouth.

CHAPTER IX

*"Love is one and the same in the original, but
there are a thousand copies of it, and, it may
be, all differing from one another."*

LA ROCHEFOUCAULD

Ben Kelham, disguised as Rameses the Great, laid a hand upon
the girl's shoulder as, passing to the left of the tent, she walked
slowly towards the door leading to the grounds, whilst sounds
of wrath came from the serried ranks of those who wished to
pry into the future.

The fortune-teller had sent word that there would be no more
reading of horoscopes or hands that evening, and had absented
himself therewith through a back entrance.

"You *have* been a long time," said Ben Kelham. He looked
magnificent as the great Sestoris, who had stood well over six
feet in the days of Ancient Egypt. "What was the man telling
you?"

Damaris was disturbed, and it was most unfortunate that,
under the spur of inquietude, he should have chosen just this
occasion and this moment to allow a hint of authority to creep
into his voice and a shadow of proprietorship to show in his
actions.

"How do you know who I am?" parried the girl coldly, as she shrugged the proprietory hand off her shoulder.

"Wellington gave you away. He followed your trail to the tent and sat growling at everybody until I came along and removed him."

"I wish you would leave the dog alone," said Damaris, with a certain amount of acerbity. "He is my custos."

"But that is not the kind of guardian you want, Damaris—you are too beautiful, you know. Let us sit here; it's lovely and warm, and the stars look just like diamonds, don't they?"

"I would rather walk," said Damaris, who was longing to sit down.

But she sat down when Ben Kelham took her by the elbow and led her to the seat; and she sat quite still when he suddenly took both her hands.

"Oh! don't, Ben," she said, when he pulled them up against his heart. "I can't stand any more to-night." And he, being over-slow in the uptak', failed to catch her in this slip of the tongue.

"I want you for my wife, dear," was all he said.

Then Damaris pulled her hands away and, removing the yashmak, looked up into his face, whilst he drew a breath sharply at the beauty of her.

"I love you so, dear! I'm a clumsy fool at speaking, but I could show you how I love you. I want to marry you and take you right away home. Do you know, I—I don't know how to explain it, but I—somehow feel you are in danger out here. I—will you—?"

Damaris looked to the right and looked to the left, hesitated and chose the middle path.

"I can't answer you now, Ben. I'm—I'm not sure about loving you, and, of course, one can't marry without that on both sides, can one?"

Oh, the blessed little ignoramus!

"Besides," she added as an afterthought, "I'm so young, and so are you."

"Oh, Damaris! Surely you don't want to wait until you find someone who's had lots of experience, which only means that he hasn't been playing the game as far as his future wife is concerned and will come to you like a ready-made suit returned from the cleaner's. The Kelhams always marry young, and our brides are always very young. That's why, I think, we're so strong and long-lived." He veered suddenly from the mazy subject of eugenics and pleaded hard, persuasively, stubbornly.

But Damaris, just as stubbornly, shook her head.

"Besides, Ben, this is unexpected. I haven't seen anything of you since I have been out; surely, if you love me so, you would have come over more often to—to—prepare the way."

She unashamedly exposed her hurt, whilst the man inwardly called himself every kind of a fool for having listened to another's voice upon a subject as vital and tricky as love.

Still he urged and pleaded, being of those who, refusing to take No as an answer, usually succeed in attaining their desire.

A wearisome process, but well worth while once in a lifetime, whatever kind of a clutter those first cousins, obstinacy, stubbornness and strong will cause you to accumulate about your feet at other times.

"I don't know enough to marry," persisted the girl. "I want to know what love really is, first."

"Oh! but, dear, I can teach you all you want to know," replied the man, in the customary all-sweeping manner of the male.

"But I want to know all about the different kinds."

"There are no different kinds, Damaris. There is only one sort."

"Then explain this to me."

It seemed that two months before the girl had left England, she had found the tweeny, Lizzie Stitch by name, sobbing over the cinders in her sitting-room grate. The besmirched little face, like a sodden little pudding, had been covered with grimy hands, and the thin little chest had heaved under the scanty cotton blouse and the stress of the tale of betrayal and desertion.

"I didn't know, miss. I didn't do it purposelike for a lark. I did think it was love, *real* love what—what is h'always pardinned. Well, miss, if you think it wise to force 'im, I'll do what you say, though it's not about meself as I'm worrying; it's 'cause I must have a father for the kid. I couldn't put it out, an' lose it, not h'ever so."

Then had come about a strange scene of transformation. Confronted by Damaris with a riding-whip in one hand, a special license in the other, and Wellington at her heels, the fox-faced young man had professed a desire to marry the tweeny on the spot.

Then had been granted a seventh-heaven glimpse of what love, real love, can be, to the tweeny maid, changing her into a veritable spitfire, who had turned and rent the fox-faced youth.

"I wouldn't 'ave you, nohow, no, not if yer were the larst man on earth, not 'alf I wouldn't. I'll get through my trouble, miss, all right, an' by meself, thanking you kindly for troubling, an' I'll wait until Mister Right comes along; that's what I'll do,

Mister Runaway."

And when Mr. Runaway had hinted that Mr. Right might kick at being called upon to shoulder the encumbrances of others, she had snatched the special license from her young mistress, torn it into bits, flung it into the foxy face and blazed into a big-hearted, big-minded, all-understanding little tweeny maid of a woman.

"I said Mr. Right, didn't I, yer bloomin' chuckhead? 'E'll unnerstand that it was all done in mistake, an' not by preference, so to speak. An' unnerstandin', he'll forgive. Lots of them mistakes are made by girls like me"—thumping of washed but still grimy hand above gallant little heart—"through swipes like you. Life's full of 'em down our way. But life's love, and love's life, and you can't get away from that, that yer can't. And I'd raver die wiv my love shut up 'ere"—more thumps above gallant little heart—"than throw it away on a louse like you, *that* I would, not 'arf!"

Ben Kelham said nothing, and there fell a silence between the two, though the Egyptian night was as full of noise as it ever is in the big cities of the East.

"What did she mean, Ben," said Damaris at last, "by that love which understanding can forgive even—even *her* trouble?"

And to Ben Kelham came the tweeny's seventh-heaven glimpse of the understanding of real love.

He rose and swept Damaris, a-thrill at the mastery, into his arms, where he held her as he might have held a child.

"That, dear,"—and he spoke choosing the simplest words, just because he knew no others, "that means that if you said you loved me, and I—if I ever found you in a—how shall I put it?—in—no matter how compromising a situation—that I should love you just the same, because I should know that, although to all appearances you—you might have sinned, yet the real you, the pure, honourable, perfect woman in you, could not show the smallest stain. Do you understand?"

"Almost," whispered the girl, as she lay still in the arms that held her as a child.

"You've *got* to understand. Listen! It may sound brutal, but you've got to understand my love for you. Supposing you disappeared, as Englishwomen do sometimes in the East. Supposing I searched, and found you, and you—you were—you were like the little tweeny girl. What should I do? Why, Damaris, unless you came to me and confessed to sin, I'd marry you, loving you, understanding you, without asking any questions."

"Without asking any explanation?"

"Yes, dear. Yes. Because I love you—"

"And you would forgive me?"

"But, dear, there wouldn't be any need for forgiveness; the real, pure you would not have done anything wrong."

Then he blundered.

Like most big men, he was diffident; he underestimated the attraction of his strength allied to a very gentle courtesy; in fact, bound up in his love for Damaris, he had never given it a thought excepting to curse the awkwardness of his body and the slowness of his speech. He knew nothing of the honesty which looked out of the eyes; the quiet strength of his movements and speech; the feeling of confidence he inspired.

He was not given to self-analysis; he loved the sun in the heavens, the grass under foot and the traditions of his house too much to waste time on that kind of thing.

So that, fearing to have hurt the girl or bored the girl, he plumped her on her feet, when he could have won her and saved her and others, including himself, a mint of pain if he had only just crushed her up to his heart and kissed her.

She stood quite still, with that dazed little feeling which falls upon one who has entered the wrong room.

"I'm not going to bother you any more, dear," he said, watching for the flash of relief which did not cross the beautiful face.

"What are you going to do?"

"There has come a report of lion somewhere near Karnak. I think I shall run down and have a look round. I thought of going on to Nairobi once I was really fit, so have got all my shooting gear with me. But, remember, you have only to send for me, and I will come. And don't try to run away, Damaris." And his voice was stern as he took her by the shoulders and drew her towards him. "You are mine! I'm letting you go now because you want to learn about life, and that you can't do if you have a man always on your heels. You will learn all right, dear, and suffer a bit, dear, but you will come to me in the end.

"I can't offer you the witchery and colouring and poetry of the East, but I do offer you the biggest love there has ever been in a man's heart for a woman and—"

A troupe of riotous guests came streaming down the path.

"One o'clock!" they shouted. "One o'clock. Masks off; masks off!"

The two walked slowly towards them.

"You *would* like a lion's skin, wouldn't you?" he asked eagerly, and stared amazed at the reproachful, hurt eyes which looked back at him just as the dancers swooped upon her.

A lion's skin! When she was craving for the strength of his arms about her, and the tower of his love behind her, from the top of which she could safely make monkey-faces of derision at Life, standing with lesson-books in one hand and a cane in the other.

She turned her back on him and entered the ballroom, and he went back to the seat in the garden, unconscious of the woman who watched.

And as the merry little crowd ran laughing into the hotel, the duchess, with mind intent on a cigarette, slipped out of another door and hurried as fast as her outrageous heels would allow her to a seat under the date-palms.

She took a Three Castles from the jewelled Louis XV snuff-box, rasped a match on the sole of one little crimson shoe, lit her cigarette, and studied the slipper.

Then she turned her head and saw a man, an Arab, standing beside the seat.

There had been no sound; just out of the dark he had suddenly materialised in the startling, silent way of the East.

Well does it behove us to remember that we have claimed the privilege of giving lessons in morality, culture, good-breeding, manners, in fact, in one word, civilisation to the world at large.

In the glaring sun of an Eastern mid-day you can sit with your feet figuratively or literally on the table, if it pleases you; it will but be accounted as one more eccentricity unto you; but in the shadows, an' you would retain the position of teacher to the world at large, keep the heels on the rail of your chair; for there are ears and eyes a-many in the shadows and behind the silken curtain.

But it took a good deal more than the sudden appearance of a native to make the old lady start.

She put out her cigarette with the toe of a red shoe, took another from the snuff-box, rasped a match—not on the sole of her foot this time—lit the fragrant weed and looked at the man, who salaamed.

"Yes?" she said courteously.

"I am the fortune-teller, great lady. In the sand, by the stars, or the lines of your jewelled hand, if in your graciousness you will permit me, I will tell you your future."

"My son, behold. I am near the sunset, the moment approaches when my tired feet will advance still further upon the bridge which leadeth me to my God and your God. What is past I know; what is, *is*; what is to be, is so near that, behold, sometimes in the stillness of the night I hear the angels whispering as they take counsel as to the moment when, one shall tap me upon the shoulder, saying, 'Come!'"

He sank to the ground just at her feet and looked up in the splendid old face with an agony of hurt born of misunder-standing in his own, so that, suddenly realising that her refusal had been taken for antipathy, she stretched out her hand, which, having first pulled a corner of his white mantle between, he held upon the back of his own.

"Tell me, then, of those I love."

The fortune-teller looked her straight in the face.

"Thy hands are full of love-flowers, white woman; thy head is crowned with them; thy feet pass upon them; thou art all love. Yea! even though there are many upon the bridge who, having preceded thee, await thy coming, yet art thou surrounded with love. And in the flowers in thy hands is there one which thou cherishest, and for which thou fearest.

"Fear not, wise woman; let thy heart beat tranquilly at dawn, at noon and at the setting of the sun; for it is written that no harm shall befall the flower, no stain shall mark the ivory petals of innocence; no rude hand pluck it before its time. Thou art not the only one to love the flower, wise woman. There is one also who loveth it and watcheth it and will pluck it in due season; there is yet another who loveth and watcheth, but from a great, great distance. If by the grace of Allah, who is God, the flower should be placed even for the passing of an hour within the hands of him who watcheth from afar, I tell thee, for so it is written, fear not, for no harm shall befall the fragrant blossom."

The old woman nodded her head so that the diamond leaves glistened, and smiled gently and lifting her hand pulled aside the corner of the mantle, and laid her hand again on his.

"Nay, touch me not, for fear I shall pollute thee, thou woman of one great race; thou descendant of one unbroken line; thou noble with unblemished shield."

Then she leant right forward, and laid both hands upon his shoulders. "My son, my son, perchance could a very wise, very old woman help thee in thy stress, for behold, she understands all things, having herself passed through the troubled waters of life."

The fortune-teller shook his head as he gripped the little hands upon his shoulders.

"For me there is no help, wise, all-loving woman. But she who loves me, she whom I love and for whom I would die, even breaks her heart through me, her first-born, in my desert home. Her beautiful eyes are full of tears, she lifts not her head, and my father, whom I honour, is far from her in her stress. Perchance in the golden mint of thy heart hast thou a few coins of patience, wisdom and love to spare."

As the old woman got slowly to her feet, the man sprang up beside her.

"My son, though thou drainest a fortune from the mint of Love at dawn, yet is it still there at eventide," she whispered as she raised her jewelled hand to his shoulders and pulled him down towards her. "My son, thou art my son, and I have faith in and a great love for thee and thine."

And she kissed him upon the forehead, whilst the tears stood in her eyes, and turned towards the house, without noticing a man and a woman sitting in the shadows at the far side of the grounds.

For the woman who watched was Zulannah the harlot, who had gained an easy admission under the secrecy of her veils and the potency of backschish.

And as Ben Kelham had sat down, she had crept quietly from behind the palms to stand, a shimmering bundle of silks and satins, in front of the man who looked up in annoyance, and then smiled.

You really couldn't be rude to anything so tantalisingly beautiful, especially when the lady of your choice has just shown a certain lamentable want of appreciation in regard to your person and propositions.

"It's one o'clock, fair lady; you must unmask."

And he uttered a cry of astonishment.

Zulannah had lifted her veil.

And the moments sped as she wove the golden web of beauty and desire and love, into which, however, the clumsy fly refused to be enticed.

But Ben Kelham, for all his slowness, was no fool, and understanding that the woman was offering him something outside her usual wares, and understanding also the danger of rousing the wrath of such a woman, he dealt with the matter as delicately as he could.

"—Come but once to my entertainments," she urged. "My girls shall dance for thee, my animals fight for thee."

The man shuddered, sick to the soul at the thought of the means by which this woman enslaved her suitors.

"Am I not beautiful?" she added.

She made her last bid; she stepped back into the moonlight and unwound her veils from about her, standing, palpitating, trembling under the possession of her strange love.

Beautiful! She was a dream—yet beside her beauty the pure loveliness of Damaris Hethencourt would have shown like the work of an Old Master beside a coarse copy.

But what will you?

Some like the snow-peaks and some the stretching plain; others the turbulent ocean, and yet others the farmyard with its rural sights and sounds. Thank goodness for it! Just imagine the lamentation throughout the world if love, like the *couturiere* set fashions for the seasons!

"Love dictates that women, this season, shall resemble the dazzling peaks of the Himalayas."

And we looking as the majority of us *do* look!

Not that we should really be downhearted about it. Not a bit. Only let the decree go forth, and every one of us, at the end of a week or so, would by hook or by crook have acquired a distinctly peak-like appearance.

But Kelham looked up, looked long, and smiled.

"You *are* beautiful—very beautiful—the most beautiful

woman I have seen—save one."

Zulannah recognised her defeat and in a whirl of rage and scented veils disappeared through the *talik* palms.

And, arrived at her house, she stormed through court and rooms and down to the bottom of the scented garden, leaving a trail of terror-stricken servants lying face downwards in her wake.

She leant over the marble balustrade and looked down into the huge pit with marble walls and sanded floor. All around it were cages in which were confined great beasts; and alcoves in which she and her guests, behind iron bars, would sit, when sated with love and feasting, to watch the animals fight to the death.

Then she ran quickly down the flight of marble steps, and clapped her hands.

From some dark corner a shape came running, ambling like some gigantic ape, maintaining an upright position by means of an occasional thrust at the ground with the knuckles of the left hand. The small eyes in his large head blinked craftily at the beautiful woman—its own mate being well-nigh as simian as itself—; it shuffled on its huge feet and pulled at its gaudy raiment with abnormally long fingers. The monstrosity had been nicknamed "Bes," after the monstrous dwarf god of Ancient Egypt, by someone—the nationality of whom is of no account—who had balanced the ardour of his studies with hours of leisure in the bazaar. The beasts, aroused doubtlessly by the scent of the thing which brought them meat, roared and flung themselves against the bars of the cage.

They were half-starved.

Unlike most of her class, Zulannah was mean. She was a niggard in things which did not concern herself.

So that, to feed his numerous progeny of repulsive simian

shape, the keeper of the cages starved the beasts. Not that Zulannah cared one iota for their hunger or suffering; it made them fight the merrier for a bit of meat.

And she sat in her ebony chair close to the bars, with a brazier beside her, and laughed delightedly as the liberated lion flung itself at the cages in which roared its wretched brethren.

And then the great beast stopped suddenly in the middle of the den, growling softly, snuffing the air. Then, with heartrending roar hurled itself straight at the bars behind which she sat.

Was she afraid? Not one bit. She was behind the bars. She laughed aloud and clapped her hands, standing just out of reach of the paw which tried to reach her.

Back across the sand rushed the animal, and then with all its might crashed against the barrier.

A look of horror swept the woman's face—the middle bar had bent. She sensed her danger, but kept her nerve. Without hesitating, she turned to the brazier at her side, carefully selected a handle well wrapped about, and, turning again swiftly, thrust the red-hot point down the lion's maw.

'Twere best not to describe the rest of the awful scene in which a woman safe behind bars clapped her hands over the pain she had caused.

But is it surprising that Zulannah's enemies were legion?

Joan Conquest

CHAPTER X

"The wind that sighs before the dawn
Chases the gloom of night;
The curtains of the East are drawn
And suddenly—'tis light."

SIR LEWIS MORRIS

The desert stretched before Damaris.

As a lover, clad in golden raiment, in quick pursuit of his love with dusky hair and starry eyes across a field of purple iris, Day flinging wide his arms leaped clear of the horizon which lies like a string across the sandy wastes. Gathering her draperies, hiding her starry jewels in misty scarves, Night fled in seeming fear, leaving behind her a trail of sweet-scented, silver-embroidered purple, grey and saffron garments, which melted in the warmth of love.

But leap he from the horizon ever so quickly, don he his most brilliant armour and pursue he ever so hastily, yet, save for two short hours when he may barely touch her hem, Night stands ever mockingly, beckoning, just out of reach.

O thrice-wise woman! How else would there be pursuit?

And Damaris laughed aloud from sheer content as she touched the coal-black stallion with her heel, and held him, fretting, eager to be away over the sand, to wherever Fate pointed.

Half-believing, half-doubting the words of the fortune-teller, this early morning following hard upon her arrival in Heliopolis she slipped from her room, wakened the astounded night-porter of the Desert Palace Hotel, and demanded a car to be brought upon the instant. And lucky it was for her that she made one of the ducal party, for nothing else would have procured her her heart's desire at that untoward hour before dawn.

With Wellington beside her, she drove hard along the deserted high-road towards the village of Makariyeh where, under a sycamore, 'tis said the Virgin and Child rested on their Flight into Egypt.

The head-lights seemed to hurl the shadows back as she raced down the Sharia el-Misalla towards the ruins of old Heliopolis, which is all that remains of the great seat of learning, the biblical City of On. And the sky lightened way down in the east as she drove along the outer edge of the fort to the Obelisk, known to the Arab as el-Misalla.

And there the words of the fortune-teller came true, for fretting and fuming in an endeavour to unseat his *sayis*, who rode him native-wise, without his feet in the stirrups, rearing and backing at the sound of the engine throbbing in the gloom, was the coal-black stallion of Unayza.

Damaris did not cast a look at the Obelisk. She had eyes only for the beautiful beast which, seemingly, she was to ride on a single rein and a wisp of a saddle. Standing sixteen hands, born of the desert, nervous and self-willed, he was no fit mount for a woman, and a gleam of anxiety flashed across the *sayis's* face as he measured the slender girl with his eye and re-adjusted the stirrup-leather.

"In the name of the hawk-headed Ra-Harakht."

The servant salaamed as he mechanically repeated the uninte-lligible sentence which had been drummed into him by his master; and Damaris smiled and replied in the servant's tongue, to his amazement, and walked up close to el-Sooltan, holding out a flat palm with sugar upon it.

It took some time before he snuffled her hand, and then only by stratagem she mounted, swinging herself in a bound to the saddle as the groom slipped to the ground on the off-side; upon which el-Sooltan wheeled sharply and headed straight for the village of Khankah, which is the outskirt proper of the desert.

For two and a half miles, at a tearing gallop, the girl made no attempt to show any authority. But once on the very edge of the desert she did, for this was the longed-for moment of her life, when alone, free, she should ride out into the unknown; and she had no inclination or intention of being hurled through that moment like a stone from a catapult. Sooltan, behaving like a very demon, tried his best to unseat the light weight upon his back by the simple and usually so effective methods of rearing, plunging and bucking; but Damaris only smiled and shouted as she looked towards the east, caring not a jot for any vagary, so content was she.

But as the sun leapt clear of the horizon, she gave one cry, touched the stallion lightly upon the neck, gave him his head, and was across the desert, unmindful of an Arab who, some distance away, which, in the desert, is really no optical distance at all, headed a grey mare, thoroughbred and of mighty endurance, in the same direction.

Where is there anything to compare to riding across the desert at dawn? At dawn, when to your right and to your left march phalanxes of ghostly shapes, which maybe are the shadows of the night, or maybe, as says the legend, the ghosts of the many long-dead kingdoms buried in oblivion and the relentless sands; when the whistling of the wind is as the shouting of men and the thunder of your horse's hoofs as the rolling of many drums, calling you through the power of past centuries and the ecstasy of the solitude in your heart, out to the mystery of the plains.

Mystery, fascination, spell, lure, call of the desert. All fine words, but hopeless to explain that which has lured more than one white woman out into the golden wilderness to the wrecking of her soul; and which has nothing whatever to do with the pseudo-psychic waves which trick us into such pitiable hysteria and hallucination.

But there is no mystery about that which called Damaris. It was the joy of youth, the salt of novelty, the exhilarating sympathy between horse and rider; she shouted as she seemingly rode straight into the massed colouring of the sunrise; she lifted her face to the golden banners flung across the sky and turned in the saddle and looked back at the hem of Night's garments disappearing down in the west.

She was still a child, for those auxiliaries, Love and Life, had not yet lain hand upon her; they had but pulled aside the veil from before her eyes for one brief second, and she, dazzled by the glimpse, had pulled it back hastily. Neither was there anything to tell her that, upon a not very far distant day, the veil would be torn from her, leaving her to be well-nigh blinded by the radiance of the greatest light in the world.

And she rode carelessly, without a thought to the passing of time or to the ever-increasing speed of el-Sooltan, who was all out in an endeavour to find his stable, also his companions, from whom he had been parted for many weary weeks.

That they happened to be in the Oasis of Khargegh, some few hundred miles down the Nile, he was not to know; he only knew that the desert was his home and that in it and of it was his happiness to be found; and it was only when Damaris turned to look at the ruins of the City of On from a far distance that she discovered that they had disappeared in a mist which was merely the combination of the distance and the waters of the oasis evaporating in the morning sun.

She tried to pull the stallion, gently at first, and then with all her might, but to no purpose; for nothing but the voice of his master or his own particular *sayis* could stop el-Sooltan once he had got the light bit between his teeth; and of the death from thirst which awaited him and his rider upon this particular venture if he continued in his obstinacy he had, of course, no warning.

"What a nuisance," said Damaris, as she looked round the great yellow plain which stretched, a carpet of level sand, to the west and under her horse's feet and broke to the east into a chain of hummocks, piled by the last sandstorm which had caused such devastation in the nomad tribes and such annoyance to the visitors at Heliopolis.

She felt no fear, only an increasing vacuum beneath her waistbelt and distress for the worry her long absence might cause her godmother.

"And Well-Well will have chewed everything chewable in the car, also the legs of the *sayis*, by the time I get back," she exclaimed. "And I can't do anything—I've irrevocably given el-Sooltan his head. It's no use slipping from the saddle, because I couldn't walk back. I can't . . ."

She broke off suddenly, rose in the stirrups and waved. And a more radiant picture of youth you could not have wished to see in a lifetime.

"A village!" she shouted. "Camels, palms, water. An oasis with tents; women and children and men. Come round, Sooltan, come round." And she pulled with all her strength, and still to no avail, for, oblivious of the peaceful, verdant patch, the mighty animal forged ahead.

"Well, I shall have to drop from the saddle, let Sooltan go, and walk over to them. They are sure to be friendly and . . ."

She had just slipped her foot from the stirrup when, clear and insistent, there came a ringing cry.

Some way off, the Hawk of Egypt had followed her from the village of Khankah, with intent, knowing the horse she rode, to watch over but not intrude his presence upon her. He had known for some time that el-Sooltan was out of hand, and had decided to call him after a mile or so more of furious exercise; but, instead, quite suddenly and instinctively, he cried, "*A'ti balak!—a'ti balak!*" which means, "Be careful—be careful," and pulled the mare to a standstill.

He too had seen the mirage of the peaceful oasis, thrown by the atmosphere from a distance of eighty miles, and with his desert-trained eyes had caught the little movement of the foot; and, connecting the two, he insistently called the stallion, knowing that a drop from the saddle at the almost incredible speed at which Sooltan was going might easily result in twisted ankles or even a broken neck.

"*Irja!*" he called. "*Irja!*" Which means, "Come back, come back!" And he called again and again as the stallion dropped from a gallop to a canter, a canter to a trot, then stopped dead; whinnied gently; wheeled sharply and stood stock-still.

"*Irja, Sooltan!*" came the cry. "*Irja Sooltan!*" And with the cry came the neighing of the mare.

The stallion lashed out, reared and stood still, ears pricked, silken mane and tail flying in the wind.

Then *he* answered, until the desert seemed filled with the calling of the noble beasts, as the girl sat with thudding heart and eyes fixed on the distant spot where fretted and fidgeted the mare ridden by the Arab.

Then something within her rebelled at this intrusion upon her privacy, causing her to be suddenly stricken with anger and confusion.

"Take me to the tents, Sooltan!" she cried, turning to look back. "Take—but—why—oh! what an escape—a mirage—a—"

But the rest was lost in the sudden bound of el-Sooltan as he raced in obedience to his master's call.

The man waited until they were within a mile of him; then he wheeled the mare and took her back along her tracks, urging her to her topmost speed. Swiftly she fled and swiftly pursued Sooltan, the man not once turning in his seat.

And as they neared the outskirts of the oasis of Heliopolis Hugh Carden Ali urged the mare so that she gained upon the stallion, and beckoned to his groom, who had run hot-foot from the Obelisk to the edge of the desert with fear in his heart for the beast but not one whit for the girl. And he caught the shouted order as his master passed him at full speed, and ran out, shouting in his turn to the stallion.

El-Sooltan, connecting the *sayis* with the bucketsful of water he stood so badly in need of, stopped short, nearly unseating Damaris with the suddenness of his decision and then with the hand of the groom upon his heaving flank trotted docilely back to the Obelisk, where Wellington, risking curvature of the spine, turned himself into a canine picture of ecstatic welcome.

"To-morrow at the same hour," said Damaris, feeding the stallion with sugar, "he will know me better."

"*Ma sha-Allah!*" murmured the servant to himself, praising the courage of this bit of a woman.

"*Bikhatirkum*," she said gently, as she moved off in the car.

"*Ma'a-s-salamah ya sitti*," answered the delighted, astounded man as he salaamed almost to the ground before such unexpected graciousness.

CHAPTER XI

*"Give me that man that is not passion's slave
and I will wear him in my heart's core. . . ."*

SHAKESPEARE

In his blindness and obstinacy and hurt Ben Kelham carried out his intention and went after lion, the report of which, for all he knew, might have been the outcome of some *fellah's* vision of a tame pussy mixed up with the nocturnal habits of the lion-headed goddess Sekhet, who, so tradition avers, prowls about ruins by the light o' the moon, seeking whom she may devour.

The moon plays havoc with the strongest-minded, out yonder!

Anyway, love-sick, he left Heliopolis, placing the panacea of sport like a poultice upon his hurt.

Shortly after, one day during the noon hours, in the cool shadows of his great palace in Cairo, there came to Hugh Carden Ali an overpowering desire to see the girl he loved amongst her own people.

She was his at dawn in the desert, although miles of sand stretched between them; his in the rush of the wind, the glory of the sky and the thunder of the horses' hoofs; but to whom did she turn at night; in the maze of the dance; the hothouse atmosphere of the hotel; the crush of the winter visitors?

So, giving a twist to the dagger of love in his heart, he tucked the dogs of Billi in beside him and drove as the sun set to Heliopolis, and, guessing that the duchess would have a table near the window, chose one on the opposite side of the dining-room, so that his presence should not be thrust upon the girl or the old woman who had known his mother.

He sat there, indifferent to or oblivious of the interest his presence aroused, unconsciously counting the vertebrae of the lady at the next table, who had evidently forgotten some essential part of her bodice.

He counted the vertebrae in the back of the lady who was dying to turn round, until the duchess and Damaris entered the room; then he clenched his hands under the table with an involuntary shudder of disgust.

It was the first time he had seen the girl he loved in evening dress, and every instinct of the Oriental in him was outraged at the sight of the gleaming neck and shoulders and hint of lace-shrouded virgin form.

She was not in full *decolletage* by any means, but the waiter's sleeve was but an inch from her satin skin when he bent over her, so that, although he had long grown accustomed in Europe to the undraping of woman o' nights, yet, because he loved the beautiful girl, he longed for the right to walk across the room, pick her up in his arms, and, smothering her in a *barku*, hide her forever from all male eyes but his own.

Later, as he sat alone in a far corner of the ball-room, he twisted the dagger of love this way and that in his tormented heart, whilst the dogs of Billi worried the life out of the hall-porter as they fretted and moaned for their master who tarried. He had never danced, himself, loathing the idea of the propinquity of a stranger's body so close to his own; of a stranger's mouth so near his own; of the animal odour of the naked body, which no perfume can hide, within his nostrils; just as he loathed the idea of a woman passing from one man's arms to another's throughout the best part of a night.

He had no desire whatever to dance with Damaris, but all the Eastern in him longed to make her dance for him; in the desert for preference; under the light of the moon; with the insistent throbbing of the drum keeping time to the rhythm of the slender feet upon the warm sand.

And he sat and dreamed under the palms, taking no heed of the sudden cessation of music, the gathering of the dancers against the walls; the half-suppressed, laughter and moistening of lip with furtive tongue and the unusual feeling of expectancy in the heavy, perfumed air.

But he came back to earth when from some corner of the room there came the faint tapping of a drum.

Three times there fell a single beat, then a gentle roll and a single beat, bringing him to his feet as he recognised the measure, just as the lights were switched off, excepting for one great beam which, striking down from some device in the ceiling, made a silvery pool in the middle of the floor.

"No!" he cried from the shadows, "this must not be. It is not seemly for the eyes of women."

But the answer to this protest came in little jeering laughs and quick remonstrance from those who feared that the whetting of their appetites should be snatched from them, and a sigh of satisfaction went up when, from the shadows, there sprang an Arabian youth, beautiful as a god, supple as a snake, quick upon his feet as any fighting stallion.

He stood for a second with arms outflung to the men and women he knew were watching his every movement outside the radius of the light, and then he sprang back with that marvellous leap which is the gift of some Arabian male dancers.

Ah me! you talk in pharisaic whispers of the Nautch girl; in righteous anger against the dainty geisha; in horror of the weaving Salomes as known in Western cities; wait, however, before you pour the last drop from your vials of wrath and indignation until you have seen an Arab dance "*al-fajr*" which, being translated, means the dawn. You can put what interpretation you like upon it: the dawn of day, or love, anything will do, but you most certainly ought not to watch it.

If, however, you persist in so doing, you should blush to the roots of your hair—you will not, because it will be the perfect poetry of motion you will be witnessing; also ought you, after the third movement, to turn your back or flee the room—you will not, again, because of the mocking sensuality which will keep you rooted where you stand; again, you ought to stuff your ears against the throbbing of the drum—but that will you not do because of the words of love which fall, seemingly reft from the dancer's lips in the rapture of his movements. It is the last word in sensual ecstasy, and should be prohibited for public exhibition to Europeans, yet it is quite impossible to point at any one movement and label it as the cause of the tumult within you.

But Hugh Carden Ali, standing under a palm, turned quickly when a little sound of distress caught his ear, and put out his hand and pulled the girl he had recognised in the dark by her perfume towards him, so that the back of her head rested against his arm; and sensing her nausea at the sight from which she had been trying to fly, and knowing the sheer impossibility of keeping the eyes shut in a theatre, he pulled his hand-kerchief from his sleeve and placed it across her eyes.

Save for the back of her head resting just below his shoulder he did not touch her, and if he bent his head so that the perfumed riot of her curls swept his cheek, should it count as a grievous sin against him?

The stone beside each of us is quite likely to lie untouched throughout our span of three-score plus ten.

At the last beat of the drum and just before the lights were switched on, Damaris was alone, with a silken handkerchief in her hand, in one corner of which, as she discovered later, was embroidered the Hawk of Old Egypt.

CHAPTER XII

". . . Hither and thither moves, and mates, and slays,
And one by one back in the Closet lays."

OMAR KHAYYAM

Hugh Carden Ali, with the dogs of Billi crushed in beside him, raced back to his palace in Cairo and with the shaggy pair at his heels passed to his side of the great house. His body-servant, as nimble as a monkey, as devoted as a dog, and almost dumb by reason of a tongue split in his youth for misdemeanour, fell on his knees at his feet.

He worshipped his young master, who had one time rescued him from a savage, baiting crowd in the bazaar and taking him into his service had made him his own particular servant; he equally loathed his master's austere bedroom and adjoining dressing-room, with simple furniture which had lately come from *Bilid el-Ingliz*, a dark, cold country across the sea, where it rains without ceasing. And he helped strip his master of the hateful, tight, hot European clothes and trotted joyfully after him to the swimming-bath, and watched him dive in and swim the length and climb out the other end, and disappear between curtains into the luxurious rooms of the East.

Having robed him, agog with curiosity and at a discreet distance, he followed the resplendent figure in his satin raiment, snow-white turban glistening with jewels and hooded falcon on wrist, and cursed the dogs under his breath when they turned and growled softly. But his curiosity was turned to a great amazement when his master passed into the court of the empty, luxuriant, perfumed harem, where once had loved and quarrelled, idled and fought, so many beautiful women.

Under the orders of the Ethiopian eunuch, giant twin of Qatim, in the service of Zulannah the courtesan, the harem was kept swept and garnished, adorned with flowers, aglow at nights with a myriad soft lights hanging from the ceiling in jewelled lamps, to which were flung the fountain's perfumed drops, to fall and break on marble floor and silken cushion, inlaid table and bright-hued birds in jewelled cage.

There does exist a different kind of harem—dirty, gaudy, ill-kempt—somewhat like the inmates—over the whole of which 'tis wise to draw a veil.

The eunuch's bankings-account—which was kept in a certain secret nook of the harem court—had become sadly depleted on account of his master's eccentric views as regarded women, but he still lived in hope, and, delighting in intrigue, as every native does, had welcomed the advent of his ebony brother primed with gossip and suggestion.

Therefore, upon the beating of the gong which had not been struck for many weary moons, he hastened to the court and salaamed to the ground before his master, who sat upon a pile of cushions, guarded by the two shaggy dogs of Billi, with the amber mouthpiece of the jewel-encrusted *nargileh* between his lips and the falcon upon a padded perch beside him.

"Bring me a woman—to dance," he curtly ordered, and the slave sped to do his bidding, with visions of a big increase in the banking-account hidden in a secret place.

And when the dancer drifted in like a flower-petal upon a breeze, Hugh Carden Ali looked up slowly, letting escape a wisp of smoke from between his lips.

The dancer wore one single garment of transparent black, hung from the shoulders by diamond bands and through which her perfectly nude body shone like an ivory pillar; her slender feet with crimsoned toes and heels were bare; the tiny hands ablaze with jewels; a huge bunch of orange-tinted diamond-sprinkled osprey was fastened in her jet-black hair; across her face there hung a short, almost transparent veil, one corner of which she held between her teeth, leaving to view the wonderful eyes, a heaven or hell of invitation—as you will.

She danced as had danced her Biblical sister to the pleasing of a king for the attainment of her desire; and she danced humming a little tune behind the veil until the movement of her beautiful body and the knowledge of a man's eyes upon her went to her head like wine, so that in the end, by force of habit maybe, she danced to conquer where she had only intended to interest.

As already mentioned, she had the morals of a jackal.

She drifted down the court towards Hugh Carden Ali and, standing before him, bowed her beautiful head to the level of her dimpled knees, laughed gently, and was gone like a bird to a far corner of the court.

She seemed to swing in the air like a lime flower caught on the end of a spider's thread, as she came slowly down once more; to be blown hither and thither like a leaf before the gale as she ran here, sprang there, to the rhythm of the little tune she hummed behind the wisp of veil; to undulate, like a field of ripe wheat beneath the summer sun as she stood quite near the man who watched her with a fraction of the interest he would have shown in the purchase of a dog or falcon in the open mart.

Her henna'd toes pressed firmly on the centre of a Persian rug of such antiquity as to render the pattern indecipherable; she moved her body from the slender waist downward not at all; the muscles of her arms and shoulders rippled, and her head moved, slightly but unceasingly from side to side.

How often one hears of the European's boredom whilst watching the Nautch Dance in which the Indian Nautch girl, fully clothed, indeed in high tight bodice and ankle-length, voluminous skirt, will drive her native audience clean crazy with the tapping of her feet and slight, undulating movements of the slender body and rod-like arms. It is indeed the dullest thing on earth to watch if you are unable to follow and *interpret* every little movement. But if you can—well! the unexpurgated version of the Arabian Nights will be as milk-and-water compared to the heady brew offered for your consumption. And the old Harrovian sitting cross-legged, upon a heap of cushions, with the smoke of the *nargileh*, drifting from between his lips, smiled as he picked up the thread of the same old story which had been spun for him when, an arrogant youth of twelve summers, he had ruled his house with no gentle hand.

Otherwise he showed little interest and felt no desire to lift the tantalising veil; neither did he turn his head, else might he have seen the ebony face of the Ethiopian eunuch peering from between a mass of flowers, from which point of vantage he watched the scene with intent to report thereon to his black twin-brother.

At last, and very slowly, and with a growing feeling of resentment in the place where her heart by rights should have been, Zulannah sped down the court upon her toes and fell at the edge of the piled cushions, causing the dogs to growl softly at her daring.

"Thou art a beautiful dancer, woman," said Hugh Carden Ali, making no movement to lift the veil. "Behold, I have passed a pleasant hour and would reward thee. What thou wilt. Money—jewels?—speak."

From behind the wisp of veil which fluttered in the dancer's quick breathing came the barely whispered answer.

"I hear thee not, woman; raise thy voice and be not afraid. I will give thee what thou desirest."

"One hour!"

The man bent forward to catch the words, and when their full import struck him, leapt to his feet and catching the woman's wrist jerked her upright, ripping the veil from before her face.

"*Zulannah!*" he cried, and sprang back, having heard of the lady's deft handling of her dagger when in the tantrums. Then he caught both wrists and held her pinioned, looking with loathing into the exquisite, furious face, whilst the great dogs, fangs bared, ruffs upstanding, sniffed suspiciously at the knees and waist, even rising on their hind-legs to snuff the slender neck of this woman who had angered their master.

For a second he held her with arms stretched to breaking-point and henna'd toes barely touching the ground, then threw her across the cushions, whilst the dogs growled softly as they prowled, belly to ground, about the prostrate figure and the ebony-hued eunuch tore at his woolly hirsute covering amongst the flowers.

But courtesans have tears as well as other kinds of women, and they use them every whit as effectively, perhaps a bit better, on account of the stoutness of their hearts.

So that when the man ordered the woman to sit up, she sat up, wiped real tears from the innocent-looking eyes, re-arranged her garments, and prepared for battle.

Tough might describe the rose-hued, satin-textured epidermis of the scarlet enchantress.

"Thou hast a great daring, woman."

The courtesan knew not the meaning of the word hesitation, and was off with the still-born desire and on with her original business between the tossing and falling of a drop from the perfumed fountain and ready with an explanation even before the man spoke.

"Thou hast misheard my words, lord. Knowing by hearsay of thy hatred of women, I entered thy house as dancer before thee, to gain as my reward one hour of speech with thee."

"Speech? Wherefore?

"Because I would help thee, and in helping thee help myself." Clasping her slender jewelled hands, across her bosom, she looked up to the gilded ceiling, and sighing softly, whispered:

"I love!"

"*Thou!*"

"Yea, lord. I love—and—thou lovest—and—nay, hear me, it is for thy advancement—and mine—and he, the man for whom my soul has turned to water, for whom I yearn—yea, if it be but for one single hour of his love—a memory of rose-time in the ash-pit of my years—he—" She stopped.

'Tis wise to approach a wounded tiger warily, especially if you are not certain as to the extent of the hurt or the power of the weapon of defence in your hand.

"Sit—and speak quickly, for I would have thee gone."

The man spoke curtly as he sank upon a pile of cushions and pointed to one on the far side of the Persian rug, upon which the most courted woman in Egypt knelt, with her eyes full of gentleness and her heart pounding in a torment of rage and fear.

"Yea, I understand."

Hugh Carden Ali spoke wearily, being stricken with love. For ten solid minutes the woman had talked round her subject. Intuitive, she scented danger; usually fearless, her whole being was sick with apprehension; desperate, she dug her nails into her flesh and essayed to reach her goal by a roundabout way.

Then she stopped, sighed, and cast down her eyes; then raised them beseechingly when the man spoke.

"Fearing to use force against the—the woman who thou sayest is loved by the man thou lovest—and may the prophet bear witness that thy tale is as full of turnings and twistings as the paths in the bazaar in which thou spinn'st thy web—thou would'st tear her from him by craft. Explain thy seemingly futile words, and hasten thy lying tongue, for behold the hour of dawn approacheth."

And the wrath in the voice was such as to hurl the woman pell-mell over the cliff of discretion down into the depths of her own undoing.

"She, the white woman, walks in the bazaar, yea, even at noon and at sunset. Perchance one evening, lured by the tale of the riches of the house of Zulannah, might not her feet stray within the portals at the setting of the sun. And behold, the key of the great door is within these hands, and—and—"

The man's hands lay quietly on his knees as he leant forward, and the shadow thrown by the flowering plants hid the twin pools of murder in the depths of his eyes.

"And—?" he whispered.

"And—" she whispered back, "would the white man, thinkest thou, take to wife her who had passed a night in the house of the courtesan? Would he not, without waiting for explanation, throw her into the filth of the bazaar, leaving her for the first comer to pick up, and turn himself to—"

She leapt to her feet, screaming, as his fingers closed round her wrist in a grip of steel; mad with fury, she tore her raiment and hair, raving obscenities in the vilest language of the lowest reaches of the bazaar, oblivious of the dogs which reared and fell and reared unceasingly behind her.

"The white woman who trapeses the bazaar unveiled," she screamed. "The white virgin who flung herself into thy arms, in the market-place, thou trafficker in foreign harlots, the—"

Hugh Carden Ali, the son of his father to the inner-most part of his being in the horrible scene, had made one little sign, and the dogs were upon her.

With a sickening scrunch one caught the side of her head in the steel jaws which stretched from the nape of the neck to the corner of the mouth; with a sharp snap the other drove its fangs into the muscle behind the dimpled knee.

They pulled her down and stood stock-still, as these dogs are trained to do; then with crimson saliva dripping from the jaws, crimson lights shining in the eyes, let go their hold and stood looking alternately from master to quarry, with slowly wagging tails.

There was no sign of anger in the man as he sat tranquilly upon the cushions, the amber mouthpiece of the *nargileh* between his lips; no sound of wrath in the gentle voice which bid the Ethiopian eunuch to remain prostrated upon the floor, until the arrival of the other slaves, who could be heard pelting through the house from every direction in answer to the summons of the gong.

"Idrabuh," he said quietly to four of the terror-stricken domestic staff, pointing to the eunuch. "Upon the soles of the feet so that he walketh not for many a day—if ever." And as the wretch was dragged screaming from the room, he beckoned to four others, and pointed to the body of the woman. "Carry that out and throw it in the street, in such wise that it is not known from whence it came. Touch not the jewels, lest thou sharest thy brother's fate."

With falcon upon wrist and blood-stained dogs at his heels, he passed out of the ill-fated court to his own apartment, and, having bathed and dressed himself, to his body-servant's grief, in hot, European riding-kit, with boots from Peter Yapp, tucked the cleansed dogs of Billi in beside him, and raced his car to the Obelisk which is all that remains upright of the Biblical City of On.

* * * * * *

The Ethiopian slave Qatim gathered up the broken body of the woman from the filth of the gutter and carried her to his hovel and flung her upon the filthy straw under which he hid the jewels he stripped from her.

CHAPTER XIII

"Best springs from strife and dissonant chords beget
Divinest harmonies."

SIR LEWIS MORRIS

As the sky lightened way down in the east and the faithful turned to prayer, the little old lady sat at her window, taking her hour of rest—her hour of understanding—with hands clasped peacefully in her lap, a little smile at the corner of her whimsical mouth and her snow-white hair fluttered by the breeze of dawn.

Bodily, mentally, spiritually, she was resting, having filched this hour in which, before donning the garish trappings of her toilet, to sit in fine cashmere night attire, covered in camel's-hair wrap as soft as satin, with her little crimson bed-room slippers peeping from under the hem and her snow-white hair confined by priceless lace; just as she had thrown aside the thoughts and worries which are the outcome of the turmoil and unrest of civilisation, to sit awhile, quietly, with her eyes upon the dazzling peaks which show so clearly when we push aside the nightmare fog we have wrapped about ourselves.

Not for her own relief did she sit at rest, for in that way rest does not come to us; but to the relieving of others by withdrawing from the lights and noises of this tumultuous planet and so obtaining a better perspective of things as they

Joan Conquest

stand spiritually, and a clearer insight into the message of the only book she considered worth studying and committing to memory.

She was no great thinker, this little old lady, neither did she store up the printed thoughts of others to repeat them aptly upon fitting occasions; she invariably mixed up the philosophers and their works; 'osophies simply bewildered her; ritual left her cold, psychology troubled her but little, save only in its practical application to the lives of those she loved. But she knew the book of life, with its tragedies and comedies, humour and crass stupidity, nettles and balm from the first chapter to the last, and could prescribe you a remedy to cure your mental hurt just as easily as she could undress your screaming baby, find the criminal pin and re-dress it for you; and every member of every Church and every disciple of every creed could have fought a pitched battle at her feet and left her unmoved, so long as the sick and sinning crept to her for help and children, rich or poor, in silks or rags, rushed at her coming to cling about her knees.

She had no fixed time for her hour of understanding. At her window in moonlight, starlight or the coming of the dawn; in her gilded armchair in the firelight or the light of the sun; in her rose-garden, in her parks, anywhere, as long as she was withdrawn from noise and strife.

Not that she did not thoroughly enjoy going out to battle upon the most mundane of material planes. A born fighter, she would plunge into the strife for the sheer love of fighting and would take the bull by the horns or the man by the scruff of his neck and lay about her right heartily with her stout ebony stick backed by verbal blows from her vitriolic tongue.

Well, if we all rested for one hour, even for one minute, out of the twenty-four during the frantic passing of modern days, what a boon we should grant our neighbours!

And as the duchess sat quietly, with Dekko the parrot fast

asleep upon the back of her chair, as becomes a well-conducted bird, Fate crept up behind and dropped the black thread of hate and the purple thread of grief amongst the others she had tossed into the old lady's lap.

She suddenly sat upright with a shiver.

Qatim the Ethiopian lifted the body of a woman from out the gutter, and the messenger from the Oasis of Khargegh strode through the gateway of the hotel and kicked the somnolent *ghafir* or watchman, who coughed discreetly behind the sleeping night-porter's back.

And when Hobson, some time later, entered the bedroom with her grace's early cup of tea, which included an egg and fruit, she said nothing of the terrible story which had run like wildfire through the servants' quarters and had turned her cold with horror.

Hobson was an autocrat in her own domain and ruled with a cast-iron rod.

"Don't you utter one word of this disgusting tale to her grace," she had said fiercely as she had sailed through the door of the ladies-maids' room, held meekly open for her by one of the under-maids, who had been caught gossiping, "or back you go to England, both of you." She turned back into the room and rattled the tray to emphasise her orders. "I won't have my lady troubled with it, d'you hear? Common circus trash! what has it got to do with you, I should like to know, if she's been killed or not? That's what they all come to, as you'll find out, if you don't take care."

She had swept from the room leaving the plump, rosy-cheeked Devonshire lasses trembling.

Many, many years ago the duchess had taken the bright, intelligent daughter of a Devonshire farmer on the estate into her service; trained her and promoted her as her seniors in the lady's service had married or been pensioned off, until she had finally risen to the post of head maid and confidential companion.

Love and marriage had passed Maria Hobson by, but she adored her mistress and constituted herself as dragon, sheepdog and buffer, so as to save her from unpleasantness or pain; at the same time issuing orders as to health and hours which her grace usually meekly obeyed—though you would not have taken a bet upon it with any feeling of security.

It is curious, the ascendancy which such a type of maid can obtain over a strong-willed mistress. Think of Abigail Hill and the influence she had over Queen Anne, which finally ousted the great Sarah Jennings, Duchess of Marlborough, brought disturbance into English politics and ruin to the fortune of the Jacobites.

But at times there was a look in her mistress' eyes and a certain atmosphere radiating from the frail little person before which Hobson quailed, so that she said quite gently, "Tea and one letter, your grace," when she found her sitting at the open window, looking out at the morning sky.

But although she spoke gently and tucked an extra shawl about the bent shoulders with a tender hand, she was thinking viciously all the same over her mistresses leniency towards her god-daughter.

"I wish the young lady could be safely married to that proper English gentleman. One can see he wants her, but she doesn't seem to know her own mind. Too pleased by half she is, to my thinking, with this country and the silly nonsense of their nasty, heathen ways!"

And she left the room with a swish of starched petticoat, when Damaris, who had just returned from her desert ride, entered to greet her godmother.

She knelt at the side of the chair and, encircling her in her strong young arms, laid her cheek against the old lady's, and knelt without movement, looking out to the desert, whilst one wrinkled old hand stroked her head and the other turned the pages of the letter.

A piteous letter of appeal from a woman whose love had brought forth the bitterest of bitter fruit.

". . . *Is* there a way out, Petite *Maman*?" wrote Jill, the English wife of Hahmed Sheikh el-Umbar. "Will you undertake the long journey and come and see me, for who knows if together we could not find a way to ensure my boy's happiness? I would come to you, only Hugh is near you, and our men in the East tolerate no interference from their women-folk. My messenger will wait for your answer. I am overwhelmed with foreboding for Hugh my first-born. If you can, come to me. JILL."

And as the sun rose the old lady still sat near the window, trying to come to a decision.

Could she turn a deaf ear to the woman she had known as a girl almost twenty-five years ago? Could she, on the other hand, go to her and risk leaving the girl at her side exposed to the indescribable appeal of the East? Should she send her back to England, or take her as far as Luxor and leave her there under the social wing of Lady Thistleton?

"Have you learned any more about the Arab who follows at a distance when you ride in the morning, dear?"

Damaris nodded.

It seemed she had overheard Lady Thistleton talking about him; his palaces in the desert and at Cairo; his stables and falcons.

The girl stopped for a moment, then continued:

"He has an English name and seems to be a millionaire, and something else which I could not catch, but by the sound of the Prickly-Thistleton's voice it seemed to be something awful!"

"This"—the old lady touched the letter in her lap—"this is from his, mother, dear, asking me to go and see her. If I do, I will tell you the whole story when I come back. Don't ask me anything until then, dear."

Silence fell between them as the hotel woke to another sunlit day.

"Something will happen to decide me," mused the old lady as, a little later, she took her mail from Hobson, who moved majestically about the room with bath-salts and towels. "From Ben," she continued, flicking a lightning glance at the face which, went suddenly rosy pink as it rested against her knee. "Written from the Oasis of Kurkur near the First Cataract. He hasn't seen lion yet, but has heard a lot about the one which is causing a panic amongst the dragomen in Luxor. Oh! how nice for him! Do you remember fat Sybil Sidmouth, the crack shot?"

It seemed that jolly Sybil Sidmouth, well known at Bisley and who had brought a thin stepmother devastated with nerves to winter in Luxor, had also fallen a victim to lion gossip, and had wired a bet to Ben Kelham that she would bring in the lion's skin.

"They are meeting at Assouan to discuss plans . . ."

"Yes?" said Damaris indifferently, and added vindictively, "Knocking about in the desert might reduce her a bit," and gave no thought to the moment of that very morning when, under some uncontrollable impulse, she had turned the stallion Sooltan and taken him back at full gallop and to within a few yards of the Arab who, in European riding-kit and boots from Peter Yapp, had raised his right hand as she had thundered past standing in her stirrups.

A woman could keep a poultry-farm till the last trump, and even then never awake to the fact that the same brand of corn is appreciated both by the goose and the gander!

And, sure enough, something happened to decide her grace before the setting of the sun.

CHAPTER XIV

"Oh! for a falconer's voice to lure
This tassel gentle back again."

SHAKESPEARE

Lunch, desultory shopping and tea with friends in Cairo had been the order of the afternoon following the dawn which had found her grace at the window trying to come to a decision about her god-daughter. They were just returning from these festivities and were negotiating the last cross-roads of the Sharia Abbas when a native policeman, waving his arm like a semaphore, stepped into the slowly-moving stream of traffic.

Resulted the usual maelstrom of motors, native vehicles, stray animals and trams, in which tossed the native pedestrian as, agile and vociferous, he slipped in and out of the block, calling loudly upon Allah in his extremity.

"A native wedding, or something," said Damaris, who was driving. "What fun!" then blushed divinely pink.

There was one gorgeous mounted figure in the laughing, happy, tumultuous crowd which came whirling across the road kept clear for it by the police.

Hugh Carden Ali had gone a-hawking in a certain part of the desert near the ancient City of On, where gazelle is sometimes seen and birds are plentiful.

Clad in orange satin a-shine with jewels, with tight-fitting Eastern trousers ending in perfect riding-boots, with diamond osprey glittering in the white turban and falcon, with jesse to match the orange coat, on gauntleted wrist, he rode serenely in the cheering throng.

His falconers with their underlings walked on either side of the roan, which fretted and fidgeted at the slowness of the pace; the dogs of Billi walked sedately and by themselves; grooms of the kennels led greyhounds on the leash; behind them, almost bursting with importance, came a Persian deftly carrying the cadge, which is a kind of padded stand upon which, hooded and fastened by leashes, the favourite birds are carried to and fro.

At the rear was the birds' van, in which are carted the birds which may or may not be required, also spare parts of the paraphernalia upon which depends the success of this sport, the sport, in truth, of kings! In the "days that are past" the favourite sport of our own monarchs, especially in the "spacious days of great Elizabeth."

The bag was good considering the district, the poles on the servants' shoulders bending under the weight of two gazelle and countless birds of all sizes and plumage.

A couple of *siyas* waving the customary horsehair fly-whisk ran shouting before their master; servants surrounded the cortege, armed with sticks which they rattled with good effect upon the shins of the more venturesome among the spectators as the procession moved slowly, as move all things in the East.

Shouting fiercely, the *siyas* stopped suddenly in front of her grace's car, arms uplifted, mouths open, then turned in their tracks and sped back to the master who had called them.

The old lady and the girl beside her interchanged never a word as they watched Hugh Carden Ali urge the mare who picked a dainty path through the wondering crowds which opened a way before her. The sun caught the jewels on the man's breast and above his turban and upon the saddle-cloth of the roan mare, and struck fiercely slantwise into the proud, handsome face with the set mouth and the eyes which never once looked in the Englishwomen's direction.

For a full minute he sat immovable, whilst the mare, freed from the fret of the crowd, stood stock-still. In his bearing, in the magnificent picture he made under the flaming skies, there seemed a subtle challenge to the two Englishwomen. All his English nature rose in revolt against the barriers that rose between himself and Damaris, daughter of his mother's race; but, curbing his passion with the self-control he had learned in British fields of sport, he remembered that he belonged primarily to his father's land, whose people had three thousand years before held the keys of civilisation in their powerful hands, whilst the people of his mother's land were just about emerging from the primitiveness of the Stone Age.

"*I am the East!*" he seemed to cry in his utter immobility.

Then he turned, beckoned, and gave a sharp order to the bewildered policeman, who salaamed almost to the ground.

Hugh Carden Ali bowed, to the saddle, as the great car shot smoothly forward. There was a smile of welcome on the face of the old woman who had loved his mother; a whole world of welcome in the outstretched hand and a little feeling of thankfulness in her heart; that at last she might get to know the man in time, and, with him, go to visit his mother, or, better still, win his confidence, heal his hurt, and so obviate the tedious journey.

But there was to be no drawing together of the man's wound with the silken threads of sympathy.

He sat like a statue, with his left hand raised in salute,[1] until the Englishwomen had passed; then, throwing his falcon, he watched the confused bird's flight in search of the quarry which was not there.

"Cry aloud to Ali the worker of wonders,
From Him thou wilt find help from trouble."

He quoted the first two lines from the *Ned'i Ali*, the formula used in the East when trouble threatens a falcon, and, touching the mare, passed down the Sharia Abbas, whilst the old lady, going in the opposite direction, came to a sudden decision.

[1]In the East the falcon is carried on the right hand.

CHAPTER XV

"When he is best he is little worse than a man;
and when he is worst, he is little better than a beast."

SHAKESPEARE

Even as the frail little old lady sat quietly looking out at the coming of the dawn, Qatim the Ethiopian sat looking with pride round his transformed hovel in the back reaches of the bazaar. Having gathered Zulannah from the gutter where she had been thrown after the dogs had pulled her down, he carried her to his hovel and, believing her to be dead, flung her body on the heap of filthy straw which served him as couch, and then stole back—in fact, six times he made the journey—to the courtesan's great house. He did not argue with himself, he had no theories and most certainly no moral standards: the woman was dead; there were certain things, beautiful, gaudy, glittering things in her house which his heart had always coveted, which had made his fingers to itch and his mouth to water; brute instinct told him to seize the bones before the other dogs fell upon them; and he obeyed the brutish impulse.

Hundreds of soft silken gowns; cushions of every hue; the great crimson cover from off the divan—all of these he made into a huge bundle which he carried to his den. The gold and jewelled toilet accessories, the silver basin and ewer, just because they glittered, he tied in a pair of emerald green satin curtains; various strange knives and things with prongs, with which on certain occasions the courtesan had conveyed food to her mouth—she used her fingers in private—with a jewel-encrusted *nargileh* of marvellous workmanship, he rolled up in a bright yellow and green Kidderminster carpet.

On his fifth journey he carried a small Milner safe upon his back, letting it drop gently upon the hovel floor without the slightest acceleration in his breathing. For five minutes he played with the knob, like a huge monkey, then grinned, rubbed his chest and bull-neck with straw, and padded off again down the circuitous streets at a gentle trot.

He looked at the sky and at the closed doors and windows of the packed houses, and grinned again. He could not tell the hour by a clock, but he knew to a second when the first of the seething mass of humans asleep on the beds and floors and stairs of the packed houses would yawn, rub the sleep from their eyes and stumble, shivering, into the street. He had still his greatest treasure to bring, and had no wish to be caught with it on his back; not because of the criminality of his proceedings—that never once entered his thick skull—but because he was scared of having the mirror reft from him. He was almost devoid of brain, but had a certain animal instinct which served him in good stead and which, in this instance, urged him to keep his part in the history of the past evening to himself. He picked up the full-length mirror as though it had been a small picture, and stood for an instant grinning cheerfully, looking round the room in which his mistress had so often kicked and threatened him.

Then he gave a little click at the back of his throat, placed the mirror on the floor and stole across the Persian carpet of an unknown antiquity and value to a painted deal writing desk which had once reposed in a shop window in Westbourne Grove; and which, on account of its little drawers and little cupboards with painted doors, had given intense joy to the woman whose wealth in hard cash in the bank and jewels in the safe was almost incredible. He lifted the slanting lid, moved a bundle of papers fastened by an elastic band, and pulled out a drawer out of which be took a cheque-book.

He had no idea of the real use of the book with the buff cover and pale pink leaves, but he knew that you had only to make certain black marks on one of the pink leaves and take it to the big house in the Sharia Clot Bey with its fierce man standing in front of the door and money would be given in exchange.

On account of his cunning, his stolidity, his mighty muscle and ferocious appearance Qatim had been made bank-messenger in chief to the House of Zulannah, and had often stood at his mistress's side when she had taken the cheque-book from the drawer and made strange black marks on one of the pink leaves. True, he had rolled his eyes and shown his teeth fiercely many a time at the interpreter who had had to be called to explain that, although he had handed a pink leaf through the bars, there was no money forthcoming; but as his mistress had not struck him for returning empty-handed he had resigned himself at last to the strangeness of the proceedings. The book meant money, that was all he knew; so he slipped it into his loin-cloth as had been his rather distressing habit when handed a bundle of notes by the bank-clerk who, with his co-workers, had never tired of gazing at the gigantic creature in white shorts, crimson tunic, huge turban and rattling scimitar.

He gave no thought to the dead body on the filthy straw; that he knew he could carry under his arm and drop into the Nile when the bazaar slept; but he pulled hard at his curly hair as a plan germinated in the sluggish convolutions of his brain.

It was a very vague and a very childlike plan, but too much could not be expected from one who had been conceived, born and bred on the animal plane.

After an hour's pondering it, however, took a fairly definite outline.

When the sun had warmed the cool wind of night he would

hide the body under the straw and visit his eunuch twin, who had really been the cause of the disaster. His silence would have to be bought. Of course it would have been better to have broken his neck at once, but it was too late now, so there was no use in worrying! Then he would go terrorise the servants, giving them to understand that he had been left in charge in his mistress's absence; he would remain in charge until he had acquired enough money to buy the coal-black little Venus who worked in the Shoemakers Bazaar; after that he would creep away with her and return to his own village further down the Nile.

And because, perhaps, of the childishness of the plan it succeeded up to a certain point.

He found his eunuch brother, who was the only one besides his master and himself to know that the dancer had been Zulannah, in the grip of such terror and physical pain as to be almost imbecile, though a look of cunning had shone for a moment in his bloodshot eyes when Qatim had inadvertently let drop a hint as to the accumulated riches in his hovel.

Anyway, they came to an understanding which ensured the eunuch's silence at the price of so much good money, paid in instalments.

Qatim had no intention of holding to his side of the agreement, nor his brother to his—as is the way of such breed of Oriental.

Then, just as he was, clad only in loin-cloth and with whip in hand, the gigantic brute strode to the House of Zulannah. Ensued a turbulent hour, at the end of which he remained acknowledged master of the house and inmates until the return of the mistress, whilst those who had mocked him went in search of cool leaves to place upon the bruised portion of their backs and those two whose heads he had cracked together for having resisted him lay quite still.

Returned to the hovel as the sun was sinking, and in high fettle, he donned red tunic, huge turban and rattling scimitar and strutted with all the negro's delight in fine feathers in front of the mirror which rested against the crumbling plaster walls.

And then he suddenly stopped and stared into the glass.

The filthy straw in the corner of the room had moved. His face went grey; great beads of sweat showed upon his chest, his knees shook, then he fell on his face and covered his head with a corner of the green-yellow Kidderminster carpet, when a voice feebly craved for water and a small blood-stained hand weakly pulled at the straw.

Zulannah was not dead.

He lay terror-stricken for some long time, then slowly got to his knees, tore off the fine feathers and flung the scimitar into a far corner; then, naked save for the loin-cloth, sat down with his back to the straw and pulled at his curly oiled hair, a sure sign in him of deep thought.

Then he grinned and, rising, walked across the floor, and, sitting down again, pulled the woman from under the straw.

No! Zulannah was not dead, nor even fatally hurt, but she was horrible to look upon when the Ethiopian had washed her clean by means of a handful of straw dipped in a broken pitcher of water.

The dog's great fangs had driven behind the ear, severing the mastoid nerve so that the mouth was pulled right up the left side of the face; it had also injured the muscle controlling the eyelid, causing it to droop and giving a diabolical leer to the once beautiful doe-like eye; it had also injured the muscle of the neck so that the head was slightly twisted; but, worst of all, the other dog had driven its terrible fangs into the muscle above the knees, injuring it so that she would never walk straight again.

And Qatim sat back on his haunches, and laughed, clapping his enormous hands.

She was not dead, and her hands were not injured, but she was too hideous to show herself unveiled and too twisted to be recognised in the street.

So all that was left to him to do was to cure her injuries—which he did, and quickly, under the advice of an old herbalist in the Silk Market,—and then sit down for the rest of his life whilst she drew strange little marks on those pale pink leaves.

CHAPTER XVI

"My faint spirit was sitting in the light
Of thy looks, my love;
It panted for thee like the hind at noon
For the brooks, my love."

SHELLEY

For some inexplicable reason, the little old lady's trust in Jill's son was unshakable. Why, she could not have well explained. It might have been because of his ability to hide his hurt or the memory of his words spoken as the fortune-teller on the night of the ball, or perhaps through his self-denial in refraining from using his mother's erstwhile friendship with the old aristocrat, as a key to the door which was locked fast between himself and the girl he loved.

After all, such marriages *had* taken place, thousands of them, so why should not his with the beautiful girl be added to the list, the outcome thereof proving the proverbial exception to the inevitable disastrous ending of all such unions?

Why did he deny himself?

Just because he loved the girl with the same all-sacrificing love his white mother had given his Arabian father.

If it had been otherwise, with never a second thought he would have lifted the girl, as doubtlessly his ancestors had oft-times lifted women in their *gazus* or raids, and left the consequences in the hands of that old beldame Fate.

So it had been decided to start the day after the morrow by private and swiftest steam-boat to Luxor, where Damaris, shepherded by Jane Coop and under the social wing of Lady Thistleton, would sojourn at the Winter Palace Hotel until such time as her godmother should see fit to return from her errand of mercy to the House 'an Mahabbha in the Oasis of Khargegh.

Thus, whilst Jane Coop slept placidly and Maria Hobson wrestled under the bed-covering in the last throes of a nightmare in which, as a camel, she packed parcels of sand wrapped in tissue-paper, in trunks which stretched across an endless desert, Damaris drove out to the Obelisk for her last ride on the stallion Sooltan.

She rode out into the shadows, the dawn having barely lifted the hem of night's purple raiment from the edge of the world; out into the desert stretching silver-grey, soundless, half-waking; just stirred by the light touch of the breeze, which, heralding the dawn, sends little spirals of sand dancing away to the east and away to the west and blows out the stars one by one.

And she rode listlessly, knowing that no desert would ever be as this desert, or dawn as this passing of the night, or liberty as this hour of freedom in the wastes of sand.

And then, when perhaps ten, perhaps more or less, miles out, she pulled the stallion sharply and sat forward, staring, whilst her heart thrilled in a most unwarrantable manner beneath her coat.

Upon a hummock of sand, with tattered robes of saffron, purple and of gold about his feet, there sat a youth.

Sideways he sat, with tips of slender feet to ground as though preparatory to flight. One fine brown hand pushed back a misty veil before the face, which shone wanly in the half-light. A strange, dreamy, cruel face, with crimson laughing mouth, hawk-nose, pointed chin, and eyes of grey-blue-green: eyes in which the pupils never close and which under the shadow of the coarse black hair a-grit with sand shone like twin pools of loneliness hidden in the rocks of Time. The other hand, outstretched, palm uppermost, held between the curling beckoning fingers tatters of the veil which, blown by the wind, twined about the slender limbs and outlined the ribbed ridges of the body thin to gauntness.

And even as she looked, the hummock showed empty, whilst, half-turned, upon tips of slender feet, with beckoning hand, he stood a mile off, perchance more, this youth of crimson, laughing mouth and haunting eyes.

One with the silver-grey and purple of the night, one with the gold and crimson of the coming day, he drew her, whilst the breeze laughed over her head and, soughed faintly in her ears, so that she strove to ride him down, only to find that he was not there; and urged the great beast further still and at his greatest speed, to see the figure ever out of reach, with beckoning hand; and little mocking laugh.

And then, with hoofs clattering in the shining bones of some long-dead fugitive who had failed to reach the oasis, the stallion reared and wheeled, and, caring naught for the hand upon the reins and with the bit between his teeth, raced back upon his tracks, leaving the Spirit of the Desert wrapped to the eyes in tattered misty veil.

Take heed!

So matter at what hour of the day you meet him; be it at the hour of noon, when the scorpion basks blissfully in the scorching sun; be it at night, when the white fingers of the moon essay to close your eyes in the sleep that perchance may have no waking; or at dawn, when heart or soul, or whatever it be, is like unto running water in its strength, beware of that gaunt figure with crimson laughing mouth.

Men bewitched as with woman have followed; women bewitched as with man have followed. You will find their bones if you go far enough or dig deep enough; and leave yours to bleach with theirs if you have not strength to resist.

Beasts see it not at all.

So that through a certain unromantic yearning for oats under his loosening girth, the stallion Sooltan raced Damaris back to the *sayis* and safety.

She had not understood the import of the apparition in the desert any more than she perceived the figure of a man standing amongst the ruins, watching her.

Hugh Carden Ali knew that it was her last ride; the last time she would feed the stallion with sugar; her last day amongst the ruins of the City of On.

The blood of his fathers, even that of the men who had swept the desert for their women, warred with the blood of his mother of a gentler breed; so that, fearing the strength of the one or the weakness of the other, he had sacrificed the last ride to the love in his heart.

CHAPTER XVII

"The hundred-gated Thebes, where twice ten-score in martial state Of valiant men with steeds and cars march through each massy gate."

There was no moon to break the shadows in the Great Hypostyle Hall of the Temple of Amnon; neither was there sound or sign of life, the winter residents and bird-of-passage tourists being duly occupied in the festivities which are the order of the night in hotel life on the Nile.

It is not actually dangerous, nor is it actually wise, to visit the stupendous ruins of Egypt alone at night. The native has far too good an eye to business to lurk behind obelisk or column with intent to spring out and demand the purse of any stray unit of the cosmopolitan hordes which bring such wealth in the winter months to the land of the Pharaohs.

Rather not! Far greater joy for him at full noon is palming off upon your guileless self the spurious scarab at a price 300% above its intrinsic worth.

Incidents of that kind do not occur in the great tourist centres—though worse, far worse happens to the foolhardy or featherheaded in the by-paths and hidden corners of this mysterious land—but if you have the vision, the terrible silence of the Past, the supreme indifference of the great ruins to the passage of Time, the wonderful repose of the mighty blocks of stone piled in the days of the great Pharaohs, are apt to give a thrill to your heart and an impression to your mind which may last a lifetime.

If you have not the vision you need not worry, for you will not want to wander from the hotel lounge after your coffee to traverse these ancient wastes.

Damaris had spent the last fortnight in helping her godmother prepare for her tedious journey.

With the knowledge that she would have a fortnight, perhaps more, in which there would be little else to do than to visit the ruins, she had rushed through the principal objects of interest in the wake of a verbose dragoman, and then given every moment of her time to her beloved godmother, to whom she had said good-bye that very morning.

Restless and irritated by the trivial conversation of girls of her own age and the amorous tendencies of the stronger sex of the same age and also a good bit older, she had spent the afternoon in the hotel grounds, waiting for the evening, when she could slip away by herself; having realised that the best time of all in Thebes of the Hundred Gates is at fall of night, when the shadows cast a seemly cloak over the vulgarity of the modern buildings, and give an air of romance even to the glittering lights of the appalling esplanade, which flaunts its tawdry modernity cheek by jowl with the quay, built by one of the Ptolemies, and in use even to the present day.

When the call of the *Muezzin* from the Mosque of Abou'l-Haggag came to her an hour before sunset she went in, bathed and dressed, and dined in her own room. Later, she stole out, ordered her car and drove herself along the broad tree-lined road and up the avenue of ram-headed Sphinxes to the first pylon of the great Temple.

There she switched off the lights, hid the starting-handle under the cushions and, tip-toeing, passed through the first pylon and up to the broken kiosk of the Ethiopian Tahraka.

She walked quietly, though assuredly her footsteps would have been deadened by Egypt's sands even if she had walked upon her heels, and stole through the vestibule to the second pylon, occasionally switching on her electric torch for fear of being tripped by fallen stone.

She had not heard of the great catastrophe which had brought the columns hurtling to the ground, due perhaps to the merciless greed of Ptolemy Lathyrus, or earthquake, or the well-known fact that temples, houses or plans built upon sand are bound to crumble; nor did she wot of the precariousness of the walls around her or the shifting propensities of the foundations.

She walked quietly because the spirit of the place was upon her, the spirit which puts a hand upon your mouth so that words shall not disturb the ghosts of the past, and which blinds your eyes so that you look back upon that hour as on a dream.

Yet, as she passed through pylon, vestibule and the Great Court, she stopped and turned, went on, and stopped again to listen.

There was no sound.

Flashing her light upon part of a fallen column, she sat down upon it, with the purple sky studded with stars as roof above her head and the sands of ages as carpet to her feet.

And as she sat, so still, her thoughts turned to the man who had said he loved her and who yet seemed so content to leave her quite alone.

A woman may refuse a man's honest proposal of marriage and have no intention whatever of marrying him, even later on, but that does not mean he need necessarily take her at her word to the extent of retiring altogether from the horizon of her life.

As for the rest, the flowers upon her breakfast-table, her rides at dawn—about that she instinctively kept her thoughts in check. It was like the cut-glass bottle of perfume which you are not allowed to use, on account of your youth; the first few lines of the first novel you filched from your mother's bookstand that afternoon she was out; the first time you put on a real evening dress and wound a fichu about your neck before you opened your bedroom door.

And as she sat there fell a little sound.

Bits of masonry as big as a bowl or as small as a marble are quite likely to fall upon your pate in colossal ruins, but, remembering the vague uneasiness which had caused her to stop and listen, further back, she sat forward and switched on her light.

Against the wall opposite her, entirely robed in black, with a glittering jewel clasping a corner of the great black mantle swinging from the shoulders, there stood a man.

There was no sign of the paralysing terror which swept the girl; her face, which had gone dead-white, was in shadow, her hands under control.

For a moment she sat breathless, then flashed the light full into the face of the man who had stalked her through the temple, then flashed it back to the jewel, then sighed—an unutterable sigh of relief.

The jewel was in the shape of a hawk, the symbol of Ancient Egypt.

Just for a moment they stayed in utter silence, those two who for all we know may have met and parted in this very spot in the days of the XII dynasty, to meet and part and meet again.

Then she tackled the untoward situation in the only possible way.

"Will you, as you promised, if the hour is come, tell me the tale of the Hawk of Egypt?"

She spoke sweetly, softly, switching out the light.

And Hugh Carden Ali crossed the intervening square of sand, which, however, being one-half his heritage, stretched an impregnable barrier between them, and sank to the ground beside her.

The perfume of her raiment was about him, the sound of her breathing in his ears; all the love and worship of his heart was hers. Yet he merely lifted the hem of her cloak to his lips.

The shadows pressed down upon them as he spoke, quietly, his voice echoing strangely in the Temple of the Gods.

"Behold, the Hawk of Egypt looked forth from the shadows of the mountain fastness, and nothing stirred in the earth or upon the face of the waters.

"Wrong had been wrought and the anger of the gods was as clouds loosened from their hands.

"And behold, as the first sun-ray pierced the fury of the storm, the mighty bird spread wide its wings, which were as of ruby and of emerald and of onyx and of gold as they glistened in the sun, and sailed upon the wind of the morning down towards the plains.

"And as he passed, glittering like a jewel in the crown of Osiris, those of his kind, screaming defiance, spread their wings and hastened west and east.

"They would have none of him, for beneath the mighty pinions showed the white plumage of another race.

"And in the radiant light of day there came from the southern plains a white bird, crossing the hawk's path as a snowflake driven by Destiny across the desert wastes; and he encircled her, lifting her upon the wind of his great pinions higher, higher yet towards the eyrie in the solitary mountain peak.

"And as they mounted, those of his kind and those of her kind, who had followed, battled with him, for he was outcast from the one and the other. And the mist, which was the anger of the gods, closed down . . ."

The shadows seemed to deepen as the quiet voice stopped.

"And—" said Damaris gently, "—the end?"

"That is on the lap of the gods."

"I do not understand!"

She had not caught the end of Lady Thistleton's chatter, else would she have been able to interpret the little story, and the man, who had thought that his parents' mixed marriage was a common subject for gossip in the hotel—which it was—sprang to his feet, The future still held the moment when someone would enlighten her as to the lowliness of his caste.

"It is late," he said gravely in English. "Perhaps if you were to ask at the hotel, someone would interpret the little tale. And now will you not return, for fear they come in search of you? It is not wise to wander alone, at night, without a companion. Your dog—?"

Damaris laughed, the echoes binding the silvery sound like a soft wrapping about the wounds and bruises Time had left upon the ruins.

"Wellington? Oh, he cut his foot badly this morning. And I—I want to go to the hall built like a tent."

"The great Festal Hall of Totmes III?"

The man made no other comment; it was not for him to offer himself as dragoman.

"Will you—take me there, if you know the way?"

"Verily would I be thy guide," came the passionate reply, "to guard thy feet against the stones which will surely be spread upon thy path."

Playing with fire! Yes, indeed!

Side by side they walked, the torch throwing a pool of radiance just ahead, until Damaris walked blindly into a column and cried aloud from the hurt of the stone against her shoulder.

It was then that she stretched out her hand for support, and tingled to her feet when sudden flames seemed to singe her finger-tips as they rested on the man's arm.

Through the Central Court and the Pylons and into the Hall of Records they went, until she tripped and crashed to her knees, and, rising, slipped her hand into the man's and stood for a moment with thudding heart when, closing fiercely round hers, it seemed to burn her whole being.

Hand in hand they stood, seeing, by reason of the gloom, vastly little of the columns which have the strange shape of tent-poles; then walked warily and still hand in hand in and out of various and dilapidated chambers.

"I—I don't *want* to go back, but I think it must be very late, so—"

They were standing near the chapel with the granite altar as she spoke, and had turned to retrace their way when she flashed her light upon a flight of steps.

Strange is the fascination and desolation of steps leading to an empty dwelling and almost as mysterious as the door ajar in an empty house.

She stood in the little room and swept the light across the walls upon which are represented the animals and flowers brought from Syria century upon century ago.

Then the light, which had been growing dimmer and dimmer, went out.

And it was the man this time who tackled the situation.

"I am your guide. I know the way in the dark."

He spoke in English as he swept the girl into his arms, carrying her like a feather down the great temple where perchance he had held her against his heart century upon century ago, even when the flowers and animals had been brought from Syria.

"May I drive you home? I should love to," he said, as he placed her on her feet near the car. He spoke in English, with an eagerness out of keeping with the trivial request, and which was merely the expression of a desire to be with her under commonplace circumstances.

"Please do. I don't think I could—I am so tired."

The *gafir* was accustomed to the strange habits of the white people, but, although almost drunken with slumber, he peered closely and furtively at the driver.

"Thank you so much," said Damaris gravely, with her hand against a mark upon her cheek caused by the pressure of an amulet made of a scarab-shaped emerald in a dull gold setting, and which Hugh Carden Ali wore night and day above his heart. "Is there anything else as wonderful to see as the Temple?"

"Deir el-Bahari."

The man spoke curtly and made no further comment; not for him was it to offer himself as guide.

"Ah! yes, of course—but people go to it in crowds, and one has to follow behind a guide in a procession."

"One is not obliged to return with the crowd, nor to listen to the dragoman, who knows nothing about the incense-trees of Punt which were planted upon the terrace to perfume the air under the light of the full moon, in the days of Queen Hatshepu."

With apparent abruptness she ended the conversation:

"I share my godmother's great faith in you. Good night."

She put out her hand as he salaamed with hands to brow and lips and heart. Perhaps that was why he failed to see it.

Or was it, perhaps, that he still felt the softness of her against his heart?

If you are dying of thirst, one drop of water will not assuage you!

CHAPTER XVIII

"A handful of meal in a barrel, and a little oil in a cruse."

I KINGS

Whilst Damaris was trying to soothe her wounded pride at Karnak, Ben Kelham was suffering the tortures of the nethermost pit down Assouan way.

His heart was not in "lion" at all, it was literally at Damaris' feet.

He had not rushed away in pique after her refusal of him on the night of the fancy-dress ball; nor with any vague idea of causing her to regret her decision in realising the vacuum, in her existence which his absence might make. He had not an ounce of subtlety or vanity in his nature. He had gone because he thought it would be the decent thing to do as far as she was concerned, and also to hide his hurt and disappointment, which were deep. The rumour of lion was genuine and the excitement, extending far down the Nile, intense. In fact, with the aid of the Oriental's prodigal imagination the one royal beast of feminine persuasion which was reported as having been seen prowling around Deir el-Bahari had been multiplied to two pairs ravaging the outskirts of Assouan.

He sat drinking coffee with jolly Sybil Sidmouth and her nerve-stricken stepmother in the lounge of the Savoy Hotel in

Assouan just at the moment when Damaris sat herself down on the broken column in the Hypostyle Hall.

"Jolly bad luck we've had, haven't we?" said Sybil.

Kelham nodded his head. The last post had come in, with nothing for him but a few letters from home.

"Yes, rotten!" he replied after a moment. "She *might* have sent me a line."

Sybil's stepmother moved restlessly in her chair.

Ridden with nerves, she was also mother of twin-daughters neurotic and plain who, sered by nature and yellowed by time and on the wrong side of the matrimonial hedge, had been only too glad to foist her on to the plump shoulders of jolly, capable, pretty Sybil and to get rid of them both for the winter.

In the last week or so a sprouting of hope had pierced the matchmaking soil in the querulous lady's really well-intentioned heart, for, like the proverbial half-loaf, a step-son-in-law is distinctly better than none at all.

But Sybil only smiled at the absent-mindedness of the young man's remark.

For weeks she had been the recipient of his confidences. He had dragged her, suffocating, down into the mud-depths of the diffidence in which he wallowed; had tugged her, gasping, to the Olympian heights from which he viewed a world of love, all rosy-red; had flung her, well-nigh senseless from exhaustion, upon the saw-teethed rocks of despair; and had taken her paddling in the wash of his vapourings.

She was absolutely heart-whole, with a firm belief in the "lion" rumour, and later, long after the end of this story, became the jolly, popular wife of the great eye-specialist to whom she had rushed when, after a soul-shaking scene with her step-sisters, she had missed the target entirely at Bisley.

As it happened, the duchess had written, but in a moment of most unusual aberration had put Khartoum on the envelope instead of Assouan, so that it was months, long after the end of this story, that the letter reached him. Strange is it how the lives of men are wrecked or made through the most trivial happenings.

The grain of dust in the eye; the mudbank in the river; the hen in the road! Just think of the outcome of such insignificant incidents.

The last letter he had received had been written in Heliopolis on the eve of her grace's sudden decision; the one that had gone astray had been mailed in Luxor, and had contained the request that, when he had shot the lion he would take the carcase or the skin as a present to Damaris at the Winter Palace Hotel and wait there until her return from the Oasis of Khargegh.

There was no doubt about the fact that he was genuinely in love.

Lion or no lion in the vicinity, he would sit dreaming for hours amongst the rock tombs at full noon or fall of evening or by the light of the sickle-moon; a perfectly absurd proceeding where big game is concerned. Food or sleep meant nothing to him, so that his usual good-temper was sharpened and his undoubted good looks enchanced by a certain romantic gaunt-ness under the cheek-bone. People seemed as ghosts to him, so absorbed was he in his love and his pain; so that his act of rising when Mrs. Sidmouth took what she thought to be a diplomatic departure was purely mechanical.

Then Sybil laughed, a jolly, ringing laugh, and laid her hand upon his arm.

"Why don't you run up to Heliopolis?"

"By jove, Sybil, that's an idea. You come along, too. Damaris would love to meet you; you're just her sort. Besides, there's nothing doing in lion here, it's only a yarn. Let's pack to-night and get off to-morrow. I'll go and see if we can get a private steamer—can't stick a public one, stopping every other minute to look at tombs!"

Sybil laughed.

"We'll go, Ben, it will be ripping. But to-morrow! How exactly like a man!"

Ben was contrite. He thought Sybil travelled with a kit-bag and her guns; he had forgotten Mamma.

Mamma protested. She was an invalid, with all an invalid's paraphernalia.

They started after the passing of a week in which Mrs. Sidmouth had a series of nerve-storms, and in which Sybil, to pass the time, wrote a four-page letter to Ellen Thistleton, which she duly received at breakfast.

They certainly did not stop en route to look at temples or tombs, but they made quite a long halt on the sandbank just above Luxor, onto which boats of all sizes and shapes so often run. The loss of time is irritating enough, goodness knows, in ordinary travelling and occurs quite frequently, but when one is love-driven and this maddening delay happens, then you have to make as big an exercise of self-control as when you rush onto the platform only to see the guard's van of your train disappearing into the tunnel.

And surely the gods laughed long and loud when Damaris chose that very day to return by public steamer from Denderah where she had been to visit the Temple of Hathor the Egyptian Aphrodite.

CHAPTER SIX

"But still his tongue ran on, the less
Of weight it bore, with greater ease."

BUTLER

Lady Thistleton's daughters were exhaustively energetic. It belied their colouring, which was dun and which, though of the same family, is distinct from mousey. It has infinitely more vim and a vast endurance and a great patience; also is it sullen and boring, but reliable.

Ellen, the elder, had been engaged to a younger son of The Inverness of Inverness. His colouring, except of course for the eyes, which were of a snapping blue, reminded one of a tomato salad dressed with chilis and smothered in mustard-sauce. His temper corresponded. They had fought over everything until they had smashed their engagement.

Berenice was engaged to a parson in Edinburgh, one of the Smythe-Smythes of London. She made a doormat of herself, loving the herculean minister, and, though longing to stay at home and get married, had, at her lover's earnest request, consented to accompany her mother and sister to Egypt instead.

To his fervent mind the loss of a few months of married life would be compensated for by the biblical discourses upon the

Land of Moses with which, later on, as his wife, she would be able to enliven Mother's Meetings.

They admired Damaris a lot, though her independence and colouring shocked them not a little. In the seclusion of the double bedroom, as they brushed or twisted their lanky locks in Hindes', they whispered about her love-affair, which had presumably gone agley, and thrilled with a distinct feeling of wrong-doing over the gossip anent the mythical Sheikh.

If they had asked Damaris about the myth, she would have told them everything quite simply and truthfully. This would have cleared up the mist but spoilt the feeling of wrong-doing.

Lady Thistleton was large and recumbent and averse to sight-seeing, but after a heart-to-heart talk with her daughters had seen to it that Damaris had no time for moping.

Damaris went here, there and everywhere; played tennis; paid duty-calls, as you must when somebody extends her wing-feathers as shelter; acted in charades; attended concerts; and was thoroughly miserable.

Jane Coop was miserable too; so was the bulldog, and, through a certain unconfessed and indefinable vigilance they both felt called upon to exercise in behalf of their beloved mistress, were distinctly nervy.

"Drat the men!" had said the maid, giving pithy verbal expression to the ragged state of her nerves as she cut the stalks of the beautiful flowers which came daily without name or message. The dog's method of expressing himself was some-what more violent; it consisted of the sudden seizure between his great teeth of the posterior portion of the nether garments of low-caste males, white or coloured.

You could almost tell the status of the male bipeds by casting a discreet eye upon their raiment, and as there was not a muzzle in Egypt big enough to fit the dog, it had ended in him being led or chained in polite society.

Damaris's table was next that of the Thistletons, who, with a vague memory maybe of their duty towards their neighbour as instilled on Sundays into their rebellious infantile heads, chatted brightly to right and to left of them at meals.

Full of the milk of human kindness, they allowed it to overflow into their writhing neighbours' jugs.

They broke through the glacial atmosphere which surrounds the Britisher's breakfast-table; newspaper propped against jam-pot was no barrier; their gladsome invitations or suggestions, dammed for the moment, would rise at last level with the paper's edge to trickle down the other side and mingle with the eggs and bacon, porridge, kidneys, or whatever trifle the plate might contain.

They read out scraps of news from the morning paper; they read out bits of home news from their stacks of correspondence, written for the most part on eight pages and in the sprawling, uncontrolled script of the woman who has nothing but trivialities with which to fill her day.

Their blood was blue, their upbringing beyond suspicion; they simply erred through a too-generous supply of the above-mentioned philanthropic fluid.

They had come home dead-beat the night before, but were first down to breakfast, as happy as could be at the thought of the strenuous day before them, and were ostentatiously comparing their books of notes or jottings when Damaris came in. They went everywhere with note-books in their hands, and made entries at the most inconvenient moments during their journey. To you or me they would have seemed but jottings, but Berenice could have read you a blank-verse love-poem in the thick markings of her fountain-pen; and Ellen a *De Profundis* from the hieroglyphics and inscriptions copied by her scratchy stylo and under which she essayed to bury the memory of the tomato-hued Inverness.

Damaris slid into her seat with an inward prayer that she might be allowed time to read her mail, which consisted of a fat letter from her godmother and a bulky one from home. "Perhaps *Marraine* will be back soon," she thought, opening the other letter first, as is a way with us perverse humans. Enclosed was an atrociously-written letter to her mother from her plain-as-a-pikestaff brother, written from Harrow.

". . . it's awfully jolly," wrote the enthusiastic youngster, "being in Ben Kelham's house. They still talk about his last house-match against Bumbles. Don't you remember I'd just got over mumps and we went down for it? Bumbles had six to win and ten minutes to do it in when Howard was bowled, and Carden, their captain, went in and drove right over the Pav. He won the match by one, don't you remember? And then Kelham caught him magnificently in the slips just as time was up."

Damaris looked at a bunch of jasmine lying beside her plate, and sighed as she opened her godmother's letter; then sighed again, more profoundly.

The duchess had arrived at Khargegh without mishap. She described the journey, gradually ascending through the desert, then down through the narrow valley of rocks—the wastes of rock and gravel—the beautiful valley—the great plain to Mahariq-Khargegh with its date-palms, its filthy lanes, its mosques, with the limestone hills almost surrounding it.

"And we can't get any further, my dear. A report has come of the appearance near here of a notorious robber gang which has infested the desert farther south for years. I don't believe it myself—Hobson is furious, as the hotel we are in is not totally devoid of—shall I call them mosquitoes?—but the authorities refuse to allow us to proceed. I have sent a runner through to the friend I was going to see."—Damaris touched the jasmine at her side and sighed. "I will tell you the whole history when I return. So sad, my child; so very tragic. She may come to see me, as the authorities have no power over her. She is staying at her eldest son's house until his return. I will let you know my movements as soon as I can. Enjoy yourself. Dekko is very quiet; he is either apprehensive or going to moult."

Damaris smiled spasmodically when, as she put the letter down under the jasmine, her neighbours let off a broadside.

The head dragoman wanted to get up a party for Deir el-Bahari on the morrow. He had twenty pairs of donkeys, all of which were so accustomed, it seemed, to going about in a bunch that they refused to move a step if one pair was missing. Nineteen pairs had been filled from the different hotels, one pair was still minus riders. Would Damaris make a couple with Mr. Lumlough?

Mr. Lumlough, who was of the raw age of nineteen and who worshipped in secret at the girl's shrine, blushed divinely salmon-pink and coughed.

Damaris shook her head.

She longed to see the Temple, as she longed to go to Denderah, but not in a crowd; also, she longed to confide all her secrets (of which her visit to the Temple of Amnon was not one of the least) to her godmother. She was just the slightest bit scared, and, being very young, felt incapable of prescribing for her burnt finger-tips.

She had only to keep away from the fire, but, as I have already said, she was very young.

"Do, Damaris! We are taking our lunch on donkeys, as well."

"But why not let the empty pair go without riders? Or let Mr. Lumlough go on one and let the other trot by its side without anyone? I'm sure it would love a holiday."

No! These twenty pairs of donkeys belonged to an asinine Trades Union. The twenty pairs went together or not at all; they went up the steep hill with a human being on their backs or not at all; if one solitary moke out of the forty trades-unionists should be asked to climb a hill with nothing on its back, it would not move one step—no, not if the most luscious carrot feast awaited it at the top; and if it refused to budge, the thirty-nine others would support it by also refusing to budge! Yes! even if they held up the whole of the tourist season for eternity and never again tasted luscious carrot in all the years allotted to the asinine race. What *is* the good of customs if you don't stick to them? The donkeys' parents had always climbed that hill heavily-laden, and what was good enough for them was also good enough for their descendants!

"I think it's horrid of you, Damaris. Besides, what are you going to do all by yourself?" said Ellen, opening a letter bits of which she proceeded to read out. "Here's a letter from Sybil Sidmouth. She and Mr. Kelham are having a very poor time sitting about in the rocks and tombs all day and half the night."

"How romantic!" sighed Berenice. "All alone with Nature in an Egyptian desert! It reminds me of Omar's Jug and Loaf verse. How does it go?" She flipped through her notebook. "Ah! here it is." And she proceeded to read, with appropriate punctuation with her tea-spoon on the edge of her saucer:

"A book of verses underneath the bough
A jug of wine, a loaf of bread, and Thou
Beside me, singing in the wilderness;
O, wilderness were Paradise enow!"

She looked up, suddenly, surprised and indignant, at Ellen, who had kicked her violently under the table; then she tried to cover up her confusion at her unfortunate *faux pas*.

"Mrs. Sidmouth, of course, is far from well," she continued. But Ellen broke in, in her high staccato and appalling French:

"*Revenons a nos moutons*—or at least, our donkeys." She looked at Damaris, who, with over-bright eyes, laughed whole-heartedly at the feeble joke. "Do change your mind, Damaris. The guide is Yussuf, the very best, you know. Besides, we *might* see the lion."

"All right," said Damaris, tucking the jasmine into the belt of her white dress, which she had never done before. "I'll come. Twenty pairs of donkeys climbing up a hill will be an awfully funny sight,—don't you think so, Mr. Lumlough?"

She smiled across at Mr. Lumlough, who was thereupon transported to the portals of the seventh heaven with a piece of toast and marmalade in his right hand.

CHAPTER XX

"I was never less alone than when by myself."

GIBBON

Next morning, with her chaperon's energetic daughters, Damaris found herself one of the herd foregathered on the Nile bank preparatory to the excursion to the Valley of the Kings, and later in the afternoon by mountain path over the ridge to that marvel of antiquity the Terrace-Temple of Deir el-Bahari.

"I don't want to go, Janie dear," she said, the preceding night, whilst the devoted maid wielded strong-bristled brushes on the burnished short-cropped hair.

"Better go, dearie. One must be polite, even if the heart breaks."

Jane Coop's literary plane swung between a three-penny weekly entitled "Real Stories from High Life" and Ouida's novels, which latter she had bought second-hand in the Charing Cross Road and kept sandwiched between her Bible and "Grandmother's Herb Recipes."

"But I don't want to go. I hate crowds, and I can't take Wellington. Every native flies from him since he got behind the Musical Colossus and growled. You remember? They thought it was the statue speaking, and the dear old darling was only trying to catch a lizard."

The bulldog loathed Egypt.

He was always either in disgrace or being talked to in baby language. He had seen next to nothing of his beloved mistress, and his digestion had been almost ruined by the amount of chocolates he had eaten out of pure boredom.

"Take me," he said, every time his beloved went out, as plainly as could be by means of his beautiful face and down-cast tail. But excursions had grown rarer and rarer and his slender middle more and more defined through grief.

"My heart isn't breaking, Janie!" Damaris declared, sitting up in bed.

"I know it isn't, dearie. There's nothing to break it over, *I'm* sure. I was just repeating from 'Her Scarlet Sin', where the beautiful heroine is torn between two stools as it were."

Jane Coop had no use for knights who left the field of combat; and as for the tales which were duly carried to her of an Arabian chief who followed her young mistress in the desert and sent her bunches of flowers and such-like trash, well! it was all you could expect if you left your own country for heathen parts!

To Jane Coop, rides in the desert in Egypt were just as much a part of the day's programme as rides on donkeys at holiday-time had been in Margate, before interfering people began to make a fuss about the rider's weight.

"You mind your own hedges, Maria Hobson, and see that your own cattle don't go a-straying, with their monkey tricks," she had said tartly and not over-lucidly, to her grace's maid, who had heard from someone who had heard from someone else that Miss Hethencourt was out at all hours of the night, here, there and everywhere. "I know what time she comes in and where she has been, and who with, and that's quite enough for me. Thank you, I can shepherd my own flock!"

She was not exactly within the confines of truth in her statement, but having learned in her youth to diagnose the hurt of dumb animals, she felt she was fully qualified to treat her beloved child's unrest without any verbal aid from outsiders.

Yet something, a warning from the future, maybe, had prompted her to speak this night as she stood beside the bed, looking down upon the beauty of the child to whom she seemed, more than anyone else, to stand in the position of sponsor.

"Will you promise me one thing, dearie?"

She stroked the red head lovingly as it leant against the motherly bosom upon which had so often rested errant lambs and stricken pullets.

"Yes, Janie darling. I would promise you anything!"

"I know things are going crosswise a bit with you, dearie, as they always do in an unknown country; but I don't worry about that, because at the crossways there is always a signpost. But now that we are in this heathen land, I want your promise that you will always tell me where you are going to when you go out—always. If it's out for a ride in the desert or over amongst them mummy-tombs, or out to a tennis-party or dance. Will you, dearie? Always?"

The insistence in the demand made the girl look up into the homely face and she did not smile as she made a little cross above her heart in the manner of children.

"I promise, Janie—cross heart. And I'm starting out early-early to-morrow morning on an excursion to the Tombs of the

Kings. We are taking lunch with us—paper-bags and remnants of sandwiches amongst Egypt's dead—tea at the Rest House and—"

She stopped for a minute, then continued slowly:

"—and if I don't come back with the rest, Janie dear, don't worry. It's full moon, and I may stay to see the Temple by moonlight."

A moment's silence; then said practical Jane:

"And as you can't take Wellington, dearie, will you promise to take your revolver? You know, they say lions have been seen in—"

Damaris laughed.

"They've left, Janie! They're all at Assouan, waiting to be shot by Mr. Kelham and Miss Sidmouth."

Jane Coop sniffed as she tucked in the bed-clothes and kissed her child good-night.

She had got to the door when Damaris spoke.

"Janie, you know all about birds, don't you?"

"Hens, dearie."

"Well!" The girl's voice came muffled, as though she had drawn the sheet about her face. "Supposing a hawk—"

"Hawks aren't hens, dearie."

"Well—hens! Supposing you had a breed of hens that were all—all—oh! any colour—"

"White Leghorns," said Jane Coop, who was beginning to get

interested in this subject so near her heart.

"Yes. Well, supposing you found that one, when it had all its feathers, had some speckled ones under its wings—"

"But it couldn't, dearie, if it was pure-bred!"

"Yes, but just supposing it had, what would be the meaning of it?"

Jane Coop hesitated, and re-tied her apron-strings. Descriptive analysis was not her strong forte.

"Well, dearie, I should say that the male bird was a—a—oh! a Plymouth Rock, or something like that. The speckled bird would be a good one, but if it was mixed it would have to be turned out of the run if you had a fancy for showing and prizes. I remember a black—But there now! what made you start your old Nannie talking about hens? Just you turn over and go to sleep, dearie. You have to be up and away early to-morrow, you know!"

She closed the door gently and left the girl alone.

"I don't understand," she said softly, and slipped out of bed to stand at the open window, with all the glory of an Egyptian night before her.

"I *don't* understand the meaning of the story," she repeated, as she watched the figure of a *fellah* wrapped in a big cloak which shone snow-white under the moon, trudging patiently across the grounds to the servants' quarters. Then, as the huge dog flung himself against her, she struck her hands together. The sudden impact sent her mind flying back to the first time she had seen Hugh Carden Ali, in English riding-kit and Mohammedan *tarbusch* in the bazaar; then in her memory she saw him dining as an Englishman; saw him riding with falcon upon fist—a very Eastern, saw him as an Arab of Arabia in the desert; again as an Englishman, save for the Mohammedan *tarbusch*, holding in the bay mare as she thundered past him on the stallion Sooltan.

In a flash she understood the tragic story of the Hawk of Egypt.

"The pity of it!" she whispered. "Oh! the cruel pity of it!" and crept back to bed.

* * * * * *

Wide-eyed and quiet, she stood very early next morning with the jostling, laughing crowd, waiting to be ferried across the Nile on the excursion to the Tombs of the Kings, which to most of the crowd ranked on a level with Madame Tussaud's Waxworks, with the difference that in the valley of desolation you could leave the remnants of your lunch anywhere, which is a habit strictly forbidden in the Marylebone Road.

Mounting the diminutive donkeys caused peals of laughter; the hamlets of Naza'er-Rizkeh and Naza'el Ba'irait rang with the cries of the cavalcade, and Damaris blindly followed Lady Thistleton's energetic offspring, as with note-book and pencil they followed the guide in and out of the regulation tombs of Biban el-Muluk, the history of which he repeated with parrot-like monotony.

Lucy Jones, lighthearted tourist, thought the lunch awfully jolly in the shade of the tomb, in fact, she made it a riotous feast, with the help of others as young and non-temperamental as herself.

After all, what did it matter?

As Lucy said, "The dead had been such a jolly long time dead," and the desolation of the valley made such a splendid contrast to the golden sunshine and violent blue of the sky.

The zig-zag path down to Deir el-Bahari occasioned more

laughter and little screams and offers of help from the sterner male, who, under an extreme insouciance, tried to hide the insecurity of his perch on the back of the humble, scrambling quadruped.

When the laughing, jostling and somewhat dishevelled crowd streamed back down the second incline and across the Central Terrace, en route for the donkeys, it left Damaris standing with dancing eyes, and laughing mouth under the blue and star-strewn ceiling of the Shrine.

And when the last sound of laughter, and clattering stone under nimble hoof had melted away; when the sky had turned the marble temple mauve and pink and deepest red, and back to pink, to mauve, to softest white; when the first star had fastened the robe of day to the cloak of night, and silence had fallen like balm upon the wound caused by raucous voices, Damaris tip-toed down the steps and out into the Colonnade of Punt.

She was quite alone.

CHAPTER XXI

"No time so dark but through its woof there run
Some blessed threads of gold."

C. P. CRANACH

It is difficult—no, it is impossible to describe the wonder of Deir el-Bahari under the moon, just as it is impossible to describe "the light that never was, on land or sea," or the Taj Mahal, or a mother's love.

To our eyes it is the picture of desolation. Just as it must have been a picture of grandeur to those of the woman who built it, Queen Hatshepu, sister, wife and queen of Totmes III.

It is built in terraces to which you climb by gentle incline; it is surrounded and crossed by colonnades; there are ruined chapels and vestibules and recesses; an altar upon which offerings had once been made to the great gods; broken steps and closed and open doors, behind which the ghosts of dead kings and queens, priests, priestesses and nobles sit in ghostly council; through which they beckon you—*if you belong.*

There has surely come to each of us, in this short span we term life, the moment when, just introduced, we look into another's face and say or think, "We have met before."

May it not have been that we once met to burn incense

together before the dread god Anubis, or to make offerings upon the altar erected to the great god Ra Hamarkhis; or was it perchance that you, if you are a woman, once waited at the temple gates to see him pass upon his return from the great expedition to the land of Punt, which we call Somaliland to-day?

Had the man with hawk-face who offers you a muffin or cup of tea to-day once brought you gifts of ivory, or incense, or skin of panther from the wonderland? Did he sweep the seething crowd with piercing eye to find the face beloved, and pass on to the rolling of drums, the crash of cymbals, the blaring of trumpets, to make obeisance to his monarch and return thanks to the mighty gods?

Perchance!

But Damaris had no thought of the past as she stood amongst the pillars of the colonnade which commemorate the great expedition; she was enthralled with the hour, the solitude, the silence, as she hesitated, wondering which way to go. Then, even as she hesitated, the silence was broken by the distant throbbing of a drum.

It came from one of the villages far down the hill and, caught by the evening breeze, was carried to the temple, to be multiplied a hundredfold in the echoing roof.

All other sounds may cease way out in the East; birds may nest and humans sleep; but the sound of the drum faileth never.

It is a message, a love-song, a lament, a prayer, and you hear it in the desert as in the jungle, in the temple as in the courtyard behind the hovel.

It is not a wise thing to listen to its call, for it can lead you off the beaten track, or over the precipice or out into the desert to die.

It caught the girl's feet in the witchery of its rhythm and set them moving upon the sand-covered floor of the Temple. Yet there was no smile on her lips as, moved by whatever it is that causes us to do strange things in the East, she danced like a wraith or a sylph, or a leaf in the wind, in and out of the columns and out into the light of the moon, and through the granite door onto the terrace where once had been planted the incense trees which had come with the spoil from Punt to perfume the air to the glory of Ra Hamarkhis.

The rolling of the drum stopped short, and Damaris came to herself with a start as she stood under the moon, then clasped her hands upon her thudding heart as she watched a man with two great shaggy dogs walk across the terrace towards her.

Save for the Mohammedan head-covering he was an Englishman, and he spoke in his mother's tongue to the girl he loved and whom he had watched since her arrival with the jostling, laughing crowd.

"The gods of the temple are good to me," he said simply. "I prayed that I might watch you dance upon the incense terrace of their house; they have answered my prayer. Come."

As they passed across the terrace to the hall of columns which is the vestibule of the chapel of the god of Death, he told her how he had watched and waited, meaning no discourtesy, until she should visit the temple amongst the limestone hills.

"Where are we going?"

Damaris spoke more to break the spell which seemed to hold her than to know the end of the walk across the sand. Bewitched by the moon and the terrific power of old Egypt, she would have followed the man blindly, fearing no hurt, even into the inner-most sanctuary which, hewn out of the rock itself, lies at the extreme end of the temple.

"To the Shrine of Anubis the god of Death, where I would

show you the Hawk of Northern Egypt upon the wall."

They passed between the great columns and up the flight of steps to the doorway beyond which lie the chambers of the Shrine, and there Hugh Carden Ali took the girl's hand as he called her name aloud, until the walls or the spirits of the gods thundered back the echo.

"The gods introduced the kings of Egypt to the sanctuary. Anubis god of Death, as you will see by the painting upon the wall, led the great queen to the door," he said in reply to a whispered question from Damaris. "I would not that the shadow of death touched the hem of your raiment. I called your name aloud so that the gods might hear. . . . Do I believe in such strange things? How can one say, I believe, or do not believe, in this land which is in the grip of a dead past which is not dead?"

And they passed in through the door and stood looking up at the Hawk of Horus painted in the XVIII dynasty upon the wall.

Brilliant in colouring, green and white, with red-tipped wings, it spreads them above the place where once was seen the painted picture of the queen who reigned and suffered and died, thousands of years ago.

"Ah!" said Damaris, as she looked up to the corner. "It is your—your crest—your—"

"It is a fantasy of mine. We trace my father's house right back without a break to the days of the Pharaohs—so, I believe, does Mohammed Ali, vendor of slippers in the bazaar." He paused, then added abruptly, with a frown and a movement of the shoulders as though he were trying to shift a burden, "If you will come with me to the inner chamber, if you are not afraid, I will interpret the Story of the Hawk to you in the shadows where it belongs."

Damaris put out her hand as though to speak, then passed into the inner room, across the threshold of which the dogs of Billi laid themselves down.

"Death is around us," said Hugh Carden Ali. "Do you believe in omens?—No? Nor I. I wish there was a seat, so that you could rest whilst I tell you—"

Damaris laid her hand gently upon his arm, and he looked down into the face shining dead-white in the reflection of the moon which had silted in through a hole in the roof.

"You know?"

Damaris looked up and smiled.

"Yes! I know. And, being the son of such splendid people, I cannot understand why—"

The gates of pain and love and sacrifice were opened and the girl shrank back against the wall as the tide of pent-up bitterness swept around her in the ruined shrine. The man's face was white, his eyes blazed in the agony of his hurt, whilst the dogs lifted their heads and growled.

". . . You do not understand! You do not understand that I love you! And, loving you, I stand a prisoner behind the bars wrought for me by the love of my parents. That I love you as surely you never have been, never will be, loved, and that I dare not, can not ask you to be my wife,—even if you loved me— which you do not. . . What? You do not see why I should not marry into my mother's race even as my father did? I will tell you why." He gripped her wrists and pulled her to him. "Because I am the outcome of their union. My father is an Arab, my mother an Englishwoman. I—I am a half-caste. I am nearer white, truly, than my father, but—but my son, although he might be white or dark,—a—a native, as you say in England—would only be a half-caste lying on your white breast, if you were my wife."

The moonbeams lengthened as the man talked on, whilst Damaris learned of one of love's bitterest mistakes.

"Oh, forgive me!" he ended. "Why did I bring you here to hurt you, to make you cry for a pain which is not yours? Why are you left alone? It is so dangerous in this land of my fathers. Your godmother deserts you whilst she goes to my mother, who is afraid for me—ah! did you not know? The man who loves you has left you to the wind of chance: my friend, Big Ben Kelham—O gods of ancient Egypt, how you must laugh!—my *friend*! Shall we meet again, I wonder?—"

Surely Anubis the god of death, Anubis the jackal-headed—who leads the soul of the departed through the underworld into the presence of the great Osiris—surely he moved upon the wall and turned to look after those two as they passed out of the inner chamber to stand beneath the Hawk upon the wall.

Or was it the shifting of the moon amongst the shadows?

"Will you"—there was no trace of the man's anguish in his voice: the Mohammedan's resignation to the inevitable may seem a weak way out to one who will kick and worry until he drops from exhaustion, but it saves a great deal of pain to others—"will you—you must surely marry some day, so beautiful, so sweet you are—will you let me give you this as a wedding-present, and will you think of me, a prisoner, when you fasten it in your wedding-gown?" He held out a jewel in the shape of the Hawk which spread its wings upon the wall above them. "It was found here, in this sanctuary—a priestly ornament? a pilgrim's offering? Who knows? Will you?—*I* have no right to it, for beneath my wings is the plumage of another race. I am not a pure-bred son of Northern Egypt."

"Will you pin it in?"

The girl's voice shook as she tilted back her chin so that her mouth was on a level with the man's as he bent to fasten the jewel in the silk.

"Will you promise me one thing? Yes!—you are good to the prisoner. Allah! how I love you, and surely, if I may not be your master I may serve you. If you should be in trouble—ever—in this land of Egypt, the very soil of which is drenched with the blood of those who have fought, and loved, and won, and lost thousands of years before the coming of the gentle prophet who said that in the sight of the great God, anyway, we are brethren—yes, if trouble should come to you, will you send me a messenger—to the Tents of Purple and of Gold? I am doing you a great wrong in lingering where I can catch glimpses of you. I love you—love you—but that is no excuse for causing you harm through the wagging of evil tongues."

Tears dropped one by one upon the jewel which glittered on her breast.

"And if I were in trouble—great trouble—if I were to come to you myself, how—?"

"My boat waits at the landing-stage from sundown to sunrise, the swiftest mare in all Egypt, as the fortune-teller foretold you, the snow-white mare Pi-Kay waits from the setting until the rising of the sun at the Gate of To-morrow, which is a ruined portal on the road of the Colossi. From there the way lies west. And fear not." He pointed to an inscription on the wall and translated it in the Egyptian tongue. "'*I have come full of joy because of my love to thee; my hands are full of all life and purity. I am protecting thee among all gods.*'"

Followed by the dogs, they walked slowly down the incline to a mound of rubbish flung up and left by an excavating party many years back; behind it they found the stallion Sooltan in the care of his *sayis*, also the one donkey which had wandered off in search of grass and got lost, and whose absence in the cavalcade had not been noticed on account of the disorder of the descent.

"Kismet!" had said Jobad the guide when he had made the discovery at the water's edge.

If the white folk could not keep count of themselves he was not going to draw their attention to the fact that one of the party was missing; he had not the slightest intention of providing an evening meal for the lion by offering to go in search of the pair. "Kismet!—Allah would watch over them!"

Hugh Carden Ali leapt to the saddle without touching the stirrups, then swung the girl as lightly as a leaf up into his arms.

Heedless of the extra burden of the slip of a girl who had mastered him in the desert and who lay so quietly against his master's heart, the magnificent black beast stood stock-still, then suddenly shivered violently, just as the dogs of Billi, belly to ground, eyes blazing, ruffs on end, growled softly.

Hugh Carden pressed Damaris back against his shoulder and turned and looked in the direction whence had come that sound, paralysing if you do not happen to be armed.

From somewhere amongst the rocky wilderness of the hills, carried by the night-breeze, had come the hoarse coughing of a lion.

"Listen," he said.

And as it came again, with shrieks of "Sabe! sabe!" the pea-green *sayis* leapt on the back of the terrified donkey, which, spurred by fear, disappeared like a streak down the hill just as the stallion, sweating with pure terror, reared and wheeled, then backed, with great eyes rolling and hoofs striking sparks from the stones.

Up he reared, until it seemed impossible that he should not fall backwards, crushing to death or hideously maiming the man who, encumbered with the girl upon his arm, could do little to calm the frightened beast, And well for them was it that Hugh Carden Ali, with his love and understanding of horses, knew that only to the sagacity of the animal could the safe negotiation of the dangerous descent down the hillside be left. He gave Sooltan his head.

There is no danger in it, goodness knows, when you bestride a diminutive donkey whose dainty little feet know every pebble on the route, but there is danger when an animal like Sooltan takes the Avenue of Sphinxes at a mad rush and slips and slithers and slides, under the impetus of his own weight, pace and terror, the rest of the way, even if he is as sure-footed as a goat.

*　*　*　*　*　*

Later, when her beloved child wakened the night-porter, Jane Coop, blue with anxiety and cold, most unhygienically closed the window and thankfully padded off to her comfortable bed.

CHAPTER XXII

"Antiquity! thou wondrous charm, what art
thou? that being nothing art everything! . . . .
The mighty future is as nothing, being
everything! the past is everything, being nothing!"

LAMB

In spite of her tongue, which was somewhat unduly inclined to gossip, Lady Thistleton was a motherly old soul and had a great affection for Damaris.

". . . I should not like either of my little girls," she was saying the morning after the visit to the Terrace Temple, "to visit the ruins or stay out unchaperoned after dark. I am responsible for you, you know, dear, and you are very beautiful and very young. Of course I know that you are a little unhappy, dear, but other girls have been the same. So you must not worry. Everything will come right. I expect you know all about my Ellen." Damaris nodded. "And everybody is so fond of you. Would you like to have a long day in bed to-day, dear, or go to Denderah with the girls? They are thinking of staying for a few days."

Damaris smiled the radiant smile which made her so attractive, and, rising, put her arms round the motherly old dear's neck and kissed her, which was an unusual thing for her to do, as she was, as a rule, undemonstrative to coldness.

"I'd love to go to Denderah, if I may take Janie and Wellington. And I'm truly not worrying; it's just a tremendous spirit of adventure which drives me to do these awful things."

So to Denderah she went, with her spirits at highest pitch at the thought of getting away from Luxor for a few days and of seeing the wonderful Temple of Hathor, the goddess of Joy and Youth.

She was in riotous spirits when she arrived at the Hotel Denderah in Kulla, where the lovely porous jugs come from; in fact, so blithe was she that Ellen, inclined to despondency and of a superstitious tendency, remarked:

"I should calm myself a little, my dear Damaris; such gaiety can only lead to depression, later on."

But Damaris only laughed.

How good it is that we cannot visualise beforehand the hour in which our tears must flow and our hearts come well-nigh to breaking!

She laughed, she sang, she visited the town, and went to bed early. She teased Jane Coop the next morning as, perilously perched on donkey-back, she headed the little procession which wended its way through the stretches of earth which later would give a harvest of corn and sweet-scented flowering bean.

She urged the panting bulldog along the three good miles, and laughed at him when, sneezing and coughing, he rubbed his great paws over his face, covered with the cobwebs which floated on the air; but she stopped laughing when she first caught sight of the great arch of crumbling antiquity which is all that is left of the edifice upon the site of which the Temple of Hathor was built; and she stood quite still in the over-powering colonnade, whilst the Thistletons, notebooks in hand, rushed inside in the wake of the guide. Jane Coop stopped dead at the outer edge of the colonnade.

"I thought you said it was a Temple of Love, dearie: all white marble, with doves and lovers'-knots and—and hearts. It's a tomb, that's what it is, and I'm going to sit outside. I don't like it; it bodes no good. Let's go back, dearie; I don't like the place or the hotel or the town. If we go quickly we can catch the first boat. Let the others stay if they want to. I'm thinking of you; my heart's telling me that you must not stop, and that if you do, harm'll come to you, or somebody."

Strange was the persistence of the usually placid woman, as she caught her young mistress by the arm and quite violently shook her fist at the sinister face of the goddess which shows on each side of the columns.

And strange it is to know that if the girl had but listened, the harm might not have befallen.

But Damaris shook her head.

"We must be polite, Janie dear, even if we are dying to go home. Besides, two or three days will do us good, and it will help pass the time until Marraine comes back. Come, Well-Well."

The dog followed his mistress up to the door, but there he stopped.

"Come along, Well-Well," she repeated.

The dog sat down, with a definite air of ending further exploration as far as ruins were concerned, on his part.

"I think you and Janie are bewitched to-day."

Damaris spoke petulantly and watched the dog waddle back and sit down beside the maid, who, busy crocheting, sat on a stone some few yards from the Temple, to which she had resolutely turned her back.

Damaris stood for a moment feeling as though the very wettest of wet blankets had been wrapped round her; then turned, listened until she heard Ellen's staccato voice coming from the direction of the antechamber in the middle of the Temple, and tiptoed across to the east side, where are to be found the ruined Treasury and Store Rooms in which were stored the incense for sacrifice or offering, the vestments and banners and other such props needful to the correct fulfilment of the rites of an ancient worship which, as far as services go, in display of wealth and sense-stirring accessories, did not differ so very much from what we see in some of our churches in this present day of grace.

She came to the stairs, up which so many years ago the mother of Hugh Carden Ali had climbed, on the day when she had fully realised that the crown of love had come to her.

Damaris climbed them, and stood on the roof, watching, as had watched Jill Carden, the clouds of twittering birds as they flew in the direction of the Libyan Hills; then she crossed to the little shrine of Osiris, stood for a moment unconsciously passing her finger over the carvings, turned as though someone had called her, and ran down the stairs.

She stood and listened until she heard Ellen's voice looming from the side chapel on the western side, then, and just as though pulled by some invisible hand, she passed quietly through the antechamber into the sanctuary where, in the days of Ancient Egypt, the mighty Pharaoh, and he only, entered to commune with the gods at the birth of the new year; and where the mother of Hugh Carden Ali, stricken with the glory of the secret revealed, had fallen unconscious to the ground, over twenty years ago.

She stood quite still, her heart beating to suffocation; then she raised her hand and pushed the hair from her forehead.

"I feel just as though the roof was pressing down upon me," she whispered to herself. "As though, through me, something awful was going to happen. I—"

She turned, and almost ran out of the sanctuary, her footsteps waking the echoes of the roof which once had resounded to the clash of cymbal, the roll of drum and blare of trumpets. She heard Ellen's strident voice calling to her, telling her to come and join them in the crypts; she paid no heed, she ran on and out into the sunshine and down to the maid, who was still placidly crocheting.

And as she left the ruin, the mantle of depression fell from her, and she laughed as she caught the great dog and forced him to walk upon his hind-legs.

"No, Janie," she said that night, as the maid tucked her up in bed. "Here I stay until I have visited the Temple thoroughly, and I'll take you down into the creepy crypts and lock you in them if you worry any more. We all got up too early and hadn't had enough breakfast—that is why we disliked the place so much."

They stayed some days, and then took the public steamer home, Damaris bubbling over with high infectious spirits, which had their birth in a secret hope that she might find a letter from Ben Kelham upon her return.

She was leaning over the rail, thinking about him, as the boat made its lazy way down-stream.

"So funny," she was saying to herself as they approached Luxor under a sunset sky. "I wonder if he will be at the hotel. I somehow feel him quite near."

And then her thoughts were distracted by the exclamations and laughter of the passengers as they rushed to the side, causing the boat to take a distinct list.

What little things serve to amuse us!

The bluebottle at the Cathedral service; the stray dog which rushes athwart the regal procession; the straw hat blown through the traffic!

The steamer was churning up the waters of the river down which Cleopatra had passed in all her power and beauty; on each side were the ruins of temples and tombs built to the glory of great god or mighty emperor; yet the tourists flung down guide-books and left their tea to shout encouragement and wave their handkerchiefs to Ben Kelham and Sybil Sidmouth, who were also having tea on the slanting deck of their private steamer, which had run aground on the pestiferous sand-bank.

Mrs. Sidmouth, in the seclusion of the saloon, was summoning all her strength for a real nerve-storm.

Damaris looked hard for a moment, then became deadly-white, and backed her way out through the crowd. She flashed a quick glance round in search of the Thistletons, and saw them leaning dangerously far over the rail, trying to attract the attention of Sybil Sidmouth, who was smiling so contentedly as she handed her companion his tea; then she turned to run to the saloon to hide herself, and ran, instead, right into Jane Coop's arms.

There was a grim set to the maid's mouth and a steely glitter in her eyes.

"I was just coming to ask you, dearie, if you'd like a cup of tea. One gets fair sick of the ruins and things one sees on this river. The young ladies can come and find you at tea if they want to."

How often had the motherly woman gone out to bring in the lamb from the storm, or hunted the fields and hedgerows for her straying chick!

Later, she sat on the edge of her darling's bed and patted the curly head resting on her faithful heart, to the accompaniment of little clucking sounds.

"There now, dearie—there now—there now! It isn't worth crying over; every river is as full of good fish as ever sailed on it in a boat that couldn't run straight. Let old Nannie dry her baby's tears. There how—there now!"

She dried the tear-stained little face with a big handkerchief, and rocked her child to the rhythm of the music which drifted from the hall, borne by the night breeze, through the open window, until the sobs had ceased.

And in the ball-room the Thistleton family nodded their heads sagely to the rhythm of the same music.

"I am sure she didn't see Mr. Kelham and Sybil, Mamma," Ellen was saying. "She was having tea when we went to find her, and looked quite all right."

"I was thankful when I saw her," broke in Berenice, patting a thick envelope with the Edinburgh post-mark. "On the *Nile*, together, it really did not seem *comme il faut* at all, and wherever Mrs. Sidmouth was, she might have countenanced the—er—the courtship by her presence on deck."

"Well, all's well that ends well," said Mamma placidly, as she secretly returned thanks that her daughters were not as others.

* * * * * *

But later, far into the night, Damaris stood at her window, with her arms round the bulldog's neck.

"You're the only one who *really* loves me, Well-Well. Everybody else run away and leaves me. I'm—I'm, so unhappy!"

Tears stood in the big eyes as she flung out her arms and cried in a sudden passionate intensity, "*Marraine*! *Marraine*! I want you—I want you! If you loved me, you would come to me, because I want you so!"

CHAPTER XXIII

"The thorns which I have reap'd are of the tree
I planted; they have torn me, and I bleed.
I should have known what fruit would spring
from such a seed."

BYRON

Olivia Duchess of Longacres stood on the balcony of the hotel, looking down at the cortege which had escorted the wife of the Sheik el-Umbar from the House 'an Mahabbah some way out in the desert and which was making its way as best it could through the tortuous, narrow, unpaved streets of Khargegh town.

The white and only wife of the great Arab travelled *en reine*; two outriders with modern rifles slung across the shoulder and brandishing throwing-spears, caused consternation amongst the spectators as at a word or touch of the unspurred foot they made their magnificent horses rear and back and plunge.

One trick or feat had caused the heavens to be rent with screams of pure joy and shouts of "*Wallahi-el-azim*," "*Ma sha-Allah*" and other references to the might and glory of the Almighty.

You do not often see this feat of strength and dexterity, and when you do, it brings your heart almost out of your body and has an exhibition of tent-pegging simply beaten to a frazzle.

A spectator of the tender age of three, clothed—as it was a day of festival—in *tarbusch* and voluminous robe girt about him with a cummerbund—on ordinary days he would have been clothed in nature and girt in dirt—toddled straight into the middle of a square, just as the outriders charged across it. There was no room for them to turn, so packed were the places where the sidewalks should have been, neither was there time in which to rein in their horses. Women shrieked and beat their breasts, men looked on at the inevitable tragedy with the composure of the sterner sex.

The babe stood stock-still.

And Yussuf the outrider, bending low on his saddle, drove straight down upon it, gathered the back part of the cummerbund and some folds of the voluminous skirt upon the point of his spear, and, lifting the mite, amidst yells and shouts and wild clamour, carried him at spear-length and top speed safely across the square.

Where the real danger comes in is in judging the exact amount of stuff to gather on the spear-head; an inch or so too much and you may get a part of the kiddie's little back; an inch or so too little and, when you have him high in air, you may cut through the cloth and cause said kiddie to make a hasty descent to *terra firma*.

Anyway, the child was safely restored to its fond mother, who simultaneously smacked it and stuffed its mouth with fly-blown sweetmeats, and became the hero for the latter part of the day.

The real cortege was headed by camels bearing gifts from the House el-Umbar to the great white woman who stood, on the balcony in a grey silk taffeta dress, a shawl of priceless lace on her head and a grey parrot upon her shoulder. Silks, jewels, sweetmeats, *bibelots* in ivory and precious metal, dates, coffee in berries, a monkey and a bushel of wheat were amongst the gifts carried by the camels who grumbled and rumbled as they stalked with swaying gait and contemptuous half-closed eyes.

Next came the armed escort, mounted on horses, with modern rifles slung and cummerbunds stuck full of the most atrocious-looking knives. They scowled at everyone, but as they passed under the balcony each one drew his knife and rattled it against that of his neighbour so that the weapons made a glittering arch in the light of the setting sun, as salutation to the old white woman who was of their mistress's race.

Came Mustapha, the Ethiopian, into whose care the Sheikh had given his wife all those years ago, when they had ridden out of the desert up to his dwelling amongst the talik palms of the Flat Oasis.

He was on foot—not that he had done the entire journey in like manner—and held the golden chain of the magnificent camel upon which his mistress rode.

She rode in a palanquin of ivory with curtains of rose satin embroidered in precious stones; on either side, also on camels, rode two slaves who waved huge circular fans on long staffs to cool the air about this woman who was so beloved throughout the land for her good deeds and loving, helping hand.

She was in silk robes of rose covered in a satin cloak of deeper shade; she was closely veiled as becomes the wife of a Mohammedan, and wore no jewels save a rope of pearls; and her steady, wonderful blue eyes, which were just twin heavens of happiness, shone with delight as she looked up at the old woman who had known her as a girl, with her hair hanging in two great plaits.

She put both hands to her forehead and spread them out in the beautiful Eastern gesture of welcome, then bowed to her knees, as she passed.

Then, turning, she pulled her yashmak a little to one side. "*Petite Maman!*" she cried. "Welcome, *Petite Maman!*" and blew her a kiss from the tips of her rosy fingers.

Arrived at the entrance, the armed escort made a circle round her with drawn knives; her camel knelt; a Persian carpet was laid across the *quasi*-clean stones; then Mustapha the Ethiopian made a sign, upon which Ameena, the little hunchback woman who loved her mistress more than her life and who had been transported with joy when she had laid the first-born, the son, in the mother's arms, came running swiftly.

Mustapha and Ameena lived one long life of secret feud; they fought like cat and dog as to who could do the most in their mistress's service; they stood shoulder to shoulder and fought everybody else in the same good cause; and the huge man scowled fiercely as the deformed little woman arranged the flowing robes and walked up the Persian carpet behind the wife of the great Sheikh.

"Well, I never!" was Hobson's comment as she peeked from behind a door. "Her grace must have made a mistake. You take that downstairs," she added, coming boldly out onto the landing to intercept the slave with the monkey. "Downstairs," and she pointed down to the entrance, surging with people, "unless you want the place to be full of feathers and fur!"

Jill stood in the doorway; looked across at her godmother, and made the beautiful gesture of salutation, then removed her veil, picked up her robes and ran across the room right into the outstretched arms.

Tears were very close as they laughed and held each other by the hand, but the laughter died away altogether as they sat in the falling shadows, the younger one with her head on the older one's lap.

Two wise women, they were fighting for the happiness of the young, as the shadows fell and the stars came out and faded before the light of the moon as she trailed her silver garments across the heavens.

Jill had risen once to her feet, in a moment of anger, and had gone out onto the balcony and stood looking down, smiling upon the crowd, composed chiefly of women, who had raised their hands and called down the blessings of Allah upon her.

The steps were strewn with gifts, ranging from live goats to masses of sticky sweetmeats and glass beads. Mothers had brought their sickly babies and laid them down amongst the goats and beads, hoping that if even the shadow of the blessed woman were to fall upon them they might be healed.

Mustapha kept guard, hurling abuse at those who tarried, helping their departure by the aid of his foot. Hobson stood like a grim sentinel outside the sitting-room door. She had made tea under the greatest difficulty—the kettle of tepid water had been flung at the salaaming offender who had brought it—and had taken it in blushing brick-red when Jill had risen and kissed her on both cheeks. Dinner had been served, hardly tasted, and been sent away, and a whole tray of cups full of burnt milk showed the perturbation of the maid's mind as she waited, and waited for the sound of the little bell which summoned her to her grace's presence.

"You are a noble-looking woman, my child," said the duchess, as she keenly scrutinised the fair face with great blue eyes and broad humourous mouth, which, but for an added serenity and dignity, was so very like the face of the girl who had been left behind at Ismailiah over twenty years ago, and who had journeyed into the desert with the Arabian Sheikh and had married him. "I'm not surprised your husband adores you. Could he not have come with you? I have always longed to see him."

It seemed that the Sheikh Hahmed had been invited to Bagdad, to some conference concerning the big Arabian question, but hoped to be able to greet her grace before her departure. In the meanwhile his dwellings, his servants, his horses and everything he was possessed of were hers.

"And he means it, *Petite Maman*; he loves making people happy. I—I *love* him." She paused for a moment; then looked straight into the stern old eyes. "My love for my son is as great as my love for his father, and I would lay down my life for their happiness."

There was no tenderness in the sad old eyes and no lines of yielding in the stern old mouth; for although her heart was aching to say yes to the mother's insistent demands for her son's happiness, her common sense had turned her into a very rock of resistance.

"I am happy, radiantly happy." Jill, who was sitting on a stool at the old woman's feet, slipped to her knees and caught the wrinkled old hands in her own. "So why should the little girl not be happy with my son, who is the finest man and dearest son ever born to woman? Tell me what difference is there? Why should my son be made unhappy? Tell me!"

She knew perfectly well. Her son's words on the roof of his dwelling under the stars were ringing in her ears; but she was hanging on to a very forlorn hope with both hands, tricking herself with the thought that, out of her love for her, the wise old woman might see things in a different light and give her consent to the marriage just because the man was her son.

But the old woman caught the mother to her breast and stroked the golden head and kissed it with a world of pain in her sad old eyes.

"Because, dear," and the words were very gentle and the voice was very soft, "just because, when we love, we think of ourselves only, and not of those to come."

The old woman sighed as Jill raised her head sharply: "Try to understand, little one. You, my dear, a white woman, married a pure-bred Arab. Ah! my, dear, my dear, forgive me, your son is—"

Jill sprang to her feet, and as she sprang caught the rope of pearls upon the arm of the chair, breaking it and scattering the jewels to the four corners of the room.

She flung out her hands, making the Eastern sign to scare away evil spirits. "The omen!" she whispered. "The omen! A broken string of pearls means—means—death."

"Come, come, child," said the old lady sharply, and to allay the unsightly terror in the other's face, and also because she believed in using an axe in felling a tree, repeated her last remark. "You are suffering now through the selfishness of love. Women who marry without giving a thought to the result of the marriage, to the good or the harm it might bring to the children of that marriage, deserve to suffer. Marry the man, if you really love him and can help him by being his wife; but let there be no children if there is anything in the union that might hurt them." She rose and crossed to the girl who was standing staring into a corner of the room, with a world of horror in her eyes. She moved back as the old woman, came towards her, holding out her hands as though to ward off some evil thing she saw in the shadows.

"I can't bear it," she whispered; "I can't bear it. I don't believe that anyone, could think *that* of Hugh. Remember how loved he was at Harrow—"

"Ah! my dear, my dear, there was your great mistake . . ."

"You're wrong," interrupted Jill harshly. "You're hopelessly, cruelly wrong. He was idolised in England; he is loved out here. It was sheer spite on the part of the—woman who told him that he was—was—" She pressed her hands over her mouth as she backed to the wall, then flung her arms out wide; her face was dead-white, her eyes blazing; she reminded the old woman of a tigress fighting for her cubs; she was beautiful beyond words in the tragedy of her motherhood. "I don't believe you—I don't believe you—I—you—"

"Listen, Jill." The old woman's voice was as cold as ice as she watched the agony in the fair face. Dear heavens! she did not want to hurt; she wanted to give in and gather the child up in her arms, but she knew what was best. "Your boy knows it, dear; he knows he is out of the running. Come over to me and listen whilst I tell you something." She sat down and pulled the suffering child down beside her, who lay across the silken knees like the stricken mother across the knees of the wise Madonna and made no sound or movement whilst she listened to the bitter words of the fortune-teller in the hotel garden at Cairo.

A little silence fell; then, very gently, very tenderly the old woman spoke:

"So you see, dear, until she is of age it will be only my duty to see that Damaris does not marry your son."

And Jill sprang to her feet and beat her hands together.

"And I," she said, "I will give my heart's blood to bring happiness to my son. Death alone shall—"

She stopped and shivered as she glanced over her shoulder out into the night, then drew herself up with a surpassing dignity and threw out her hands in the Eastern gesture of resignation.

"You say 'I will not,' I say 'I will,' but it is God who decides." With a little sobbing sigh she relinquished the unequal struggle, just as Hobson walked boldly into the room and stood inside the door, like a graven image of intense displeasure, when her mistress, unable to withstand the unspoken disapproval, consented, after a promise to Jill to have another long talk on the morrow, to go to bed.

But there was to be no long talk anyway in the town of Khargegh on the morrow.

She lay in bed, propped by pillows against which, divested of its mask of red and white and blue, the dear little old face shone brown. A priceless bit of lace hid her own white locks, free for the night of the outrageous perruque which covered them by day and which lay at the moment hidden in its box.

A pair of crimson bed-slippers peeped from under the bed, another pair, absurdly small, outrageously high-heeled, buckled and crimson, made a splash of colour near the dressing-table. Her little hands were gently folded under the ruffles of priceless lace of her cashmere night-attire as she lay quite still, trying to find a way out through the jungle of pain and grief which seemed to spread round and about so many she loved; whilst Dekko, puffed out with sleepiness, sat on the back of a chair, muttering incoherently to some fanciful image of his weird brain.

Hobson lay fast asleep in the next room, which had a communicating door with that of her mistress. Knowing nothing of nerves or of temperament, she had dropped asleep as soon as her head, with scanty locks tortured into a *chevaux-de-frise* of steel pins, had touched the pillow; her strong hands were clenched on the frill of her stout calico nightdress; her powerful face looked grim in the dim light of the moon, which, high in the heavens, flung a silver shaft through the open window straight across the bed. There was absolutely no sound when, just as, so many miles away, Damaris made her passionate appeal, as she stood by the window, Hobson, dour, stolid, unimaginative, yet with a streak of Scotch blood in her veins, sat straight up in bed. Her eyes were wide open as she stared in front of her, then she passed her powerful hand over her grim face and flung the bedclothes to one side.

"She's in trouble." She spoke very clearly, sat for a moment thinking, then reached for a puce dressing-gown trimmed mulberry. "I'll go and tell her," and the infinite love in the pronoun was good to hear. "She'll understand."

The duchess turned: her head as the door opened slowly, but made no movement, although her heart suddenly quickened its beat.

"Yes?" she said quietly.

Hobson walked up to the bed and took one of the little old hands between her own powerful ones.

"Miss Damaris wants you, ma'am." She spoke with certain conviction; then added, "I've had a dream, ma'am. I saw nothing, but I heard Miss Damaris calling you. It woke me up. '*Marraine*,' she said, 'I want you.' That was all. And she does, ma'am."

She stood patting the hand of her mistress, who lay for a moment quite still; then the faithful creature put a Shetland shawl round the bent shoulders as the old lady sat straight up in bed.

"Would you please find Miss Jill's maid," (she used the term of the past, when Jill Carden had stayed at the Castle and had teased Hobson to death) "and ask her to tell her mistress that I should be pleased if she could find it convenient to come to my room for a moment."

Hobson found the aged body-servant lying asleep outside her mistress's door.

Ameena had learned a few words of the English language in the last twenty years, but not enough to allow her to understand the terrifying person who stood over her; so that she shook her head whilst Hobson repeated her request over and over again, and ever more distinctly, until it ended at last in a veritable shout which brought Jill, who had not slept for the ache in her mother-heart, to the door.

For a moment she stood, a beautiful picture, with big questioning eyes and two great plaits of auburn hair hanging down over her satin wrap; then she ran down the corridor and into her godmother's bedroom.

In an hour those two forceful women had made their plans, acting without hesitation upon what might so easily have been the outcome of digestive trouble on Maria Hobson's part.

Fully clothed, the two maids entered her grace's bedroom, the one carrying the tea-tray and the other a plate of biscuits.

"Ameena," said Jill, who was sitting on the end of the bed, "please go and find Mustapha. Tell him to go to the station, find the station-master and give him this letter. We want a special train as soon as possible. Mustapha is to bring me a written reply from the station-master."

She spoke with the authority of the Eastern potentate and took no notice of the maid when she knelt and kissed the hem of her satin wrap.

"Give me a cigarette, Hobson," said her grace, in the depths of whose eyes twinkled the star of humour. "We shall be starting as soon as possible, maybe directly after breakfast, for Luxor."

"Yes, your grace. I will begin the packing," said the imperturbable Hobson, placing the tray on the table beside the bed. "And when you have had your tea, ma'am, will you try and get a little sleep? You can leave everything safely to me."

But special trains do not grow like blackberries upon a side line in the East, so that many weary hours passed before they set out upon the return journey, which was rendered infinitely tedious by the never-ending mistakes which got them shunted into sidings to allow the ordinary trains to pass.

CHAPTER XXIV

*"The watchmen that went about the city found
me; they smote me, they wounded me; the keepers
of the wall took away my veil from me."*

SONG OF SOLOMON

The night before Ben Kelham's return to Cairo, Zulannah sat on a pile of cushions, with her back to the crumbling plaster wall, in the filthy, smoke-filled hovel.

She had completely recovered, and save for the excruciating pain caused by the shrunken muscles when she moved, was as sound as a bell, and likely to live to a ripe old age, slave to her whilom servant, who sat on his heels, inhaling the fumes of the jewel-encrusted *nargileh* which his heart had always coveted.

It is useless writing about the hell through which the woman had lived from the moment she had returned to consciousness. Besides, there are some things which words cannot describe, and which in any case are best left alone, not even to the imagination.

She was absolutely in the power of the negroid brute. With the destruction of her beauty she had lost everything save what she had in the bank, and from the ever-growing heaps of little canvas bags in a corner and little piles of banknotes under the straw, she knew that some day that, too, must come to an end.

She had loved her jewels, loved the shimmering pearls and sparkling diamonds, and had found her greatest joy in dipping her hand into a leather bag filled with unset stones. How often had she sat in the luxury of her bedroom, revelling in the trickle of the rubies, sapphires and emeralds from between her fingers into her lap.

Even those she had lost.

The Milner safe stood open, showing empty shelves, and she shuddered yet at the memory of the frightful scene which had followed her refusal to open it.

She loved jewels; wanted them for their beauty; had fought the negro for them; but there was one thing she clung to even more, and that was life, so that when the huge hands had slowly, so very slowly pressed upon her neck, she had given in and setting the combination, had swung the door slowly back.

And Qatim, grey-green with fright, thinking that it had been worked by the power of a *djinn* or devil, had flung her out into the night, and having scraped a hole in the foetid earth under the straw, with fervent prayers to whatever he worshipped, had withdrawn the jewels, hidden them, and called the woman back.

Yes! she clung to life. Strange is it how we do, even when youth and beauty and health have passed from us. How, crippled and unlovely, twisted of temper or limb, with failing senses, in bath-chair, or propped on sticks, we hang on to the last thread, when surely we ought to be so thankful to snap it and be away to whatever our lives here have prepared for us over the border.

> "Were't not a shame, were't not a loss for him
> In this clay carcase, crippled, to abide?"

Well might old Omar ponder upon this.

But Zulannah had a good reason for clinging to life, in spite of the greatness of her debacle.

The metal of which had been wrought the one love that had come to her in her short life had not been able to withstand the crucible of physical pain. For hours and days she had writhed in the agony of her physical injury, with no one to care if she suffered or starved, except the Ethiopian, who, when her senses had come back to her, had twitted her upon her failure in her love-affairs; had tormented and mocked and laughed, until a great wish for revenge had taken the place of her former love for the Englishman. Revenge, above all things, on the girl who had been capable of inspiring love in two such men; revenge on the white man who had really been the primary cause of her downfall, but a lingering, hellish revenge, if she could only think of one, for the man who had given the order to the dogs just because she had reviled the white girl, Damaris.

So she sat on the pile of cushions, smoking the cheapest cigarette of the bazaar, whilst her cunning brain wove plots around the astounding news Qatim had just imparted.

They were perfectly free from interruption. The door was barred and the small aperture which served as window was too highly placed in the wall to allow of eyes to peep; but it was superstition that really kept them safe and proved far more potent as a barrier against their neighbours' curiosity than any spike-crowned wall.

Qatim had given out that the woman was bewitched, and that death, instantaneous and horrible, would be the fate awaiting anyone but himself who should speak to her or look upon her unveiled face before the setting of the sun—some of us Christians refuse to walk under ladders—and, although it entailed much fetching and carrying and marketing on his part, still, it ensured them solitude.

"And you saw him?"

She spoke with a sibilant intaking of breath, caused by the twist to her mouth.

"Yes; with a beautiful white woman—another. They have come from Assouan by the boat."

"Not the girl who rode in the desert with—"

She touched the purple angry marks on her cheek.

"Nay, woman; I have told thee, *she* walks in the blackness of the ruins, with the man who caused thee thy hurt. She drives with him," he spat, "she should take thy place in the bazaar, O Zulannah of the thousand lovers."

The woman paid no heed to the jibe.

"Who told thee?"

"Behold, the night-watchman of the big hotel upon the edge of the water sent me word."

"Why?"

"That is no business of thine. Tell me what scheme thou hast in thy head. Dost desire the death of the three?"

Zulannah shook her head and turning it so that the wounds and distortion were hidden, leant against the wall.

"Not yet!" she said, loosening with filthy hand the uncombed masses of jet-black hair, which still retained something of the perfume of better days. "Not *yet*! Let me think awhile."

And she paid no heed to the man, who sat staring at her, breathing heavily.

The right side of her face, untouched and perfect, showed in all its beauty against the dirty whiteness of the wall; her hair served as a mantle to the perfect figure in the soiled satin wrap; her crippled limbs showed not at all in the foul room lit by a wick floating in a saucer of oil.

The light went out suddenly.

Oh, Zulannah! surely your cap of misery was full to the brim!

CHAPTER XXV

"He that has patience may compass anything."

RABELAIS

Ben Kelham sat near the balustrade on the verandah of Shepheard's Hotel just after breakfast, pretending to read the morning paper, whilst trying to make up his mind.

Sybil Sidmouth and her mother, owing to lack of accommodation, brought about by the crush of visitors in the huge caravanserai, had gone to the Savoy; for which the man was secretly thankful.

He wanted to eat out his heart all by himself in the appalling loneliness which had overwhelmed him when, on ringing up Heliopolis the night before, he had learned that Damaris and the duchess had transferred themselves to Luxor.

And you simply cannot indulge in your particular brand of *malaise* or dolour with an extreme optimist sitting opposite you at meals, or adjacent to your elbow at most other times.

He anathematised the postal system of Egypt; his own haste in accepting the girl's refusal; the oriental imagination which magnified cats into lions; but, above all, the wash of that steamer (upon which Damaris had returned from Denderah) which had re-floated his own craft and sent him racing full steam ahead for Cairo.

Another hour of the infernal wait on the sandbank, and he would have transferred himself to one of the scores of small boats and been ferried across to Luxor, where he would have dined at the Winter Palace Hotel, whilst waiting to catch the express to Cairo, and perhaps have seen his beloved in the dining-room, or have heard that she was staying there.

He was thoroughly irritated as he pondered in his deliberate way as to the best thing to do.

Should he take the first train back to Luxor, or, as the duchess had not seen fit to acquaint him as to her movements, should he stay where he was, write her a letter, or send a telegram and wait for an answer? Anyway, he was irritated enough to scowl at the commissionaire who was rating a woman whom he had seen hanging about the street, doubtless with intent of soliciting a nickel coin from one of the great white race as he— or she—descended the steps to stroll along the street.

She made a few choice remarks upon the undoubted inclusion of a pig in the commissionaire's parentage, in a curiously sibilant voice, then limped away with a distressing swing of her body from the hips.

"Can't you keep those people quiet?" Kelham demanded angrily, as he moved a chair further back, and lit a cigarette.

An hour had passed, in which he had come to no decision, when Fate, in the shape of a page-boy, offered him the just-arrived, local morning paper, which he took and read, with only half a mind upon the gossipy contents.

"By Jove!" he suddenly exclaimed. "If that isn't a bit of luck! Here's the very excuse for getting down there without kind of thrusting myself upon them." He flattened out the paper and again read through the paragraph which gave a most extraordinarily detailed account of the immensely wealthy Hugh Carden Ali, his career at Harrow; his travels; his stables in the desert; his birds and a hundred and one other details calculated to interest those who like reading about other people's most intimate affairs. It ended: ". . . Being a great sportsman, the strange story of lion which is causing such uneasiness and is likely to do harm to the Luxor season, has taken him to his Tents of Purple and Gold, one of the wonders of modern Egypt and which lie in the desert a little distance from the well-known Colossi."

He did not frown this time as he folded the paper and turned to watch the commissionaire in conclave with a coal-black Ethiopian who, clad in crimson tunic, enormous turban and with scimitar rattling at his side, tendered an envelope.

"Yes, yes," said the hotel servant. "I will see that it is delivered into the gentleman's own hands. And, tell me"—he lowered his voice as he winked his eye—"has she returned from Alexandria?"

Qatim was caught in a quandary, and he cursed the vanity which had urged him to don his most resplendent garments upon his errand to the great hotel, to which he had come after a violent argument with Zulannah.

With a heart full of hatred, and agony in her twisted limbs the woman had hung about the streets in front of the hotel until she had seen the man for whom she had felt such a sudden and fleeting love, and who was the primary cause of her disfigurement.

Hurt him she must, if only as a balm to her own physical and mental agony; and in what better way than by destroying his faith in the white girl he loved?

Hence the letter, written hastily in the hovel and consigned to the care of the Ethiopian, who, in return for his assistance, had demanded backshisch in the shape of a pink leaf covered with strange black marks.

The woman's presence in the great city in her deplorable state was the last thing he wanted to be known; so he lied—clumsily.

"Nay; she is in Alexandria," he blurted out.

The commissionaire slowly winked an eye.

"Perhaps," he said; "perhaps not," and chuckled as the negro turned hastily and strode away in the direction of the bank.

And thus came it to be known in the bazaar that Zulannah the courtesan had returned to the great city.

And a little later, Ben Kelham felt no tweak at the string with which Fate had hobbled him to his destiny, when, on hearing his number called, he took the letter from the page-boy, turned it over, and looked at it on each side, as we do when curious, but not over-interested; then he opened it idly, read it and crushed it in both hands.

It was written in the execrable English Zulannah had picked up in her few years of cosmopolitan intercourse with different nationalities; it was in vile hand-writing and was as despicable a method of revenge as an anonymous letter usually is.

It ran after this fashion:

"If you want to find your white woman go and look for her in the ruins of Karnak, at night, in the arms of her half-caste lover, Hugh Carden Ali."

And the woman who had limped back to the street, sniggered behind her veil as she watched the man tear the letter into shreds, while he sat and thought out an answer to this second problem.

"It's a damnable lie. My Damaris and good old Carden! I expect they've met, but who—" He sniffed at his hands suddenly. "Pah! Now, where have I smelt that scent before?—filth!" He sat with his hands to his nose, then frowned as, under the suggestion of the perfume, the picture of a lovely woman clad in silks and satins and wearing rich jewels rose before him.

"My God!" he said slowly, as the full significance of it all dawned slowly upon him. "Of course! She—she invited me to—to visit her—and I refused. By all that's clean and decent, if I don't make her pay for this! And it's Carden, too, who can tell me the best way to set about it. The harlot! I wonder if I shall have to wait until evening for a train." He clenched his hands until the knuckles showed white, as he unseeingly watched a woman limp down the street. "I'll make her sorry she was ever born."

He need not have worried on that point. Fate was dogging those unsteady feet back to the hovel.

The spreading of a prairie fire is slow compared to the speed with which news runs through the bazaar. The servants in the big house in the big garden went sullenly about their various tasks of tidying and clearing up the courtesan's home, whilst little knots of people, composed principally of women, stood about in the vicinity of the gate.

It was the first time the tyrannical woman had been absent upon a long journey, and the relatives and friends even unto a most distant generation of her servants had taken advantage of it to visit the house and examine its, to them, surpassing luxury.

The Ethiopian, with his mind fixed only upon the bank, had taken but little interest in the house itself, and had visited it but rarely, and then only for the sake of appearances; so that the visitors had become more and more brazen, as the days passed, fingering the satins, sitting upon the cushions, feasting on the floor.

Bes, the monstrous keeper of the lions, had become prime favourite with the men, and the neighbourhood had resounded with the roars of the brutes at night as they fought for their food.

Also was there something savage in the way the women visitors had fingered and touched everything, and had visited every corner of the building. They were fat or thin, plain or passably good-looking; they were all hideously poor, and in their heads they had the echo of the gibes their menfolk had cast at them, when, returning with empty pockets, they had boasted of great conquests.

Which boasting the sillies had believed, thinking, as all women think, that their own particular male has been specially favoured of the gods and is therefore an Adonis in the eyes of every other woman.

There was an indefinite air of trouble in that quarter of the bazaar which increased with the heat of the day. Household matters were neglected, whilst the women foregathered to talk; words were few, but gestures were quick and expressive; the servants, wondering at the absence of the Ethiopian, grumbled as they worked; they had been paid no wages in their mistress's absence, and were on the verge of mutiny.

Brave words! When they knew that they would fall flat upon their faces at the first swish of her satin robes.

They waited all the day, and no definite word came of the woman's return. They waited until the stars twinkled and they still waited with the terrible patience of the East. Why they waited they could not have told you. They dared not set upon her if she passed in her litter; she wielded too great a power through her beauty and wealth for that; but as the hours passed, they moved softly to and fro, as moves the wretched beast in his cage at feeding-time, whilst a look of cunning allied to cruelty shone in the soft brown eyes.

It only required a spark to start the conflagration.

CHAPTER XXVI

*"And the dogs shall eat Jezebel . . . and
there shall be none to bury her."*

II KINGS

The station was bathed blood-red in the after-glow of the
wonderful sunset, which, being a daily occurrence, is hardly
ever noticed by the winter visitors in Cairo; a star or two
twinkled in the pale grey hem of the coat of many colours
which Day was offering to Night, as the evening breeze lifted
the edges of the veils and blew refreshingly around a woman
who descended awkwardly from a native cart and limped her
way across the station yard. The porter trundling Ben
Kelham's luggage caught her by the shoulder and likening her
to the cross-eyed offspring of a clumsy she-camel, flung her to
one side. Rage incarnate glared from her eyes, bitter
vituperation flowed from behind the yashmak, until, noticing
that a swashbuckling member of the native police was making
his menacing way towards her, she quieted down and limped
to where she saw, standing, the station porter of Shepheard's
Hotel.

Strange is that power which has led so many a criminal to the
gallows by dragging him irresistibly back to the scene of the
crime.

It was some such force which had held Zulannah throughout

the day. She had nothing further to gain by looking upon the man who had unconsciously been the cause of her ruin; she had done her best to retaliate by blighting the love she had herself tried to gain; but she had been mastered by a morbid desire to look just once more upon Ben Kelham, hoping to be able to trace in his face some sign of his mental hurt.

The suffering of innocent people and animals had always given her intense pleasure. How much greater, therefore, her satisfaction if she could bring, and gloat over, bodily or mental pain to someone who had made her suffer?

She hung about until she saw Ben Kelham arrive, and stood quite close to him, chuckling inwardly at the tale told by the grim set of his mouth.

Zulannah was dirty; her hands were ill-kempt; her fine muslin veils filthy and torn; but there still hung about her the faint odour of the perfume she had always used in the hey-day of her success. The passing of a barrow piled high with luggage disturbed her veils, and as the rush of some excited natives disturbed the air Ben Kelham swung around.

He had suddenly scented the perfume of Zulannah the courtesan.

He looked to right, to left and all about him, eyed with disfavour the dirty woman so close to him, who stood crookedly, with an evil leer to one eye; frowned and walked away to the platform from which the train starts for Luxor. All stations in the East are invariably and most uncomfortably crowded with natives who either stray hopelessly after the manner of lost sheep, or stand stock-still, as hopelessly incapable of movement, or rush pell-mell hither-thither at the sound of clanging bell, or shriek from locomotive; but the station was unduly crowded this evening, owing to the return of hundreds of pilgrims from a visit to a certain shrine in the countryside and an influx of their friends and relations from the bazaar to greet them.

The strong electric lights were blazing, intensifying the vivid colours and modifying the dirt upon what was intended to be the white portions of the natives' picturesque raiment; they shone down also upon the disfigured woman who, with a certain amount of satisfaction in her heart, brought about by the grim look on Ben Kelham's face, was limping towards the exit. She had just reached it when her veil was caught on the rough wicker of a basket containing hens which was being carried on the back of a man whose mean hovel—which yet had been his home—had been razed to the ground to allow of the building of the courtesan's house.

He had stood the best part of the day, with heart full of vengeance, amongst the little knots of people loitering outside the courtesan's gate, and had only been induced to leave the spot to go and claim the poultry waiting for him at the station.

Just as the veil caught in the wicker he moved a little to one side to escape a group of laughing, joyous pilgrims; swung right round to shout them a greeting and in so doing pulled the struggling woman in front of him, tearing off her veil and exposing the right side of her face which, having escaped injury, was still wonderfully beautiful, in spite of the dirt. The basket of hens crashed, to the ground and, bursting, liberated the birds, as, with a yell of "Zulannah!" the man leapt straight at the woman, who dived under a porter's arm and disappeared through the exit.

There was a sudden mad rush to the exit by the inhabitants of the bazaar, who, jamming together in a shouting, yelling pack, gave the woman a few moments' grace.

"Stand on one side, sir. Come back, miss!" ordered the station-master, seizing the arm of an indignant Britisher. "It's no use trying to stop them; they go like this sometimes, quite mad, generally when they've sighted a thief or somebody against whom they have some grudge. Let them pass, sir; let them pass."

The station-yard was packed with vehicles, motors, omnibuses, and scores of rattling, racketing native carts.

Straight into the middle of them fled the woman, terror lending her an incredible speed which agonising physical pain augmented. She dived under horses, she squeezed through vehicles, she twisted and turned, caring naught for the native drivers, who, indifferent to the daily sufferings of their wretched little horses, lashed at her with their whips, with shouts of "*Shima-lak!*" "*U'a-u'a!*" "*Riglak, riglak!*" "*U'a-u'a!*" and peals of derisive laughter.

Headed by the man who had carried the hens, their eyes blazing, helpless victims of the indescribable blood-lust which sometimes seizes the mob, the inhabitants of the bazaar, with those who, understanding nothing of the cause of the tumult, had joined in merely for the sport, were after the woman like a pack of hounds.

If it had not been for the limp caused by the shortening of one leg, and which became more noticeable the more she ran, she might have escaped in the crowd in the Place Rameses and been alive to-day. But the pack, as they ran, shouted, "A lame dog, a lame dog! Who has seen a lame dog?" and those who had rushed to door or window to watch the fun pointed her out with yells of laughter. She found a few moments' respite when she tripped and fell over the neck of a recumbent camel indistinguishable in the gloom of the side street into which she had turned as she headed for her own house.

She had no distinct plan in her head; she was too exhausted to think; she only knew, as know all wounded animals, that home is the place to get to when stricken unto death. If she had just sat quite still on the kerb, pulled a bit of stuff across her face and pointed way down the street, with peals of laughter, the mob would have swept past her and she would have been safe; but she blindly ran for home. If she had stayed where she had fallen, behind the camel which lurched to its feet as the pack ran by, she would even then have been safe, but she lay, face down in the filth, only long enough to regain her breath, which sounded like a whistle as it shrilled through the twisted mouth. With breath regained she was up and away, with the secret door in the wall—which had been discovered in her absence—as her goal, just as the human hounds, doubling on their tracks, tore into the street, to see the fluttering end of her dress disappear round a corner.

She ran with a twisting, shuffling lope horrible to see; she looked like some wounded animal as, bent double, she paused again for breath, just for one moment, with face to the wall. She ran on; she stumbled and regained her footing; she fell on her crippled knees; then onto her face in the dust, where she remained, breathing like a far-spent horse, with bloodstained foam flecking the corners of her mouth. A great shivering shook her as she listened to the shouting, yelling mob questing this way and that for the lost quarry. She did not pray; poor Zulannah! she knew nothing of a God of Love or Pity to pray to; she lay still, burying her fingers in the sand, clinging desperately to what remained to her of life.

They swept round the corner, those men and women, screaming vengeance on her who lived in luxury whilst they starved; who hung herself with jewels and neglected to pay the trifling debts of the bazaar; who lived in a house built on the site of their demolished homes. They rushed past and over her lying begrimed and foul, one with the dust of the ill-lighted street They drove her face into the dust; they marked her beautiful body with the shape of their feet; but they did not kill her.

She wanted to live.

The pack passed on to the bazaar, carrying with it the definite news of the return of the woman Zulannah; and if you had looked close you would have seen the cunning in the eyes of the man who had carried the hens; if you had listened to his whispered words you would have shivered at the ferocity of his counsel.

In the passing of ten minutes you would, if you had walked that way, have walked through empty streets in the vicinity of the courtesan's house, and there would have been nothing or nobody to whisper to you of the men, women, children, and dogs standing packed in the rooms and passages and courtyards, waiting for a given signal.

The moon looked down on a peaceful scene as Zulannah, wrapped in filthy garments, crept stealthily from shadow to shadow.

Had she been more observant, she would have wondered at the intense stillness of the bazaar, which, no matter at what hour of the night, is full of little sounds; the song of a woman, or her laugh, or her cry; the crack of a whip; the baying of dogs.

If she had looked back she would have seen the stealthy opening of doors, the craning of a furtive head as quickly withdrawn.

She paid no heed.

She was so near, so very near the place in the wall hidden in the shadow of the *talik* palms and in which was the secret door which opened on the pressing of a certain brick in the third row from the top. And once in the house, with a veil across her face, a whip or dagger in her hand, she would show them who was master, cripple or no cripple, fool that she had been to have submitted to the black Qatim, but thrice fool he, who knew nothing of that other bank in which one-half her fortune and one-half her jewels were kept in safe custody against such a rainy day as this.

She cursed herself for the blundering, feeble way she had set about revenge; she cursed the moon; the agony of her limbs; the stretch which lay between one shadow and another; but she laughed, though no sound issued from the gaping mouth, as she stood in the last patch of shadow which was separated by some few yards of silvery path from the black blot upon the wall which covered the secret door.

They had hunted and harried her, and walked upon her body lying in the dust, but they had lost her and had gone back to their hovels to eat and sleep, and maybe once more cast up the reckoning of the money she owed them, the which—she swore the most horrible oath—she would never pay.

She gathered up her dust-ridden garments and stole swiftly across the moonlit space; she had just touched the edge of the shadow, she was almost home, when, with a mighty shout, they were upon her. Out of the houses, out of the courtyards, down the streets they swarmed, children and women falling, to be jerked to their feet by the men who ran silently, urged on by the fanatic who for years had hugged the idea of some such moment of most horrible revenge.

And then to the sinister sound of the rushing feet there was added the baying of many pariah dogs which, from every conceivable corner and from miles away, raced like a pack of wolves upon the Steppes, to join the hunt.

Blind with terror, shaking in agony, Zulannah fumbled helplessly for the special brick; it lay, she knew, in the third row and had as mark a jutting piece of mortar in the middle.

She passed her hand wildly up and down, too mad with fear to count; every brick, to right, to left, and as far as she could reach above, below, had the jutting piece of mortar; the wall was as high as the heavens; the third row was here, beneath her hand—no! high above her head—no! one, two, yes, here—her fingers touched it—it was gone.

It takes a long time to write or read in inky words, but it was really only a few seconds before the door swung open.

She gave a scream of terrible relief and rushed into the blackness and as she rushed a dog leapt straight at her shoulders.

She screamed again and swung-to the door with all her strength; it shut upon the dog, breaking its back; it remained ajar to her pursuers.

There still was hope. She knew the way; they did not. Could she but get to her bedroom behind the massive doors, could she but reach the telephone, the instrument she had regarded as her finest toy, she would soon have the police running to the rescue. She fled down the narrow passage which led to a jumble of small rooms; she even paused for a moment to listen to the cursing of those who ran behind her, stumbling in the narrow way.

She fled through the farthest door; she was free; there but remained the shallow flight of marble stairs to the suite wherein her bedroom lay.

Then she stopped, and, shrieking, flung out her arms.

To right, to left and upon the flight of stairs, there stood her servants.

The men and the women she had flogged and kicked, thinking to heal their wounds and bruises and dim their memories by throwing gold amongst them on the morrow.

They made no movement, they simply stood and stared.

Her head-veil and mantle had gone; her under-garments were torn to shreds, leaving exposed the slender body which leaned sideways like a tree which had been struck by lightning. Her matted hair fell far below her waist; it made a frame to the horrible face, one side of which was as that of an old, old hag, and the other, grimed with dirt, flecked with foam, was yet as lovely as a jewel.

They shrank back and still further back; they made the sign to scare away the spirit of evil; thinking her possessed of Eblis, the devil, they would not have touched her for a gold piece.

They turned their heads at the sound of rushing footsteps; they motioned her to move on; believing her mad, they gave her a chance, for in the East you dare not turn your hand against the mentally afflicted.

She ran.

And after her came the pack in full cry.

Across great rooms, lit by hanging lamps, scented with brasiers of perfumed wood, she fled, slipping upon chinchilla rug or glaring monstrous hearthrug of Berlin wool, in her desperate haste to quit the house.

Out into the air she must get; under the trees in the garden; under the moon; down the broad paths to the wall at the end.

There was no wall too high for her to climb in her extremity. Her face was grey; her eyes sunk in black: orbits; her nose pinched, with nostrils which blew and flattened like bellows to her laboured breathing.

A hand clutched at her streaming hair and missed it as she sped down the garden; they were upon her heels, dogs jumping at her face as she ran.

She was blind, deaf, almost dead when the great gorilla-shaped arms of Bes closed about her.

She made no sound as she hurtled through the air. Mercifully perhaps was she dead, as she crashed down into the pit at the bottom of which great shapes prowled hungrily.

They did not stay to watch, not one of them.

Shouting and laughing, men and women ran back to the house, which in one hour they had stripped bare.

Just before the dawn a great flame shot skywards, an orange

ribbon across the purple robe of dying Night.

*   *   *   *   *   *

Requiem

"There was an awful row in the Bazaar last night," said Mr. Ephraim Perkins to his spouse facing him across the breakfast table. "They killed a woman and burned her house down."

"Really, dear?" said Mrs. Ephraim Perkins, rasping butter on a piece of toast. "These natives want a firm hand over them. Poor thing! They usually stab each other in the East, don't they?"

"Yes; I think so. But they threw this one into a lions' den."

"Now, that's exaggeration, Ephraim." The knife never stopped its rasping. "They would not be allowed to keep wild beasts in a populated quarter."

"Stranger things happen in the native quarter, Maria," misquoted Mr. Perkins, "than are dreamt of by the Government official."

True words!

If we dared penetrate the labyrinths of the bazaar and stir with foolish finger the dust which lies thick upon immemorial custom, what should we not find?

But having a meed of wisdom in the full measure of our imperial insularity, we do not pry with foolish fingers; guessing, even knowing of the wild beasts in those labyrinths, we draw a glove upon the hand and walk delicately in the opposite direction, with half-closed eyes.

"I repeat, it is an exaggeration," stubbornly replied Mrs.

Ephraim Perkins, as she stretched for the marmalade. "And I do hope the fire-engines arrived in time."

CHAPTER XXVII

"A tale-bearer revealeth secrets; but a man of understanding holdeth his peace."

PROVERBS

It was the night of the full moon.

It was also the night of the cotillon given by a certain princelet of unpronounceable name and great wealth, who hailed from one of those countries in Europe where quasi-royalties abound.

The cotillon-favours were to be of extraordinarily fine quality. Rumour spoke of gold cigarette-cases and other such trifles, for both sexes; the supper was to be a Bacchanalian feast; every invitation had been accepted—*ca va sans dire*. The hotel was like a disturbed wasps' nest, and the buzzing of the chatterers and the gossips well-nigh deafening.

Damaris had decided to go to the ball; in fact, since her storm of tears on her return from the unlucky visit to Denderah she had taken the broad view of the situation and had decided to give her neighbours no cause for comment and to continue the festive life, as led in the winter season on the Nile, until the return of her godmother; after which she would, as soon as possible, shake the dust of the land of the Pharaohs from off her feet.

In fact, so gay was she, so full of life and high spirits, that she appeared to have forgotten her lover completely, thereby giving the Thistleton family cause to congratulate themselves in the seclusion of their bedrooms.

"I told you so, Mamma," had said Ellen, this night of the full moon, as she had pondered before the mirror upon the effect a headache-bandeau in the shape of a royal asp would have upon a certain retired colonel who seemed inclined to find solace for his long widowhood *en secondes noces*. "She evidently did not see Mr. Kelham and Sybil on the sand-bank, and I honestly do not think she cares for him a bit."

"No," broke in Berenice, whose hair clung to her head like wet seaweed to a rock; "I am sure she does not. Do you think if Ambrose had—had courted me and then neglected me, that I could have danced and laughed and—"

"Well, I'm thankful," broke in Mamma. "Looking after any girl as beautiful and—"

"Erratic," supplied Ellen, who had decided on the headache-bandeau.

"—erratic as Damaris, is certainly no—"

"Sinecure," supplied Berenice, who, in the fervour of her affection for her herculean cleric, gave no thought to such trifles as head-dresses, and not much to the rest of her attire.

Giving a final pat to her offsprings' toilettes, Mamma shepherded them downstairs, tapping at Damaris's door as she passed, inviting her to join them in the Winter-Garden, where they were going to sit and look at the dresses, and watch the arrival of the guests from the less select hotels.

Damaris looked radiantly beautiful as she stood for a moment at the window of her godmother's sitting-room, into which she had gone to fetch a fan.

True, her eyes looked over-big in the violet shadows that surrounded them, and her cheek and collar-bones were unduly prominent, but then, however well you hide the fox of uncertainty which tears at the vitals of your common sense and sense of humour, you cannot completely hide the outward signs of the inner agony which tortures you.

"You're a perfect picture, dearie!" said Jane Coop as she tied the ribbons of the simple, heelless, white leather shoes in which the girl always preferred to dance. "Let me look at you just once more."

Like a slender lily Damaris stood under the electric light. The soft white satin seemed to cling like a sheath to the slender, beautiful figure; her arms were bare; the bodice cut low enough to show her gleaming shoulders. She was dazzling, virginal, remote as she stood quite still, looking down at her maid.

Her eyes looked intensely black; her red hair flamed; she wore no jewels save for a massive jewelled brooch in the shape of a hawk which glittered in the bodice just above the waist-belt where, thinking the bodice too low, she had pinned it hastily.

"I don't like that brooch, dearie," said the maid. "It's a waste of money, I think, to buy these heathen things. But there! you and her grace know best. And don't forget your cloak, darling; it's too chilly to sit out in the grounds without one, Egypt or no Egypt. I'll be real glad when we run into Waterloo station, that I shall."

Damaris laughed as she took the satin cloak with broad sable collar, then kissed her Nannie and walked down the corridor to her godmother's sitting-room, followed by the bulldog.

"I don't want to dance, Well-Well; I'd much rather stay up here with you and read."

"Humff!" said the dog, as he followed his beloved onto the

small balcony, where he stood as close as he could to her as she leant on the rail, and looked up at the moon and out to the other side of the river, where ruined temple and ruined tomb shone white.

"I'll come up and see you both," she said, looking down into the hideously-beautiful face, with its honest eyes and beaming expression. "But I can't take you down with me, you know. You might hurl yourself into the middle of a fox-trot to find me. I'll bring you up a cake or a chocolate, if you'll stay in here and not go after Jane to worry her with my night-slippers. Good boy; stay here and wait for Missie."

"Take me with you," said Wellington, as plainly as he could with eyes and tail. "Take me with you."

"Can't, old boy. Look"—she reached inside for a book she had been reading, and laid it on the ground. "Keep that for Missie until she comes back."

She smiled down at the great brute as it placed both forefeet upon the volume, but she sighed as she leant for a moment on the rail, then suddenly drew back as she heard her name mentioned by someone who, hankering after a cigarette, had wandered out to the canvas rocking seat directly beneath the balcony.

". . . Well!" said the masculine voice, "I think it's damned hard lines on Miss Hethencourt, that's all; and a man wants a damned good hiding for being a knave as well as a fool."

"Of course it's not gospel-truth," replied the voice of the hotel's biggest-gossip-bar-none, who, on account of her abnormal interest in other people's affairs, had earned the sobriquet of Paulina Pry, "but some people I know who were at Heliopolis and have just come from Assouan told me that Mr. Kelham is engaged to Miss Sidmouth—you know, she is the crack lady-shot—and that they are on their way home now. The engagement, I should think, will be announced shortly."

"Well, all I can say is that I'm infernally sorry that Miss Hethencourt has been made the butt of gossip and scandal through a cad's behaviour, and I think that you and I ought to be shot for discussing her and her very intimate affairs. If—"

Damaris waited to hear no more.

White as chalk, she stumbled back into the room and crouched down upon the floor beside a chair, burying her face in her arms. For five of the longest minutes of her life she knelt, burning with shame, trembling with rage; then she sat hack on her heels.

"Is there nobody to help me in all the wide world? Nobody I can go to?"

And clearly, as though it was in the room, she heard the echo of the words spoken in the Shrine of Anubis, the God of Death: "Allah! how I love you, and if I may not be your master, I can at least serve you. If you are in distress, will you send me a messenger to my Tents of Purple and Gold? . . . My boat from sunset to sunrise waits at the landing-stage . . . the mare Pi-Kay waits from the setting until the rising of the sun at the Gate of To-morrow."

She acted on the impulse of her outraged pride; she gave not one thought to the mad thing she was about to do; she stayed not one instant to question the trustworthiness of the man who had so strangely shadowed her since their meeting in the bazaar; she decided in the flick of an eyelid.

She would go to him; she would tell him everything, and if he were then willing to make her his wife, she would go to his English mother, and from the shelter of her arms proclaim her engagement to the world.

Yes! she would run away.

In a flash she thought of her beloved old godmother and the loving arms always held out to her, and the loving sympathy and counsel which never failed.

But she shook her head.

To silence the scandalmongers her engagement must be made known before that of the man who had treated her so shamefully; who, if only she had known, was racing towards her at that very moment as fast as train could take him.

"Wait for Missie; you shall come to her," she whispered as she knelt and kissed the dog; "you and Janie."

She sprang to her feet.

What about her promise to her old Nannie? Had she not crossed her heart and given her word that she would always let her know where she had gone?

She moved swiftly to the writing-table, took a sheet of paper and hastily wrote a line; then looked round for some place to leave the message.

Wellington whimpered as he stood with his fore-feet on the book.

She ran to him and twisted the folded paper into the steel ring of his collar, hugged him closely, and turned away.

With a lace veil over her head, concealing her face, with the sable-trimmed cloak wrapped close about her, she slipped from the hotel without being recognised, and down to the quay.

Almost uncanny is the intuitive power of the native.

Without hesitation, a boatman stepped forward and salaamed

to the ground before her.

"By the sign of the Hawk-headed Harakat."

He repeated the phrase his master had taught him, and which he had repeated over and over again for many days.

And Damaris never once looked back as the boat crossed the blue-green Nile, which, for all she knew, would stretch forever, an impassable barrier, between herself and those she loved.

Acting as in a dream, she could never clearly recall what happened until she stood at the Gate of To-morrow. She had a vague recollection of crossing the great river, and of being helped out of the boat, and of four gigantic Nubians who stood near a litter and salaamed as she approached; she remembered, too, that the litter was lined and hung with satin curtains and piled with satin cushions, and that she had been carried some distance at a gentle trot which had in no wise disturbed her.

Then it had been gently placed upon the ground, and she had been handed out, to find the *sayis* of the stallion Sooltan standing salaaming before her, with his hand on the bridle of the snow-white mare, Pi-Kay, the glory of Egypt.

CHAPTER XXVIII

*"He made the pillars thereof of silver, the
bottom thereof of gold, the covering of it of
purple, the midst thereof being paved with
love . . ."*

SONG OF SOLOMON

Accustomed to the flowing robes of the Arab, it is not as
difficult as it might be imagined to break a desert-trained horse
to side-saddle; but the mare, Pi-Kay, spoilt and sensitive,
behaved like a very demon whilst the *sayis* exchanged the
ma'araka, which is the native pad without stirrups, for the
lady's saddle. She was not really bad, not she! She was simply a
spoilt beauty and inclined to show off, so that every time her
big, beautiful eye caught the sheen of the girl's satin cloak, she
backed and reared and plunged, but more out of mischief than
wickedness. For many days she had been ridden alternately
astride and side by the *sayis*, who loved her better than his wife
and almost as much as his son; ridden from the Tents of
Purple and Gold—and not over-willingly did she go—to the
Gate of To-morrow at sunset, to be taken back at a tearing
gallop to the Tents, without restraining or guiding hand upon
the reins, at sunrise.

It was not sunrise now, and she did not like the person in the
shimmering satin who had, in some miraculous way, swung to
her back and stayed there; but she was headed in the direction

of home, and the moonlight was having just as much effect upon her temperament as it has on that of humans.

A moon-struck horse or a moon-struck camel in the desert is a weird picture and it were wise, as they are for the moment absolutely fey, to give them an extremely wide passage.

"Guide her not, lady," shouted the *sayis* to Damaris, who answered to the movement of the mare like a reed in the wind, but otherwise seemed to take no notice of horse, or man, or moon, or untoward circumstance; he hung on for a moment to the silken mane and stared up into the girl's unseeing eyes; then, with a ringing shout, let go and jumped nimbly to one side.

There was no backing, no rearing, or vagary of any sort now; the mare started on her journey; broke into a canter; broke into a gallop; then, silken mane and tail flying, thundered back at a terrific speed along the path marked out by her own dainty hoofs, and the relentless feet of that hound, Fate.

Damaris turned in the saddle and looked behind, and then to her right and then to her left.

She was alone in the desert.

The sands, stretched like a silver carpet in front of her and like a silver carpet with the black ribbon woven across it by the mare's feet behind; to the east and west the sandy waste seemed to undulate in great fawn and amethyst and grey-blue waves, so tremendous was the beast's pace; the horizon looked as though draped in curtains gossamer-light and opalescent; the heavens stretched, silvery and cold, as merciless as a woman who has ceased to love.

And then, just as on the far horizon there showed a mound which might have been a hillock of sand or a verdant patch, outcome of precious water, or a slowly-moving caravan of heavily-laden camel, the mare Pi-Kay increased her pace. You would not have noticed it, for it would have seemed to you that she was already all out; but you would—as did Damaris—if you knew anything about horses, have *felt* it, had you been riding her. It was that last grain of the last ounce by which races are won; the supreme effort of the great sporting instinct, which lies in all thoroughbreds, human or animal; and Damaris, thrilled to the innermost part of her being as she sensed rather than felt the quiver which passed through the mare, leant forward and touched the satin neck.

That which distance had given the appearance of a mound grew more and more distinct. It was no mound nor hillock, verdant patch nor slowly-moving caravan of camel.

Three tents showed at last distinctly, and the following is the short explanation of their origin.

As it is not good for the Oriental youth to stay under the same roof as his mother, once he has come to man's estate—which is at any age after eleven in the lands of intense sun—the building of the House 'an Mahabbha near the Oasis of Khargegh had been begun within the first year of the birth of Hugh Carden Ali.

Owing to the entreaties of his English mother, the boy had not been affianced in extreme youth to a little maid of two or three or four summers, upon whom he would not have set eyes until the night of the marriage.

His mother had idolised him and he had worshipped her; he obeyed her, he would willingly have died for her; later, at her request, he even left his country of sunshine and vivid colouring for hers, so cold and bleak; but before that and at the age when other high-caste youths of Arabia settle down in their own house to contemplate seriously the taking of the reins into their own despotic hands, he had absolutely refused to go to the House 'an Mahabbha, built for him as his father's first-born.

Perhaps also it was the English blood in his veins which at that age filled him with the spirit of adventure.

A desire for solitude, a desire for something sterner than the everyday existence of his luxurious life had driven him out into the desert, where, bewitched, as it were of woman, he had followed the Spirit which ever held out her long fine hand with beckoning finger.

A mere boy? Absurd! Ridiculous!

Not at all; for the high-caste boy of twelve in the Orient is oft-times as much developed physically and mentally as the Occidental of over twenty.

He had followed the Spirit where she had beckoned, and, an Arab through the blood of his father, had caught her and crushed the body, slender to gauntness, in his arms; had twined his fingers in the coarse, black hair and pulled it back from the different-coloured eyes; had sought the crimson mouth until his lips had rasped with the kisses a-grit with sand; slept with his hands clutching her tattered robes of saffron, purple and of gold; torn the misty veil from before her face and dreamed with her cool breath, which is the wind of dawn, upon his face.

He loved her and to her had pitched his tents.

He prayed that he might be with her when he died, and, convinced that his prayer would be answered, he had pitched him a funeral tent between those of Purple and of Gold.

Bewitched of the desert, the colour of the tents resembled those in which she decks herself in the passing of a day and a night.

Outwardly they were just ordinary Bedouin tents, the tan and brown of camel-hide; flat-roofed and square, giving a full-grown man room in which to move and stand to his full stature without the fear—as in the peaked affair called bell—of bringing the whole thing down upon his crown. They lifted at each side to allow the desert wind to enter at any hour it listed; or the moon to pierce him with silvery spear; or the stars to blaze like jewels before his eyes, as he waited for sleep on a rug upon the sand.

The one in which he slept was hung inside with satin curtains of deepest purple, with here and there a star of silver, which glittered in the light of the cut-crystal lamp which hung from the cross-pole. The Persian rug upon the floor was grey and old rose and faintest yellow, and glistened like the skin of woman; of the ordinary furnishings of an ordinary bedroom there was no sign—you would have to go much farther afield to find the tent with all the paraphernalia of the toilet. Just as you would have to go still farther and towards the west, to where were pitched the stables, and the quarters of the specially-chosen servants he took with him in his desert wanderings; just enough—and they had their work cut out—to look after the dogs and birds and horses. The camels, upon whom depended the supplies, were right out of sight, and any one of the servants would have preferred death by torture to approaching within a mile of his master's tents until he heard his call.

In the other tent he ate his bread and dates and drank his coffee or received the humblest of his passing brothers; those who, scorched with heat, tortured with thirst or hunger, and blinded with flying sand, yet would not exchange one minute of their own free desert life for an eternity of soft couches and the most succulent effort of a *cordon bleu* in the cramped surroundings of a crowded city.

It was hung with orange satin; cushions of every hue were flung upon a carpet of violent colours; the lamps of bronze with wicks floating in crimson saucers, hanging from the crosspole, were rarely lit; the satin curtains hid a smaller room behind filled with dates and coffee-beans, sweetmeats, beads and other things which bring joy to the grateful heart of the wandering Arab and his family.

The sand outside was marked and pressed, down with foot-prints of men and women and little children.

They had not to ask in order to receive.

But no foot but his had ever trod the fine matting of the tent between the other two.

Firmly convinced that his prayer would be granted and that in the desert he would find the answer to the many questions which had occurred to him to ask of life, he had sought for a covering under which he could lie after death until naught but his bones should be left for the wind of chance to play with.

He had all a Mohammedan's belief in the hand of destiny, but the English blood in his veins filled him with horror at the thought of being torn to pieces by vultures after death; his desert blood filled him with an equal horror at the thought of being weighted down by the regulation tomb of bricks and mortar.

And so it came to pass on this night of the full moon, when the girl he loved was racing towards him and Fate was disentangling the threads she had knotted so grievously, that he lay stretched upon the block of wood which stood three feet high in the centre of this tent. He lay face downwards, with chin in hand, looking out through the lifted flap in the direction of Mecca, whilst the moon hung as a silver shield above him, and the desert enfolded him on every side.

Outwardly the tent was as that of any Bedouin; tan and brown, the colour of the camel's hide, of which it was made; square-roofed, with one side only which lifted, the side which was towards Mecca.

Inside it was lined with a copy of the queen's funeral canopy of softest leather; stretched square; to the touch as soft, supple and fine as velvet.[1]

True, this copy had not taken year upon year to make, nor had scores and scores of nimble fingers stitched and stitched for days and months to finish it, as in the days of the XIXth dynasty. The panels in the copy were of one piece of hide stitched finely by machinery, with the emblems painted upon them after the stitching; in the original they are made by the stitching together by hand of thousands and thousands of pieces of gazelle-hide, each of which had been painted either pink or blue or green or in various shades of yellow before the stitching.

Look up with Hugh Carden Ali as he lifts his head to gaze at something far beyond the tent-roof.

You will see a copy of the central square which, divided into two, rested upon the top of the shrine which covered the dead queen who died about one hundred years after the siege of Troy. One side of the panel is sprinkled with yellow and pink rosettes on a pale-blue ground; the other side shows the vulture, the emblem of maternity, holding in its claws the feather of justice; six there are in all.

That is the ceiling.

The tent walls are lined with a copy of the flaps which hung down on each side of the shrine of the funeral-boat of the Egyptian queen who, some thousand years before Christ, crossed the blue-green Nile, followed by other boats filled with her priests and princes, her officers, her mourning women. North and south, the flaps are of chess-board pattern in squares of pink and green; behind one of which was hidden the small room which held naught but a crystal pitcher and crystal basin, filled to the brim with water for the ablutions at the Hour of Nazam, which is the Hour of Prayer.

Near the top the sides show bands of colour, red, yellow, green and blue, almost as bright in the original as on the day the paints were mixed, one thousand years ago. Beneath the bands upon one side you will see the signet-ring of the priest-King Pinotem—whose son Queen Isi em Kheb espoused—; also the royal asps and the scarab, the emblem of life out of death.

Upon the other wall you will see the lotus-flower, which opens at the rising of the sun and closes at its setting; the enigmatic double-headed ducklings and the picture of a gazelle, which is doubtless the representation of the pet which, bound in mummy trappings, was found beside its royal mistress in the tomb. Across the lotus-flowers, like a silver shaft, there hung a light throwing-spear.

A very technical description, taken down in rough notes at the museum, of a specimen of patchwork—even like the patchwork counterpanes of our great-grandmothers—stitched together by dusky slender fingers in the days of the great King Solomon.

And to Hugh Carden Ali as he lay in this tent, looking towards Mecca, there came the sound, from a great distance, as of a horse running at full speed.

[1]This is a description of the funeral-tent of Queen Isi em Kheb, contemporary of the wise Solomon, mother-in-law of the Shishak who besieged Jerusalem and "carried away also the shields of gold which Solomon had made." (II Chron. 12.)

It served as a pall to cover the royal lady upon her last terrestrial journey, when she crossed the Nile in the funeral boat from her palace in Karnak (?) to her burial-chamber in Deir el-Bahari.

CHAPTER XXIX

"La vie est breve:
Un peu d'espoir,
Un peu de reve
Et puis—Bon soir!"

MONTENAEKEN

A great light shone in his eyes as he rose from the couch of wood upon which his dead body, with feet turned towards Mecca, was to lie.

The light from the lamp of bronze and cut-glass shade of deepest orange tint struck down upon him, throwing shadows from the snow-white turban which outlined the fine face to beneath the eyes, and round about the hawk-nose, and the mouth of which the gentleness was so belied by the dominant jaw; it gave an ivory shade to the snow-white satin of his raiment; it glistened on his only jewel, an amulet carved from an emerald in the shape of a scarab, set in gold and hung from a fine gold chain about his neck.

His beauty was of the East, but it was male; there was no trace of that effeminacy which so jars upon the sensibilities of those who are bred in colder climes and brought up on sterner lines than the luxurious dweller of the East.

He stood listening to the far-distant sound, then threw out

his arms.

"By the mercy of Allah, God of Gods, I am found worthy to serve thee, O my beloved! Within the hour, yea! in but a little over the passing of half one hour, before the shadow of my tent shall reach yon rope, I shall have looked upon thee."

He knew!

His heart told him who was coming to him out of the night; his knowledge of the desert enabled him, by the drumming sound of the hoofs upon the sand—a sound which has not its semblance in the world—to know to a second when the mare would stop before the tent.

It was not the Hour of Nazam, the Hour of Prayer before dawn, the dawn which was to see his questions answered, but he turned and, pulling back the velvet-soft leather curtain, entered the small room lighted by a silver lamp hanging just above the crystal basin full to the brim with water.

No! it was not the Hour of Nazam, but filled with the Oriental's mysterious premonition of that which is to befall, he performed the prescribed ablutions of the Hour of Prayer. Three times he washed his nostrils, his mouth and hands and arms to the elbow; the right first, as ordained, then the head and neck, and ears once and feet once.

He stood erect, with his hands above his head, for five full minutes, whilst the drumming of the sands sounded nearer and nearer, then emptied the water in a circle upon the desert sands, refilled the crystal basin with water from a crystal pitcher and passed into the tent and out upon the sands across which, and even as a speck upon the horizon, he saw the mare Pi-Kay racing. And he threw his hands heavenwards with a great cry:

"Allah be praised! Oh, Allah, unto thee I give thanks!"—the prayer of thanksgiving uttered by his own father so many years ago.

It was a sight to watch, that of the snow-white mare Pi-Kay stretched out, flying like the wind, ridden by a slip of a girl with her gleaming cloak streaming like a banner behind her; but the look upon the man's face was still more wonderful to behold as he stood motionless, sharply outlined against the orange light behind him.

The mare slackened not her pace one whit; like a thunderbolt she hurled herself right up to where stood the master she loved with all her great equine heart; then she stopped short, fine fore-legs spread wide; then reared until it seemed she must fall backwards; then crashed down to rear again, until the loved voice bade her stand.

With the strange frozen look in her eyes which gave them the appearance of ice-bound lakes, and which had been there since she had crept from the hotel, Damaris slipped from the saddle into the arms of Hugh Carden Ali, and there she rested, trembling from head to foot with the stress of her ride, whilst the white mare whinnied for some recognition from her master. And he pulled her forelock from about her gentle eyes and pulled her small ears, and stroked the arched neck; then with a sharp word ordered her to her stables, and, turning to lead the girl into the tent in which no foot but his had trod, gave no more thought to the mare Pi-Kay.

She obeyed him, with mighty little zest, yet lingering not one moment, even though her delicate nostrils showed wide their crimson depths, and her satin flanks heaved like bellows through the speed in which she had covered so many miles.

She moved away at a gentle trot, then stopped and looked back along her satin flank towards the tent, in a vain hope of seeing her master just once more; she did not turn completely round,—she obeyed where she loved—she just looked back along her flank; then, doubtless recognising her defeat, gave a little flick of her heels and trotted off again.

She was just midway between the tents and her stables when she stopped dead, with ears pricked forward.

Save for the silvery mane and tail blown by the night-wind she might have been a statue carved out of marble, so still was she.

Then she suddenly backed and reared a foot or two, then backed again; wheeled; started towards the tents; stopped and wheeled again.

She trembled from head to foot, the beautiful terrified creature; great eyes rolling, little feet sending the sand flying as she moved continually on one spot.

There was nothing to see as she stood, looking east; the tents were behind her, her stables in a straight line from them to the west; there was absolutely no sound, none at all until she neighed.

She neighed until the desert rang with the sound, neighed until the horses in the stables some miles away pulled at their halters and lashed out on every side; then she reared and wheeled as she stood straight on her slender hind-legs, then, crashing to the ground, with a convulsive leap was off into the desert.

Neither did she return for many days; nor was she seen until that dawn when her *sayis* found her in front of the middle tent, snuffing at the closed flap.

*   *   *   *   *   *

But the flap was not closed this night, as Hugh Carden Ali sat on the couch of wood and looked at the girl who sat beside him.

She stared down at her hands, which pleated and flattened and re-pleated the satin of her skirt, and her face was as white as her neck and her arms, which shone like lilies kissed by the sun, under the light of the orange lamp.

He waited for her to speak, for it was not for him to guide or influence her in any way by spoken word.

He led her to the wooden couch, which had perforce to serve as seat as there was none other in the tent, and took her cloak, passing his hand gently across the sable collar which encircled her throat; and he glimpsed the hurt of her heart down in the depths of her eyes when she looked up at him and put out her hand and stopped him when, murmuring something about coffee, he turned to the entrance.

"I could not drink it, thank you," she whispered. "I—I want—" and stopped and looked down and pleated the satin over her knee and flattened it with her palm.

She was terrified at the desperate step she had taken—and well she might be. She was strung to a great pitch of nervous excitement through the exhilaration of her tearing ride; she was stubbornly determined to prevent the finger of scorn from pointing in her direction; but she was finding a subtle salve to the smart of the wound to her pride in the romantic setting of the wonderful picture made by the man beside her.

In faith, I see no real excuse whatever in exoneration of her mad impulse, unless it be in her education—or, rather, want of it—and in the fact that she was younger than her years.

Educated in the hugger-mugger way in which are educated the girls who will not have to use their knowledge to earn a livelihood; with, it must be confessed, the great and rare—in these days—asset of perfect manners and courtesy towards all mankind, yet had she never been taught the rudiments of self-control and deliberation. She had a heart of gold, truly, but she leapt to conclusions with closed eyes.

With her to think had always been to act. So that, having leapt far out into a morass of incertitude, she sat perplexed, for 'tis no easy matter to say, "Please will you marry me?" to a man, even if you know that he worships the ground your shadow falls upon.

He sat silent, with his eyes upon her hands, waiting for Fate to point out his path.

Little by little, bit by bit, her surroundings began to affect her. The blood came slowly back to her cheeks so that they glowed like the wild rose in the hedgerow; and her eyes began to lose that set stare which hides the perturbed mind, and to soften behind the heavy fringe of lashes, and her hands to cease their nervous plucking at her dress.

She lifted her eyes to the strangely-painted tent side, looked at the silvery spear and tilted her head back until her throat gleamed like an ivory pillar, to look up at the ceiling with the painted vultures—the emblem of maternity.

The man looked up, then looked down upon this woman of his mother's race whom he loved, and longed with all the intense passion of his father's race that he might see his first-born upon her breast.

She was trying to find words, and they came to her when she clasped her hands upon the jewelled brooch in the shape of the Hawk of Egypt.

She looked at him suddenly and a little shiver swept her at the strange beauty of this silent man; and he as suddenly turned his hands palm upwards in an uncontrollable gesture of Eastern prayer to Fate who had so much to give him, or, perhaps, so little!

"You said you—you would help me if—I came to you—in trouble." She tripped and stumbled over the words. "I have come to—to—"

"Ask my help."

The words were as cold as stones dropped in the beggar's hand, but Damaris leant back quickly when she looked into the man's eyes and saw in them the reflection of the fire she had kindled.

"What is the help you need of me? I know nothing of the ways of women, but I do know that it has been the storm which has swept you from your safe harbour out towards a shore upon which are piled the wrecks of many souls."

She twisted the brooch between her fingers.

"My wedding gift," said Hugh Carden Ali softly, then watched the crimson dye the white neck and surge across her face. "You come—to—*me*—for help." He repeated the words slowly. "Then you, of course, are—are free—ah!" He leant forward and caught her hands. "You have run away—from what? No, do not speak, I can read your answer in your face. You have been hurt." He lifted the little ringless left hand, then pressed it against the other between his own, whilst a great light flamed in his eyes. "You have come to me, and there is but one meaning for me in that you have come to *me*. Is it—" His voice dropped to the softest whisper as he crushed her hands down upon the wooden couch so that she swayed towards him. "Is it that I may fasten my own wedding gift into the bridal robe of the woman I love and will take to wife—*is* it?"

Damaris bowed her head so that the curls danced and glistened in the light, as the torrent of his words, in the Egyptian tongue, swept about her like a flood.

"Hast thou come to me in love, thou dove from the nest? Nay, what knowest thou of love? I ask it not of thee—yet—but the seed I shall plant within thee shall grow in the passing of the days and the nights and the months and the years, until it is as a grove of perfumed flowers which shall change to golden fruit ready to the plucking of my hand."

He pressed her little hands back against her breast so that the light fell full upon her face, and held her thus-wise, watching the colour rise and fade.

"Allah!" he whispered. "Allah! God of all, what have I done to deserve such signs of Thy great goodness? Wilt love me?" He laughed gently. "Canst thou look into mine eyes and shake thy golden head which shall be pillowed upon my heart—my wife—the mother of my children? Look at me! Look at me! Ah! thine eyes, which were as the pools of Lebanon at night, are as a sun-kissed sea of love. Thou know'st it not, but love is within thee—for me, thy master."

And was there not truth in what he said? May there not have been love in the heart of the girl?

Not, maybe, the love which stands sweet and sturdy like the stocky hyacinth, to bloom afresh, no matter how often the flowers be struck, or the leaves be bruised, from the humdrum bulb deep in the soil of quiet content. But the God-given, iridescent love of youth for youth, with its passion so swift, so sweet; a love like the rose-bud which hangs half-closed over the door in the dawn; which is wide-flung to the sun at noon; which scatters its petals at dusk.

The rose!

She has filled your days with the memory of her fragrance; her leaves still scent the night from out the sealed crystal vase which is your heart.

But, an' you would attain the priceless boon of peace, see to it that a humdrum bulb be planted in the brown flower-pot which is your home.

And because of this God-given love of youth which was causing her heart to thud and the blood to race through her veins, she did not withdraw her hands when he held and kissed them and pressed his forehead upon them.

"Lotus-flower," he whispered so that she could scarcely hear. "Bud of innocence! ivory tower of womanhood! temple of love! Beloved, beloved, I am at thy feet." And he knelt and kissed the little feet in the heelless little slippers; then, rising, took both her hands and led her to the door; and his eyes were filled with a great sadness, in spite of the joy which sang in his heart as he took her into the shelter of his arms.

"I love thee too well," he said, as he bent and kissed the riotous curls so near his mouth. "Yea I love thee too well to snatch thee even as a hungry dog snatches his food, though, verily, I be more near to starving than any hungry dog. What dost thou know of love, of life, in the strange countries of the East? For thy life will be a desert life, my love, if once thou art my wife. Look up; look around thee." He pointed to the stars, he pointed to the dim horizon of the desert over which at that very moment was padding that hound Fate. "Wilt thou be content with that, and with me and thy children? Wilt thou not yearn for the comforts of thy heated rooms, the company of those who will point the finger of scorn, maybe, at thee as they have pointed it at my mother?"

He spared her not one jot as he made plain to her what might be the result of her marriage. She would not be marrying the pure-bred son of a splendid race, as his mother had done; she would be the wife of a half-caste, the mixed off-spring of two great races; her children would be half-castes, outcast from their rightful heritage of the sons of the East and the West. The women of her race would not own her, the women of his father's race would not permit her children to play with theirs. Wealth, palaces, camels, horses, jewels would be hers; a place for her children in the seat of his fathers, or her fathers, *never*.

"I should be strong, I should be strong, for in my heart something tells me that I am thinking of my happiness and not thine."

"Your mother," whispered Damaris, so softly that he had to bend, his head lower still, so that when she moved, in the pain of his arms which crushed her, her cheek brushed his. "*She* is happy—everyone says so."

Happy! Yes, she was happy, his beloved, most honoured mother; at least she had been, until there had come the question of her child's happiness, her half-caste child!

Then he laughed, joyfully, stretched the girl's arms wide, then crushed her hands above her heart.

"Of course! of course!" he cried. "They are at my House 'an Mahabbha, the House of Love, even now, where they have met to see if they, the dears, thy wise old godmother, my beautiful wise mother, can find an answer to this very question."

They were not. Sick with suspense, they had landed on the far side of the Nile, on their race with Time to the Gate of To-morrow.

"We will go to them to-morrow, thou and I. To the Gate of To-morrow, thou with the mare Pi-Kay, I with the stallion Sooltan, who will well-nigh kill thy mare, my woman, in jealousy. Yea!" He bent and whispered in her ear so quietly, so coldly as to cause the girl to tremble. "As I will kill anyone who looks at thee when thou art my wife."

Then he laughed like a boy as he swung her round and held her at arm's-length by both hands. "We will start to-morrow to meet them, when we will lay the question before them. And then—and then—why—?"

Damaris, with all the smart of the wound to her pride revived, had shaken her head.

"I want you—I want you—to—"

Hugh Carden Ali understood by the grace of intuition.

"We will start for Khargegh to-morrow," he continued after a little pause. "And at the same time—if it will please thee, with thy consent—I will send my swiftest runner to Luxor, where he will despatch by cable the news of—oh! my beloved!—of our engagement—Allah! what a word to describe the opening of the gates of Paradise—to all the great cities of my country and of thy country. Have I thy consent?"

Incapable of speech, Damaris nodded; having cast the die, she trembled like a leaf; and at the sight of her, white, with big, frightened eyes staring at him and teeth driven into her lip, he took her in his arms.

"Thou art mine, beloved, mine as thou hast been in all the past, as thou wilt be in all the ages to come. All mine, thy heart, thy soul, thy body. I ask to gather no pebble from the path nor flower from the tree; I will have the jewelled necklace of thy beauty to hang above my heart, and the grove of thy sweetness in which to take my rest. I love thee, and for the agony of the hours passed in the ruined temples I will take my reward. I love thee, love thee, love thee!"

She made no sound when he bent and kissed her hair, but in the glory of the love which is that of youth, which is as a bud at dawn, the full flower at noon and a few petals at dusk, and of which the fragrance stays with you down all the ages, she raised her face so that he kissed her on the mouth.

And he kissed her closed eyes and the pillar of her throat and the whiteness of her shoulders, and her crimson mouth again and yet again, in the wonder of this, his hour of life, granted him by Allah who is God; and then raised his head and stared out across the desert.

From a great distance there came to him the drumming of a horse's hoofs upon the sand.

CHAPTER XXX

*"The true, strong, and sound mind is the mind
that can embrace equally great things and small."*

SAMUEL JOHNSON

The two wise women had long since left Khargegh.

By special train, by special boat, by aid of runners, telephone
and telegraph, but above all by the magic of the Sheikh el-
Umbar's name and his wife's unlimited distribution of gold,
Olivia Duchess of Longacres and her maid and Jill el-Umbar
and her maid arrived at the hotel on the night of the full
moon.

They would have arrived before sunset if it had not been for
the mistake made about the special steamer which had kept
them waiting at the quay; they would not have arrived until
twenty-four hours later if they had made use of the ordinary
train and boat.

"Can't we go faster, ma'am? Can't we get there quicker?"

It was Maria Hobson, stolid, solid, dour, big-hearted woman
with a streak of Scotch blood in her veins, who worried
outwardly. If you had watched her out of the corner of your
eye you would have seen her shake her fist at the desert; if you
had walked behind her on the quay you would have heard her

say, with a world of entreaty in her voice, to some terrified, non-understanding *fellah* who quaked at the knee: "Can't you get a move on, somehow? You're only a heathen, to be sure, but if you'd heard the tone in the young lady's voice you'd do something instead of sal-aaming."

She said very little to her beloved mistress, but to Jill she poured out her heart, and Jill who with the intuition of a mother's love had connected the dream with her son let her repeat her tale over and over again.

". . . Just as though she was standing on a precipice and frightened of falling over was her voice like, Mum, Miss Jill—may I call you Miss Jill? It's more familiar-like and—homely, and I know you will excuse me, Miss Jill, if I say that I can't get used to you in those clothes, pretty as they are and becoming to you. It seems to me like fancy-dress, you with a veil over your face, if you will excuse me saying so. You are just the same to me and my lady as when you came to stay with her grace; and glad I for one shall be when I see the barouche waiting for her at Victoria, with Whippup and his powdered head on the box. I don't mind that young chauffeur with one leg lost in the war, but I don't like that wicked-looking red vermilion motor-car of her grace's, though the slum-folks do, and you should hear them cheer, Miss Jill, when it goes down Shadwell way."

This conversation took place on the quay whilst her grace was absent, trying to still the unaccountable fear with which her heart had been filled by her maid's dream, by talking to the little brown urchins who swarmed about her the better to view the bird.

"What do you think of them, Dekko old fellow?" She took him on her wrist, at which he spread his tail, rattled his wings, and puffed his ruff, whereupon the children fled, yelling. "Come now, say something nice to the poor little things. You've frightened them. Ask them if the boat is ready."

Dekko gave a sudden piercing screech:

"You damned, dirty lot!" he yelled. "You—"

And some doubted the bird's sojourn on a sailing-vessel in the full-rigged, full-mouthed days of 1840!

Her grace rapped the razor-edged beak sharply and returned to the other two just in time to hear her maid's answer to some question:

"Sergeant O'Rafferty of the Irish Guards, Miss Jill. He demeaned himself by marrying a *bar*maid, miss."

As already mentioned, love and marriage had passed Maria Hobson by.

Arrived at the hotel, their spirits went up with a bound.

What had come to them out there in the desert town? Had they all been stricken with some dreadful depression? Of course the child was safe in this laughing, dancing, happy throng, and at the sight of her god-mother she would leave her partner and run to her; would throw her arms about her, and hug her in her loving way.

Owing to the crowds of people and the crush of cars, little if any notice had been taken of their arrival; the luggage was coming up later.

"Wait a minute here, Hobson," had said her grace. "Jill, come and see if you can recognise Damaris by the picture you saw of her—the prettiest girl in Egypt!"

They stood at the side door of the ballroom and scanned the laughing couples sitting in rows in the throes of the cotillon. Ellen Thistleton, with the royal asp of ancient Egypt with a slight list to starboard above her heated countenance, stood alone in the middle of the room, with a glass of champagne in one hand.

Before her stood Mr. Lumlough and the colonel for whom the gilded asp was being worn at such a rakish angle.

She stood for quite some seconds in her conspicuous position, as though debating within herself upon the choice. As Mr. Lumlough subsequently remarked to his panting partner, in his customary slang, "She had a nerve!"

Then, with head on one side, she coyly handed the Veuve Clicquot to the thankful young man, and allowed herself to be gathered to the heart of the portly, jubilant colonel, who, loving her, saw the jaunty gilded asp as a nimbus around her head.

Of Damaris there was no sign, and the old lady's heart, through some unaccountable terror, seemed as if it would sink into her small crimson shoes, though outwardly she showed no sign of the fear that gripped her.

"I expect she has gone upstairs, or out into the grounds to give Wellington a run—I don't see him anywhere. Come, Hobson; give me your arm to the lift."

A deep growl welcomed them as the maid opened the sitting-room door and switched on the light as the ladies entered. Wellington lay near the balcony window, head on paws, with the book his mistress had given him between his teeth. He rose slowly, very slowly, eyes red, ruff bristling round the spiked collar, growling menacingly.

"My dear," said the duchess quietly, "just stand still. Damaris has gone away. He is always like this when she has left him. Hobson, go and see if you can find Jane Coop. I hope to goodness you don't."

She walked across the room and passed close to the dog, who turned his head and, growling savagely, watched her as she moved. Then she came back and sat down quite near him, and leaning down arranged the buckle on her shoe, whilst Jill stood perfectly still, filled with admiration for the old woman, who was not acting out of bravado but simply tackling the situation in the only possible way.

Once let a bulldog on guard know that you do not want to take away or touch his carefully-guarded possessions, and that you are not in the least bit afraid of him, and all will be well.

"Come over here, Jill."

Jill, who had removed her veil and satin mantle, crossed the room and sat down on a stool at the elder woman's feet. She took the wrinkled little old hand and patted it; then they sat still and silent, hand in hand, waiting for the maids' return.

What was there for these women to make such a fuss about? Cannot a girl be allowed to sit out perhaps a dance, or a whole cotillon even, without the world coming to an end?

What made them all three fret, and fuss, and fear?

The great love they had one for the other, perhaps, for love has been known to pierce the mental fog we each one of us weave about ourselves and so allow us to help one another, sometimes even at a great distance.

Maria Hobson knocked and opened Jane Coop's door, who rose and came quickly towards her; and as her grace's maid involuntarily glanced round the room, old Nannie peered over her shoulder with the hope of seeing her young mistress in the corridor.

"Isn't she here?"

"My young lady? No; she's dancing." She paused, and put out her hand. "Isn't she dancing? Isn't she?"

Why did Jane Coop fear as the others feared, and why did her bonny face go suddenly white?

Because she, too, was one of the happy, limited throng who know what real love is.

"My mistress would like to speak to you, Miss Coop."

"What's wrong? Maria Hobson, tell me what's wrong."

Hobson allowed the unlicensed use of her Christian name to pass unnoticed; she closed the door behind her and spoke gently, as she took the other woman's hand and shook it, which was her somewhat masculine way of showing sympathy.

"I don't know; none of us know that anything *is* wrong. As Mike O'Rafferty used to say. 'We may be afther barking in the wrong back-yard,' but I had a dream, Jane Coop. Sit you down whilst I'm telling it you."

They sat on the sofa, hand in hand, strangely like their mistresses as they sat in the sitting-room near the suspicious bulldog.

At the end of the story of the dream, Jane Coop rose.

"Thank you, Miss Hobson. I thought my young mistress was dancing. I was hoping she was forgetting a bit, with the music and young folk. There's one thing, I shall know where she has gone to. My dearie wouldn't break her word. Come along." She opened the door and turned and spoke over her shoulder.

"Drat men!" she said briefly and emphatically.

"Yes, *drat* 'em!" replied Maria Hobson, even more emphatically, as her memory leapt clear across the gulf of years to the time when she had walked out with a certain Sergeant of the Irish Guards.

Jane Coop dropped a curtsey to the gentry and stood just inside the door, up in arms, ready to fight anyone at the first word of condemnation of her young mistress.

"Come over here, Coop, please, and tell me everything you can about Miss Damaris. I have an idea—mind you, I am not sure—that she has gone out alone, and we must be as quick as we can in finding her, because Egypt is no place for a white girl to be running about in by herself."

Jane Coop took up a corner of the big white apron she insisted upon wearing, and pleated it between her fingers as she told her grace everything with a surprising lucidity.

". . . She came in here to fetch her fan, your grace, and in here somewhere she will have left me a message. I've never known my baby to break her word, and I'll look for it, if I may. She'll have written it on a bit of this block and with this pencil. It's been thrown down in a hurry. Miss Damaris is that tidy, she can put her hand on anything she wants in the dark, which is more than most of the slipshod, take-off-your-dress-and-leave-it-there young ladies of the present day could do."

The anxious maid hid her fear in a never-ending, *sotto voce* invective against the Pharaohs and their descendants down to the present generation, as they all hunted vainly for the bit of paper; then she stood helplessly in the middle of the room and apostrophised the dog:

"*You* know where your missie's gone to. Why don't you help us, instead of lying there growling?" She stood scowling at him, then suddenly walked across to where he lay. "I wonder if she put it inside that book," she muttered; then gave a little cry as she caught sight of the paper twisted in the steel ring of the spiked collar. "I've got it!" she cried. "I've got it!"

The duchess, who was quite near her, put her hand on her arm.

"Take care, Coop. The dog is really angry. Let me get it."

"Not you, your grace. No, not ever so, bless you."

Wellington was standing on the book, great tusks gleaming, eyes glaring, a hideous picture of rage; but love casts out fear, even the just fear of a dog who would never let go until you or he were dead, once he got his teeth into any part of yon.

There was no haste about Jane Coop as she knelt beside him. "Missie wants you," she said. "D'you hear?" The rose-leaf ears pricked at the sound of the beloved name, but the whole tremendous body shook with his growling response. "You don't love her, you brute, else you'd have picked up the book and been ready to start at the sound of her name. I'll teach you to be so slow." With a sudden lightning movement she caught hold of the loose skin just under the jaw, firmly, grimly, with her left hand, holding him amazed and for a moment helpless as she pulled the paper out of the ring; then she let go, and pointed to the book, just as the dog was about to spring.

"Missie told you to keep it for her."

The room vibrated with the thunder of his fury as he placed both feet on the book and glared about him.

"I know," said Jill as she read the message over the old woman's shoulder. "She has gone to my son. To his tents in the desert." She spoke quietly and with a certain dignity and authority which checked all questions. "He will take her straight to me. Shall we go back to Khargegh, or shall I go to them, to his tents?" There was no sign of the triumph in the mother-heart at the thought of the happiness which was to come to her first-born; neither had she a single thought for the others.

A mother's love is the most surpassing of all loves; it is the eighth wonder of the world; it is a mystery before which that of the Sphinx shrinks to insignificance; it is the one love which asks for so very little in return for all it gives.

Blessed, sanctified refuge against all harm!

Five minutes of quick discussion; rapid weighing of the pros and cons as to the best way to keep from the ears that which would serve as a whetstone to the tongues of the scandalmongers; a sharp, clear understanding and decision.

The manager of the hotel salaamed deeply in the doorway before the high-born women, and showed no surprise at the tale—which he believed, perhaps—of Miss Hethencourt, who had gone to meet her grace and having undoubtedly mixed up instructions, had either gone up to Kulla to meet her, crossing her on the river, or had crossed to the other side, thinking, as her grace had suggested doing, that the return from Kulla would be made by camel on the far side of the Nile.

Good gracious! no. He had long since given up showing or feeling surprise at anything any of the great white races might elect to do. He had harboured them for several winters in his hotel, you see.

Certainly everything should be ready in the quickest possible time. A hamper and some brandy; the boat; and upon the other side the swiftest camel from the hotel stables for her Excellency the wife of the Sheikh el-Umbar; the swiftest men to carry a litter—ah! two litters, as her grace's maid would join in the search. Not Miss Coop; she was staying behind, of course, to have everything in readiness for Miss Hethencourt, who would doubtless be very tired and a little frightened.

"There is nothing to fear," he added. "Nobody has ever really been lost in Egypt, and as Miss Hethencourt will not want a crowd of friends to meet her on her safe return, not one word shall be said about the little expedition of relief."

He salaamed and retired, leaving the duchess looking after him.

She had her doubts about his belief in one word of the story.

*   *   *   *   *   *

Wrapped in her ermine cloak and leaning on her ebony stick, Olivia Duchess of Longacres stood near all that is left of the Gate of To-morrow.

Hugh Carden's mother looked down at her from the back of her camel, on which had been fixed the padded seat which is perhaps the most comfortable of all saddles.

Wellington, with the book between his teeth, sat next her, firmly secured by a rope through the steel ring in his spiked collar to the back of the seat.

"Take him, your grace," had urged Jane Coop, whose own heart was nigh to breaking at being left behind. "Take him; he'll find her if we should happen to have made a mistake. Missie calling you, Wellington. Take the book to Missie; she wants it."

And the dog had obediently picked up the book in his teeth and waddled in the wake of the search-party.

Maria Hobson stood close beside her mistress; the indifferent *fellaheen* stood some little way apart. They, too, have long since become accustomed to the vagaries of the great white races.

"Let me go alone, dear. He is my son!"

The mother had pleaded for the sake of her first-born, and the old woman, understanding, had given way.

"Goodbye, dear. I will wait for you here. Hobson will look after me. Besides, as long as we save her good name, what matters anything else? Thank God for the moon, Jill. You will easily follow the track of the two horses. Give them both my love, and tell them I'm waiting. *Au revoir*."

She stood and watched the camel slither across the desert at that animal's almost incredible speed; then turned, sat down on the edge of her litter, took out her bejewelled Louis XV snuff-box, rasped a match on the sole of her crimson shoe, and lit a Three Castles with her eyes on the track left by the hoofs of two horses.

Yes! Two.

Just an hour before they arrived, Ben Kelham had started from the Gate of To-morrow to find his school-mate, Hugh Carden Ali, at his Tents of Purple and of Gold.

CHAPTER XXXI

"Sweet is true love tho' given in vain, in vain;
And sweet is death who puts an end to pain."

TENNYSON

Hugh Carden Ali, quite still and strangely unwelcoming, stood just inside his tent; as Ben Kelham flung himself off his horse; neither did he put out his hand to take the outstretched one of his old school-fellow.

Pretending not to notice the seeming lapse in courtesy, Kelham turned to hitch his horse, only to find that that product of the bazaar had cleared for the horizon.

It were wise when out in the desert, if your horse is not desert-trained, to hang on to the bridle until you have hobbled or hitched your steed, lest peradventure the vultures, at a discreet distance, should assemble about you later, as you lie raving upon the sands, only waiting until your ravings cease altogether, to approach quite near to you.

That the omission was intentional never crossed his mind. He remembered his friend's religion and the strictness with which he adhered to its tenets, and thought that perhaps the shaking of a fellow-creature's hand was forbidden at certain hours.

So that he did not offer his hand again, but his eyes shone with

Joan Conquest

all the affection, which might be termed love, he had had at Harrow for the man who had met him so often as opponent in the cricket-field, and as a friend in his rooms.

He stood quite still for a minute just outside the tent, the moon shining down upon his splendid six-foot-two, and a little shadow of doubt swept across the face of the Eastern as, so strong was the moonlight, he noticed the set of the jaw and the honesty of purpose in the steady grey eyes.

This Englishman might make a mistake, might blunder in the slowness of his deliberate way—there was the faintest suspicion of a smile on Hugh Carden Ali's face as he remembered, even at this critical moment, how, having won the toss, it had taken Ben Kelham so long to decide, at the foot of the Hill, whether to put his side in or not—but that he would deliberately behave like a cad to anything so beautiful and desirable as Damaris, or in fact to any man, woman, child or beast on earth, no! that thought was not to be entertained for one moment.

Come to think of it, what a blessing it is that the cad cannot efface the mark of Nature's branding-iron.

He may be an Adonis, a diplomat, a *bon viveur*, a good sort, a real sport; he may have a brain and a personality and a gift for choosing and wearing his clothes; his blood may be cerulean, red or merely muddy; but just watch out. One day he will forget to shoot his linen, and you will catch a glimpse of the mark of the beast.

And in the second of time which it took this little analysis of his friend to flash across his mind the hands of Life moved slowly towards the hour.

He put his hand to his turban, then stood on one side.

"Come in, Kelham. Who ever would have thought of seeing you! Jolly decent of you coming all this way out to see me. I thought you were after lion, but I see you have no gun. I'm afraid I can only offer you coffee. No pegs in a Mohammedan's tent, you see."

They each advanced one step and their hands met and gripped across the little dividing-line, on one side of which, one of the two stood under the stars which belong to all men, and the other inside the desert dwelling.

Such a faint line, this one of racial distinction, yet which rises as a barrier higher than the Himalayas, deeper than the ocean, and stronger than steel between the men of the East and the men of the West.

Kelham laughed as he sat down at the end of the wooden couch to which, without making any apology for the bareness of the tent, his host had pointed.

"Jolly seeing you again, Carden. I had an idea you were travelling round the world, and only discovered through the morning paper that you were quite near. The paragraph gave a full description of you and these tents, so I took the first train—I was in Cairo—enquired about you when I arrived at Luxor station, where they seemed to know all about you, hired that horse which has gone off on a survey into the middle of the desert, got ferried across, and came straight here. I don't mind telling you that lion is rather a sore point with me at present." He laughed again as he took his automatic Colt, which lay cosily in the palm of his big hand, from his pocket and released the safety-catch.

"I'm like darling old Aunt Olivia; she refuses to be parted from hers, once she has sighted Port Said. By Jove, Carden, you've absolutely got to meet her, if you haven't met her already. She knew your mother well. But of course you stayed at the Castle—no! you didn't though; you had measles. Well, you've got to meet—"

He stopped suddenly as the thought of the abominable

anonymous letter flashed across his mind; turned a dull red under his tan, and looked round the strange tent, and then at the man who sat on the opposite end of the wooden couch, dressed in all the picturesque simplicity of the East, with the stars and the far-reaching desert as a background.

He sat quite silent, staring at his friend, who yet in some indefinable way seemed such a total stranger.

"By Jove, Carden," he said at last, "I didn't know you had—" He stopped, confused, horrified at the words which had almost escaped him.

"Turned native, Kelham? I haven't. I am an Arab, a Mohammedan by birth. This"—he looked quickly at the leather curtain at the back of his friend—"This is my natural environment. Harrow was a—a loving thought on the part of my honoured mother, and—" He paused, and raising his voice ever so slightly, looked steadily at the curtain which seemed to move, perchance blown by the night wind—"and a great, a terrible mistake. Yes, Kelham, a terrible mistake. Did you ever think of the risk I ran, I, an Arab, of meeting some white woman, whom I might love? Supposing I had met such an one, and had loved her, and had wanted to marry her, tell me, you, all white as you are,—*could* I have done so?"

He took a simple wooden cigarette-case from his cummerbund and held it out to his friend; they lit their cigarettes and sat smoking in an intolerable silence.

There was no real need to ask the question, because it had been answered even whilst the Englishman had swung himself from the saddle. In a searing flash, by the sound of his friend's voice, the way he moved, the whole Western look of him, Carden Ali had understood that this man, born of the moors, the bracing climate, the cold skies, the snows and springs of England, was the true mate for beautiful English Damaris.

But, to turn the knife in the wound in his heart, he repeated the question, and Kelham, who knew it could be answered only in one way, wrenched at his collar and got to his feet, and crossed to the wall, to finger the throwing-spear with his back to his friend.

"Well, you know, old man, I—well, don't you think it's best —as your father is an Arab—well!—well, you know what— who was it said—something about East and West?—I— don't—" He passed his hand over the wall, then exclaimed, in an effort to change the subject, "By Jove! it's leather! Why, I thought the wall was velvet."

Carden laughed and lit another cigarette as he watched Kelham out of the corner of his eye as he walked slowly round the tent.

Keeping something from each other, they were ill at ease, where, under ordinary circumstances, they would have talked without ceasing upon the good old days at Harrow; of Houses and masters and schoolfellows; of Ducker—the swimming-bath—and Lords and Bill—the roll-call.

They talked, instead, disjointedly upon things which, though they interested them mightily, were not near their hearts as is the Hill to the Harrovian. They had both come to a decision, which, however, left them in nowise comforted.

Ben Kelham decided as he walked about the tent that not a word about the anonymous letter or the courtesan should pass his lips. How could he ever have thought of mentioning the matter, even if it had been only as a safeguard for the future in finding out the best way in which to silence the woman's lying tongue? Besides, if Carden, he thought, had met Damaris or the duchess, he would most surely have said so—which only showed that he knew nothing whatsoever about the Oriental.

Hugh Carden Ali had come to his decision even as he had realised that honour bade him give up the girl whom he had held so close to his heart in his one hour reft from life; on the pretext of want of accommodation, with promise to meet in Cairo or elsewhere as soon as possible, he would send Ben Kelham back upon the track to Luxor, and by a circuitous route would take the girl at dawn to a spot from whence she could ride to Kulla, and get from there by boat to Denderah or back to Luxor.

None save the *sayis* knew she had come to the tents this night, and he was faithful and as dumb as a dog. Besides—the Oriental had shrugged his shoulders—if he should prove to be otherwise, what easier than to silence him for all eternity?

And if a life barren of love stretched as bleak and limitless as the desert before him, what then? Life was short, and if children of mixed races were to suffer the hell he must suffer through honour, well, surely praise should be offered to Allah in that he would never see his man-child upon the breast of woman.

"Kismet!"

He whispered the Oriental's supreme submission to the inevitable and caught his breath, then lit another cigarette.

Ben Kelham placed his hand upon the chequered curtain, which swung back at his touch.

"Is this where you sleep, Carden? I never thought you had another room behind."

"It is the room in which I make my ablutions prescribed by Mohammed the Prophet of Allah who is God, at the hour of prayer."

The words, which were in truth a prayer for the safe keeping of the woman be loved and had renounced, rang sonorously through the tent, causing Ben Kelham to turn and look at the Oriental, who had risen to his feet as he prayed.

The two fine men stood looking at each other across the tent; then the Englishman moved forward and sat down on the end of the wooden couch as the other moved back and leant against the wall, with his fingers upon the little amulet above his heart.

"Have you ever been in love, Carden?" Kelham asked abruptly, unable to control the question.

"There is no have-been in love. You either love or you do not love. Do you?"

Ben Kelham nodded his head.

"Then, if you do, why, in the name of Allah who is your God as well as mine, are you here? Why are you not at the feet of this woman, stricken with wonder and humility before the gifts the great God has given you? Why do you leave her exposed to the temptations of the East, where has been wrecked the soul of many a white woman? What is the killing of wild beasts compared to the look of the woman's eyes? Where are your eyes, the eyes of your soul? What is this love you speak of which lets you drop the jewel from between your fingers as you would drop the half-consumed cigarette upon the ground?"

It was the prisoner's last despairing cry as the prison-door swings to, shutting out the sun, the song of birds, the voice of children; it was the beggar hungering for a crust, crying against the wasted abundance of the rich man's table.

"What is this love you speak of, this love which lets you pass your days in the shadow of another woman, a woman brown as a burned cake, as comely as a stuffed pillow, who lies in wait to kill the king of beasts? Yes! I know; in the East all things are known. I know whom it is you love, and it is for her that I dare speak as men should not speak of woman. Go to her; tarry not; go and heal the wound to her pride, her heart, her love, lest in her pain she should fly to the first hand for succour."

Ben Kelham sprang to his feet.

"Do you think, if my love was returned, Carden, that I should be here?"

"Love!" The man's voice was not raised one tone, but the tent vibrated with the passionate words. "Are you such a coward that you run away at the first hurt? When the ball struck you in the face at Lords, did you retire—hurt? No; you stuck it, and scored a century! Are you such a dullard that you cannot read beneath a woman's yes and no? Love! Do you know what love means? What would you do for love? Could you forgive in love?"

Kelham stared at the man who, word for word, repeated, the question Damaris had asked on the night he had proposed to her.

"If you heard tongues gossiping out of jealousy of the woman, you loved; if you found her in a situation which could not easily be explained; if she, hurt, wounded, had run like a little child to another to beg for balm for her wound,—tell me, would you forgive her? Tell me!"

There was a strange insistency in the repeated question and a deep anxiety in his eyes, which passed as Kelham laughed.

It was the genuine, honest laugh of the man who loves and is willing to shoulder the burdens, great and small, which love brings in her train.

"You say there is no 'have-been' in love, Carden. I say there is no question of forgiveness in love. You love, and there is no room anywhere for anything else but love."

A great silence fell; the silence of two strong men who for one moment had broken through the barbed-wire of convention, to be their natural selves; the silence heralding the birth of a new day.

There was no sound, as the hands of Fate pointed to the full hour.

It all happened and was over even as the hour struck.

There was a shout from both men as the tawny shape leapt out of the night through the opening of the tent; the crashing report of Ben Kelham's revolver as he fired; the coughing of the wounded lioness as, spitting blood, she recoiled to spring; a ringing shout from Hugh Carden Ali as he flung himself in front of his friend just as he fired, and the great brute, with a mighty roar, turned and disappeared into the night whence she had come.

There was a look of great wonder on the face of Hugh Carden Ali as he stood looking beyond his friend; then he suddenly turned in the direction of Mecca.

Slowly he raised his hand to his turban, whilst a look of ineffable peace swept across his face and stayed, as a little red stain like a crimson rose showed just above his heart.

"*Here, Sir!*"

The answer to the roll-call rang out across the desert he had loved so well, and was carried by the breeze of dawn up through the stars to the Head Master whose justice and mercy take no account of race.

Then the old Harrovian crashed face downward, dead.

CHAPTER XXXII

"Millions of spiritual creatures walk the earth
Unseen, both when we wake and when we sleep."

"Spirits that live throughout Vital in every part. . . ."

MILTON

The light from the silver lamp shone down upon the water in the crystal basin and upon the girl's red head as she crouched upon her knees against the leather curtain.

Well might she crouch, well might she have put dust upon her head as do the Easterns in their grief and shame; well might her voice have wailed out across the desert in sorrow for the young life broken by the careless fingers of her heedless youth.

But she knelt without movement, with her face in her hands, the hands which had so lightly played pitch-and-toss with a man's heart and a man's life, and prayed desperately, silently, for forgiveness.

Let it be granted her on account of her years, for youth is ever blind, and the young are ever selfish, giving never a thought to the years they must spend, when, grey-haired and wise, they will try to repair with their shaking old hands, the tatters and rents they had made in their thoughtless, grasping youth.

Strange it is that the old in years, in sorrow and knowledge, will sit darning the rents and patching the bad places with their trembling hands, as their wise old heads nod and their dear old mouths murmur a prayer, and yet be unable to teach the young how to keep the fabric of life whole, or safeguard it with the lavender of love and good-will pressed between its folds.

Until the drumming of the sands had sounded like distant thunder and the shape of the horse and its rider had become distinct to the desert-trained eye of her desert lover, Damaris remained apprehensive and silent in the safe refuge of his arms, which crushed her to his heart; then he lifted her and carried her swiftly to the little room of prayer lit by the silver lamp and, wresting a promise from her to keep her presence hidden, no matter what she might hear through the curtain, kissed her hands one and twice and yet again and left her, drawing the curtain close.

Horrified, she heard the voice of Ben Kelham; like a statue of fear she stood, with her ear close to the curtain, for the half of an hour, the thirty short minutes in which she came to understand at last, clearly, definitely, that there was only one man in the world for her, and that was the Englishman who sat with clenched hands under the lash of his friend's words; and her hand trembled so that the curtain shook as though blown by the night-wind as she held it back just wide enough to look through without being seen; and her eyes were soft with gratitude when she understood the greatness of the sacrifice the man of the East had laid on the altar of his honour and his friendship and his love.

But her youth had gone from her forever and her heart had been stamped with the seal of an everlasting regret; her eyes had been filled with a great questioning which was never to be answered on this earth, when her scream had been drowned in the crash of the report as the man she loved had fired, and killed his friend.

Had Hugh Carden Ali really feared for the safety of his friend and flung himself between him and the wounded beast, or, understanding that in that way only could peace be obtained for all three, had he deliberately sought death?

Allah, who is God of all, alone knows the answer, so let us leave it with Him.

And then, being untried and very young, she slipped to her knees and fell unconscious, with her face upon her outstretched arms. And there she lay whilst the silence of the coming dawn fell upon the earth, and wrapped itself in a soft winding-sheet about him who lay asleep upon his couch of death, at the foot of which stood his friend, looking down upon the peaceful face.

Only a few moments had slipped into eternity when Damaris shivered and, bewildered, not knowing if an hour or a second had passed whilst she had lain senseless, rose to her knees.

There was no sound.

She sat back and pushed the hair from her forehead; then rose and tiptoed to the curtain. She put out her hand, and drew back; then, urged by a desire which clamoured for definite knowledge, parted the curtain and looked in. She looked for just one second, then staggered back and back as far as the crystal basin filled with the clear water which was used in prayer; and she stood with her arms outstretched, and fingers spread between her eyes, and the picture she herself had painted in the thoughtlessness of youth, and then swung round, with her back to the Tent of Death and looked down into the water, and, as though a veil had been lifted from before her eyes, looked back along the past, and forward into the future.

As in a flash she saw the wreck she had made of her life by throwing away the substance of a good man's love for the fantastic conviction that, as she was not as other girls, she must therefore go a-venturing through the world's mazy high-ways and by-ways until she had found her own particular niche.

She saw the picture of herself proclaiming it to her life by throwing away the substance of a good man's godmother's letter of invitation to Egypt. She saw the girl's lips moving. What was she saying?

"I want to find my own nail and hang for one hour by myself, if it's on a barn door or the wall of a mosque—as long as I am by myself."

Then the picture faded, to give place to another in which she saw herself sitting in the moonlight beside Ben Kelham; the honest, slow, lovable man standing at that very moment a grim picture of despair, divided only by a curtain from her, through whom, indirectly, he had killed his friend.

What was she saying to him in this dream-picture?

"I don't know enough to marry; I want to know what love really is, first . . ."

What was he saying in reply?

". . . You will learn your lesson all right, dear, and suffer a bit, dear, but you will come to me in the end."

She suddenly knelt and plunged her hand down into the water, breaking the smooth surface into a thousand miniature waves which turned, as she stared, into the mocking smiles of her acquaintances and friends; and she knelt quite still until the surface was once more smooth, out of which, as she stared, looked the tragic face of the dead man's mother and the grief-stricken, shamed face of her beloved godmother.

The gossip, the scandal, with her name linked as lover to that dead man; the chuckles, the sly lifting of eyebrow and pursing of lips when it should be known that the other man, the dead man's greatest friend, had come upon them unawares, alone in the tent at night?

The story of this struggle, the shooting of the treacherous friend—for who would believe the story, told by the principals in the drama, of a wounded lion which had turned and disappeared into the night?

There would be the inquest, the inquiry, the arrest for murder and the trial, in which she and all those she loved would be pilloried, through her fault, in the eyes of the world.

She stared down at the water, which seemed to hold her hands in the icy grip of death—her hands—look! what was that?—what had happened to them?

They were spotted with red!

She tore at her handkerchief and rubbed them; under the water, rubbed hard, rubbed frantically, but the red spots were there on her hands, on her handkerchief, on the water—the red she had seen when she had looked . . .

She flung the handkerchief from her and rose to her feet, shaking convulsively from head to foot.

Poor child! Half-crazed from horror, light-headed from fatigue and want of food, she had mistaken the reflection of the jewelled Hawk she wore at her breast, thrown by the lamp upon the water, for the stain she had seen and which had looked like a crimson rose above the heart of Hugh Carden Ali, as he lay asleep, with his feet turned towards Mecca.

"God!" she prayed. "You Who alone can save me and—every-one—from shame; You Who can hide me from—Ben—show me a way out—show me a way out!" And as she repeated the words, the answer came.

"Of course," she whispered. "Right out in the desert, out on the sands, alone with my shame, where, when this has been forgotten, perhaps all that will be left of me will be found by some wandering Bedouin, who will bury me deep in the sand."

She was genuinely remorseful and horrified at what she had done, but also was she, as are so many of us who do not really feel deeply, pleasurably thrilled at the thought of the dramatic picture in which she should be the centre figure.

If only men knew it, that is why so many women create such terrific scenes over nothing at all—it gives them a chance of donning their most effective gown and pulling their hair—if their own—down about their shoulders.

Not even then did she grasp the full meaning of love!

She parted the curtain at the back of the room of prayer, and looked out across the desert and behold! standing upon the tips of slender feet, wrapped about in binding cloths of grey and white, there stood a figure.

And the wind of dawn, upon whose wings are wafted the liberated souls into the safe keeping of Allah, who is God, lifted for one instant the veil from before the face.

Just for a moment she looked upon the eyes alight with no earthly happiness and the tender mouth smiling in farewell, and then the wind lifted the soft cloth of grey and white and bound it across the hawklike face.

Half-turned, the figure stood with beckoning hand outstretched. And to the girl was granted the Vision of the Legions at Dawn.

There was no sound in all the limitless desert, yet the air was filled as with the tramp of feet, the thunder of horses, the rumble of wheels.

They came from nowhere, those countless legions, from out of the shadows of the spent night. They walked in phalanxes, the uncountable spirits of dead kingdoms, with eyes uplifted to the dawn; spears raised, mouths open, with their shouts of welcome to the break of day, they rode their horses thundering down the path of Time; they drove their four-horsed chariots straight towards the cup of gold which rested on the rim of the world.

They come from nowhere, those countless legions, from out the shadows of the spent night; they journey over the ordained path which they have trod since the beginning of time, which has no beginning, and which they will tread unto the end of all time which shall have no end.

And, laughing or sobbing, hoping, despairing, we shall fall in as our line passes and go marching along with them, marching along, until we came to the place where "*the shadow of the God is like a ram set with lapis lazuli, adorned with gold and with precious stones.*"

"Wait for me."

The whisper was just a part of the shadows, as the girl turned her face to the East.

Wrapped in her satin cloak, she walked wearily on and on. Her eyes were wide open, staring in a terrible fatigue; she saw nothing; her heelless slippers were torn to shreds, her feet were bleeding; she felt nothing. Not once did she look up or back or round. Had she done so, she might have noticed that her footprints in the sand were describing a circle, as our footprints do when we are lost in the bush or the desert.

The shadows had gone, and the sands stretched a carpet of rose and grey and gold before her; the sky a canopy of blue and grey and purple above.

Like a lighthouse of Hope, Day was flashing his golden beams across the sky, a message to the weary who have toiled through the night.

And then, with one great leap he sprang clear of the horizon, just as Damaris stopped.

She looked back in the direction in which she thought she had come. There was no sign of the tents; there could not be; they were not out of sight, but merely wrapped in the mist which, sometimes rises as a fog in the desert at dawn.

"Let me die soon! let me die soon!"

A great sob shook her as she prayed the prayer of the weak. How much easier is it to stand at the window, with the police battering at the door, and, stimulated by its morbid interest, blow out our brains before the gaping crowd—which will, by the way, take exactly the same morbid interest in the shooting of a horse in the street—than to retire into the silence of the prison-cell or seclusion of the tideless backwater, and there work out our salvation amongst those who do not know if our name is Smith or Jones or Brown—and much less care!

In the intensity of her prayer she clasped her hands upon the jewelled symbol upon her breast and looked up.

From out of the west, cleaving the air like a thrown spear, flying straight towards the sun in greeting, there came a hawk. Up, up it sped, as though to pierce the very heavens; then hovered, wheeled and swooped downwards above the girl. She flung out her arms as its symbol struck through her clouded senses, and unconsciously called the "Luring Call" she had heard but once, when she had first seen the man, who lay asleep in the tent, in the market-place of the Arabian quarter in Cairo.

Sweet and clear her voice rose through the morning air, rising until the bird caught the sound and, just as she swayed and fell, swooped.

Down it came, straighter than a shaft of rain; swept across her like the wind; rose; and sailed away.

There was no call to bring it back now. The falconer who had thrown it, as was the custom, at sunrise, was upon his knees with his forehead upon the ground, in sign of a great grief, taking no notice of his master's favourite *shahin* which he had petted and trained. It flew towards the rising sun; it flew away; it was never seen again.

Perhaps, after all, had it heard its master's call?

CHAPTER XXXIII

"Good-night?. . . . . . .
Let us remain together still,
Then it will be GOOD night."

SHELLEY

Ben Kelham sat on the ground, with his head resting on the edge of the wooden couch so that his friend's satin coat touched his cheek.

Save for his hands clenched round his knee there was no sign of the grief which was well-nigh breaking his heart; which had drawn great lines across his face and had turned him in one hour from a youth, into a grave man, with steady, sorrowful grey eyes.

There was no sound as he sat staring in front of him as the light of the lamp grew dim in the coming light of day, there was no movement anywhere save for the chequered curtain behind his friend, which stirred as though blown by the wind of dawn; they seemed to be alone, quite alone in the desert, these two who had been known as David and Jonathan in the care-free days on the Hill.

And he turned his head and looked at the wonderful beauty of the calm face, and in the soft light it seemed that the brown eyes were looking at him from under half-closed lids, and he stretched out his hand and laid it on the arms which were folded across the breast in an attitude of surpassing dignity.

"Carden, old fellow," he said, "wake up!"

As his friend slept on, he spoke more clearly, repeating the line out of the school-song, which had acted like a charm in those days when love, and pain, and death had been mere words to them:

"Carden," he called, "Carden, *it's a quarter to seven, there goes the bell.*'"

And when there came no answer he turned and buried his head on his arms.

So he sat and kept his vigil with never a thought to the outcome of it all. Servants there must be somewhere, he knew, but time enough to explain things when they appeared; time enough to face the world with the terrible tale; time—oh! a whole long life in which to regret. And he ached with a great longing to look upon the girl he loved; he longed passionately to be able to tell her everything before he must tell others; he threw out his arms in a vain hope that perhaps he could reach her, and drawing her to him put his head down upon her knees and tell her of his love for his friend, which had almost equalled his love for her; his one moment of doubt when a vile hand had linked their names together; his happiness when the friend he had doubted had lashed him with words, and told him bluntly to try again.

Then he sat up and turned and looked out into the desert and got to his feet, but his hand did not go to his hip pocket as he watched something which came running fleetly through the shadows.

Iouaa and Touaa, the dogs of Billi, were racing home to tell their master of a surprising adventure which had befallen them, ever so far out in the desert, where they had gone for an evening stroll before taking up their posts as sentries outside his tent for the night.

And if only He had not shaken his head when they asked him to go with them—and He had had his riding-boots on and all—He would have seen for Himself that there was every excuse in the world for them being out so late at night.

What matter if they were a disgrace to look upon, with their shaggy hair matted with sand, and what looked suspiciously like blood? What if one of Touaa's ears hung limp and Iouaa's tail hung down? The lioness was dead, and they were coming just as hard as they could pelt to ask Him to come and see.

They knew exactly what He would say and do when they rushed upon Him. He would hold up His hand and say, "You disgraceful-looking pair of disreputable tikes"—He always did—and pull them to Him—Touaa first, because she was a lady—and would run His hands over them to feel for bumps, and turn back their ears and lips and look at the pads of their feet, and give them a good cuff, and lead them off, if they were scarred with battle, right away to another tent. And there He Himself would wash their faces and their wounds and brush the sand out of their coats and—but of course this was a deadly secret—would prize open their mouths and wash out all the remains of whatever they had been chewing or chasing with a long-handled ivory finger-nail brush.

Of course He would not do all this to-night because this was a special occasion, and they knew exactly how to make Him come out of the tent and send a certain call ringing across so that their friend the stallion Sooltan would come racing, with native pad and halter, riderless towards them.

This is how they worked it. First Touaa, because ladies always come first, would pull his coat and then go out and point in the direction of the find, growling softly, then give a short yelp and give up her place to Iouaa, who had just pulled the coat, to come and point and yelp, whilst she returned, to pull the coat.

It sounds complicated, but it's really as simple as simple and had never been known to fail.

Of course He would throw something at them and tell them He was coming because He was sick to death of them and their silly ways; but they knew better. He was really just as keen as themselves—besides, He belonged to the desert.

And tonight they would take Him first along the path where they had chased their own shadows and show Him the very spot where they had stopped and crouched, belly to ground, as the wind had brought a most unusual scent to their keen noses; then they would take Him further along the path and show Him how fast they had gone by the marks of their pads in the sand; and then—and then! they would show Him the scene of the great and glorious fight. Why, the field of battle stretched for yards and yards and yards. And they could show Him the marks where the wounded lioness had lashed with her tail in rage, and the very place where they had taken off as they leapt upon her. And He would really have to take care where He walked, because the place was in a really terrible state, and He would have to keep his hand on the halter because horses, even stallions, were most foolishly upset at the scent of lion.

There was the spot where Touaa had rolled after her side had been ripped, and the place from which Iouaa had leapt to fasten his fangs in the lioness's muzzle from which she had dislodged him by rolling on her back and ripping his chest and throat with the claws of her back paws, which somehow had savoured of hitting below the belt.

Then they would show him the place where the great tawny beast lay dead—she was quite dead; you could go and touch her, they had seen to that—and you could see by the churned-up state of the sand how she had beaten off attack after attack. And they had leapt again and again to pull her down, until the great fangs had met in the side of her neck and worried and gripped until the end.

Whose fangs?—Oh! well, of course ladies have to come first.

And they raced across the desert as the dawn broke, to tell Him of the great victory they had won for Him; and then, within twenty yards of the tent they stopped dead, threw up their fine heads, eyes red and glaring, ruffs standing, and sniffed the mingled scents which came to them on the wind.

They sniffed the ground at their feet and growled and, belly to the ground, crept a few yards to their right. The lioness had passed that way! Would their great victory be not such a big surprise for Him after all? Had He seen the beast already? And that other scent—a mixed scent of humans, the humans that were not of the desert! Humans meant noise. Where were they? Why was there such a strange feeling, such a strange quietness about the place? Did He sleep so soundly that He did not hear and whistle them?

They stood quite still, still as though carved, out of stone, looking at the light which showed dim in the coming dawn, and which, when they hunted across the desert, had always been to them as a beacon of happiness.

Then they growled, the deep, unforgiving growl of hate. Somebody was standing looking at them from inside the tent, and that somebody was not Him, nor in any way like Him.

Their great faithful hearts, leapt in a strange fear for their master, and the hair on their backs rose stiff and straight as they moved slowly forward, side by side.

Up to the entrance they went, growling softly all the while; then with barks and yelps of joy they leapt inside.

They had seen Him asleep; their hearts were at rest. How could He hear or whistle them if He lay asleep?

One on each side, tails wagging, eyes gleaming, they stood with fore-feet upon the couch and bent to sniff Him who was so dear to them. So they stood for just one uncomprehending moment; then dropped, to the ground, shivering, as Touaa gave a little whine. Then they walked slowly round the couch, whining and sniffing as they went, and Touaa stayed a moment to lick the hand which had so often pulled her silky ears, and Iouaa rose for an instant upon his hind-legs, and scratched at his master's boot, as he had so often done when impatient to be up and away across the desert.

Then, side by side, they crossed to where the man stood watching, with nails driven into the palms of his hands and tears in his sorrowing eyes.

Touaa wagged her tail once, Iouaa drove his head fiercely against the clenched hand, it was their only way of asking what had happened to make Him sleep so very soundly.

And Ben Kelham bent down and, putting his hand under their mighty jaws, lifted their heads so that their sorrowful eyes looked into his, and slowly shook his head. And they turned and walked close against each other to the outside of the tent, and there they sat upon their haunches and lifted their heads and howled.

Three times the despairing cry, the Last Post of the faithful friends, rang out across the plain; then they turned and walked slowly back, close together, and, separating at the foot, went up to the head of the couch and sat down upon their haunches one on each side of Him; immovable; as though carved by grief out of stone.

Ben Kelham, with the one thought of shutting the tragic picture, if only for a moment, from his eyes; of hiding his grief if only from the great dogs, blindly pulled back the curtain and stumbled into the silent room of prayer lit by a silver lamp.

He stood staring down at the water with which his friend had so lately prepared himself for the hour of prayer; he stooped to pick up the white handkerchief he had evidently dropped.

And he stood and stared and stared as he turned the little lace-trimmed square over and over in his hand. It was wringing wet, it smelt faintly of the perfume the girl he loved had always used; it had her initials woven in one corner.

"My God!" he whispered, as he looked round the little room; then crossed to the spot near the curtain where the sand had been disturbed, and then followed the prints of small feet across the floor to the further side.

"My God!" he repeated. "I understand." He turned his head and looked back at the curtain which divided him from his friend. "Carden, old fellow, I understand what you gave your life to make me understand." And his heart beat with a great love and a greater gratitude as he parted the curtain and went out into the desert. He did not once turn to look back, else might he have seen a speck on the horizon, moving at the incredible speed with which a camel can race as it slithers across the sands.

CHAPTER XXXIV

"In Rama was there a voice heard . . .
Rachel weeping for her children, and would not
be comforted, because they were not."

ST. MATTHEW, II

"Hugh!"

As she called to her son from her high seat upon the camel the
woman was the only living thing to be seen in the desert. In
her simplicity, her colouring, her solitude, she was biblical; she
might have been a woman of the Old Testament asking for
succour or sanctuary at the tent of Abraham pitched between
Beth-el and Hai; she might have been a woman fleeing from
the wrath of Moses, who gave unto sin its strength when, out
of sheer solicitude for the soul-welfare of the masses, he made
laws about things to which in the innocence of their hearts
they had, up till then, never given two thoughts.

Leave that corner piece of pasture unhedged, and it's odds on
that not a single soul will tramp or want to tramp over it, from
one year's end to another; hedge it, close it with padlocked
gate, prop up the warning *re* trespassers and see if you don't
find a wide track of footprints across it in the morning.

Yes; the picture was biblical.

Rebecca must have worn exactly the same fashioned clothes as this woman, and doubtless Leah had become pink-eyed through the tears of vexation she had shed over the ancestral humped quadruped she had ridden; and most certainly Lot's wife, Ruth, Solomon's wives and appendages, Jezebel, and every other woman mentioned in the Bible once watched just such a dawn rise across just such a desert.

We change our fashions, our fixed opinions, the colour of our hair and the pattern of our socks when the fancy seizes us, but neither time nor man has changed the desert—so far. Thank heaven for it, there is still one place left in which we can go to die or be re-born—in seemly solitude.

The grief of Rachel was shadowed upon the face of Jill, the wife of the Arab, as she sat quite still, looking down at the pool of orange light flung from the tent out onto the sand; then she sighed, the little sigh of the anxious heart which, like the wind that springs up and sweeps over your dwelling, and is gone, heralding the storm, is the forerunner of the grief which will ere long overwhelm you.

She knew!

The lover, the wife, the brother, the friend, can temporarily blind themselves with the blinkers of false hope and can blunt the stabbing spear of hideous fear with sharp-edged reasoning, but the *mother*—never.

You cannot deceive her with a smile, nor can distance hide your distress from her; you cannot, if you could be so minded, conceal your joy from her, nor can you hurt her with a wound that will not heal.

Go to her with your hands swelling from the sting of the wasp you found in the stolen fruit, or stained with crime; or your shoes wet through with the mire of the by-ways in which you have been straying, and what will she do? She will sit you down in front of the glowing fire of her love, warm your straying feet, wash away the stain in the bitter waters of her tears, and then dry them with her smile.

And you can go on straying—if you could be so minded—until seven million seventy-times-seven, and you will find her just the same.

It is not forgiveness; it is Love.

And it was Love which, when there came no answer to her call, urged Jill to get her camel to its knees.

Over twenty years had passed since Jill Carden, the English girl, had first tried her 'prentice hand upon the obstreperous camel. She had ridden out into the desert under the stars with her desert lover; she had, strong in a great love, fearlessly climbed the high wall of racial distinction crowned with the spikes of custom and convention; she had watched the seed of happiness burst and blossom until it had grown into a great tree; but she had forgotten that no tree, however deep its roots, however strong its branches, is safe, so long as Fate, in senile jealousy, can tear the heavens into ribbons with her hellish lightning.

The camel, lurching and groaning, staggering and heaving, got to its knees in just the same way as Taffadaln had done over twenty years ago; just as the camel will do twenty centuries hence, if it has not become extinct through some button, or wire, or wave, or ray which will have turned the desert into a kind of international piazza into the middle of which, for our post-prandial coffee and cigarette, we shall be conveyed in a few moments by means of something wireless, for so much cash down in advance, which will include the tip to the Bedouin waiter.

One can see empires and deserts disappearing, but the tipping system—never!

And as Wellington would not let go of the book his mistress

had left him as guarantee of her return, so as to grip the back of the seat in his powerful jaw, he came nigh to being strangled as he lurched and swung and bumped as the camel got to its knees, which seemed to be legion as it tucked its legs under and untucked them, and did it all over again with vociferous lamentations until it had got them all neatly folded up; and once standing four-square upon the sand, he wrinkled his nose in disgust and removed himself some yards from the odour of this unpleasant complaining brute which hailed undoubtedly from the bazaar, and gave disgusting and crude imitations in its throat of water being poured out of a small-necked bottle.

He wanted his mistress, and her only, so, having no use for or interest in this woman who had brought him, for no apparent reason, upon such an uncomfortable journey, he simply took matters into his own big head and without a with or by your leave waddled off, book in slobbering mouth, to look for his beloved, whom—his olfactory powers not being of the keenest—he felt to be somewhere in the neighbourhood, perhaps playing at hide-and-seek behind the tents, as she did on wet mornings at home behind the Chesterfield.

Jill dismounted and stood facing the desert, which seemed to stretch as one vast purple pall; and as she stood she wrestled with a mighty fear which held her so that she could not turn and go towards the tent through which shone the orange light.

She did not say to herself that her son had gone out with his horses and his dogs; she did not try to trick herself with the thought that perhaps he slept in his purple tent, and for that reason had not rushed out hot-foot across the desert to meet and lift her from the camel.

She knew that she had only to turn and walk the few yards to the tent to have all her questions answered, but she also knew that all she wanted to do was to stand on and on and on, just as she was, with her face towards the night, and her back to the dawn of another day, and definite knowledge.

She loved her other sons deeply and dearly; she loved her little daughter; but her first-born held equal place in her heart with the Arab his father, and her love for him was beyond words and almost too great and too holy a thing to be written about here.

Tears and laughter, the moon and the stars, the mystery of the Sphinx and the desert at dawn, at noon, at night, bound them both to her heart with golden chains of a surpassing love.

She had said no word of what she had suffered in all these years he had been gone from her; she could not have told you, an' she would, of her joy at the thought of his home-coming at last.

And she lifted up her hands and cried aloud:

"He is my son! He is my son!"

Then turned and walked slowly to the tent.

She made no sound, she gave no cry, she just stretched wide her arms in stricken motherhood, as the great dogs sat immovable at their master's head, like images of grief carved out of stone.

The cloak slid from her shoulders and fell about her feet, as she crossed to the foot of the couch with out-stretched arms, where she stood, such a slender and beautiful mother, looking down; and her silken veils filled the air with a gentle whispering as she moved to his head—such a desolate mother,—looking down at the little crimson mark which showed like a rose above the heart.

"Hugh!" She whispered, as she touched the long lashes which hid the eyes which had always been so full of tender love for her. "My son!" she whispered as she stroked his cheek and, with slender fingers and a little smile, tucked back the stray lock of brown hair which never would stay under the turban.

She patted his chest and arranged the full skirt of his satin coat into folds, and stroked his hand as mothers do; and she knelt at his knees and laid her cheek against his boots, and smiled a little, nodding her head, just to let him know how wonderful she thought him.

She did not know she was doing it; she did not fully understand—how could she?—she was just holding back the door which was closing.

She lifted the amulet in the form of a scarab, of which the base was in the shape of a heart, and which just touched the mark that looked like a crimson rose.

She was not very good at reading inscriptions, but she always tried her best, because it pleased him and made him laugh—so lovingly—at her funny little accent. And to please him now she tried; she did not know she was doing it, but there was not much more than a crack left open through which she could see.

"My Heart, my mother; my heart, my mother; my heart whereby I came into being."

And if great tears dropped upon his heart as she slowly read "the words of power," they surely made a very fitting insignia with which to enter into the presence of Allah, who is God.

She kissed his hands, and kissed the closed eyes, and tender mouth which smiled as he slept.

She moved round the tent, pulling the curtains straight, having promised faithfully to carry out his wishes—ah! how she had smiled when she had given that promise; love of his wife and his children, she had thought, would soon oust the idea of death from his mind—and looked up at the lamp, to see if it was well filled with oil, and gently took down the spear from the wall, whilst the great dogs sat immovable as images of grief carved out of stone.

And she laid her hand upon their heads and, taking the corner of her veil, wiped the sand from their jaws; but they growled softly—not angrily—just to let her know that no hand but that of their master must touch them.

She went to the entrance and called them, but they growled, just to let her know that they would answer no voice but that of their master, and that for the sound of that beloved voice they would wait for eternity.

Of course she did not quite understand them—how could she—not knowing that the love of a dog surpasses that of a friend, and equals that of a mother?—so she lifted the chequered curtains at the back just to let them know that there was a way out, and looked down at the footprints of small feet and of heavy feet, and across to the lifted flap through which she could see the day dawning.

And if her whole being shook with anguish as part of her question was answered; and if her heart was stabbed with sudden pain at the thought that strangers had plucked her crown of glory from her and trampled upon it; and if she suddenly threw out her arms and questioned the Almighty upon the wisdom of His ways, can we blame her?

She passed through the lifted flap of the Room of Prayer, and mounted her camel, and rode out to the west; and at the sight of the woman with the light throwing-spear in her hand the servants, who had been watching the tents, rushed out to meet her and, at the sign she made, bowed their heads to the sands.

And their dirge swept across the desert as they answered as she called:

"Thy Master, O my people, has started upon a long journey. Allah receive him at his journey's end into His safe keeping!"

"Our Master," they answered, "is absent upon a long journey. Allah guide his feet into eternal joy."

They brought her two camels and watched her depart, then turned to make all things ready to lead their Master's horses, and dogs, and birds down to the river.

She rode her camel some distance from the Tents of Purple and of Gold and of Death, and hobbled them, and returned on foot across the sands, which were gold with the beams of the risen sun.

She lifted the lamp in the Tent of Purple and spilled the oil upon the floor, and let drop the wick upon the oil; and she crossed to the Tent of Gold and did likewise, and as the flames shot up on each side, she crossed to the Tent of Death, and entered.

She bent down over her son and kissed him, on the forehead and laid her cheek just for the last time against his, and stood for one moment at the foot of the couch, with arms outstretched in stricken motherhood, looking down.

Then she turned and went out, and called softly to the dogs, who growled, not angrily, but just to let her know that they could not come.

And she looked at her son Hugh Carden Ali, with his two friends like images of grief carved out of stone to guard him, then, dropping the curtain, went out as the door closed.

And just as the *shahin* flew straight to the sun in answer, perhaps, to his master's voice, she raised the spear and drove it through the corner of the tent into the sand, so as to let those who passed know that the owner was absent upon a long journey.

Joan Conquest

CHAPTER XXXV

"But in the night of Death Hope sees a star
and listening Love can hear the rustling of a wing."

ROBERT G. INGERSOLL

The south wind shouted with joy at the glory of the new day; the sky hung like a canopy of radiant colours, with little clouds of pink dropping like rose-leaves towards the sands which stretched, as a golden carpet, from east to west and north to south.

The south wind shouted far above Ben Kelham's head, it chuckled like a laughing child at his elbow, and buffeted his sad face gently until it saw a ray of light spring up in the steady eyes; then it ran laughing away—you could hear it distinctly on all sides of you—like water singing in a barren place.

The sun is the lamp of the world, and night is its cloak; but the wind is the voice of its heart and you have only to listen to catch its message, and to watch even in the beat and burden of the day, to see the leaves move as its sweet breath touches them.

Take your burdens to the rock in the storm; take them to the depths of the pine forest, and open your heart to the wind.

You will learn many things before you reach home, and

amongst them how to loosen the straps which gall your shoulders.

Big Ben Kelham walked slowly, with his eyes upon the faint track of little feet which had moved in a circle, and not once did he look behind, else would he have seen the smoke of the burning tents. He moved slowly, not because he feared or because he did not want to run, but because he knew, and wanted time in which to reason with himself, to decide if he had the right to take the joy which was waiting for him.

He stood for a moment with his hands in his pockets, the strong, silent, lovable man that he was, and shook himself just as a spaniel does when it comes out of the water. He had been nigh to drowning in the depths, and out of his pocket, to be lost for ever, had fallen the jewel of youth; but somehow he had managed to scramble to the bank and to pull himself out, and he made a step forward and swept the horizon to see if his journey was at an end; then hesitated—remembering.

He stood quite still and looked at a slender figure wrapt about in a mantle of gold which stood some distance off, with hands outstretched toward him and with beckoning finger. And the wind, with a laugh, lifted the veil from her face, and dropped it, and lifted it again, and swept the mantle so that it clung to the slender, supple figure, then spread it out behind like gleaming wings.

She put one finger to her mouth, and opened wide her eyes of knowledge shaded with the fringe of tears, which come from pain, and just as much from joy.

"Follow me," she whispered, and the south wind seized upon the golden tones, and flung them to the west wind, and to the east, and to the north wind, so that the message was carried right across the world: "Follow me—I am Hope."

And he plunged his hands still further into his pockets and scrunched up some keys and small change and a most cherished pipe, just out of gratitude, and walked on.

He found her; in fact, he would have seen her ever so much sooner if she had not been lying face down on the sands, with her head buried in her arms. He did not hasten, knowing that the whole of his life stretched before him in which to heal her hurt. She did not hear him because he walked lightly, as those delightfully big men do; and he stood over her, wondering how to rouse her without frightening her, and frowned when a little sob shook her.

Then he smiled.

Strange is it how, in the very middle of the most dramatic situation, a little thought will push open the lid of its own little brain-cell and creep out to touch our risible nerve. It really ought to know better, because empires and marriages and business contracts have been upset, if not lost, on account of its freaky humour; and it twisted the corners of the man's mouth into a distinct smile as he involuntarily thought of the drizzling November afternoon when Damaris, in brogues, tweed skirt and mackintosh, had announced her intention of going out to join in some demonstration which had to do with the upholding of the rights of her fellow-sisters, and had only been dissuaded therefrom by the opportune arrival of tea and muffins.

Little Damaris! Just one of those women who creep right into the hearts of men on account of their gentleness and apparent helplessness; who are born to be put into a glass cupboard before which those who love them spread themselves like door-mats; who rule with a rod pickled in their apparent helpless-ness, which is stronger than a whip of steel, and who are quite closely related to the barnacle and mollusc to which the tide regularly brings tit-bits out of the ocean, whilst the more mercurial eel has to go out and thresh about in the mud for what it requires to keep it going in its fight for life.

Anyway, the eel has the advantage of getting about a bit!

Then the smiled faded, and he knelt, because he could not stand the sound of that little sob any longer, and he put out his hand and stroked her hair.

"Damaris, darling, it's I—Ben!"

She stiffened under the shock of the words, and flung her hands over her head.

The terrible hour had come!

She would have, out of very decency, to tell him everything: why she lay where he had so miraculously found her; how she had promised herself to his friend; how she had . . .

She clutched her bonny curls in both hands and pressed herself hard to the ground, longing that it should open and swallow her up. She could not get up, she could not turn round to meet the eyes of the man she loved with all the strength of the love of which she was capable; she could not watch the love in his eyes change to a look of disgust; she simply could not do it.

And then she felt his hands on hers, and his fingers unfastening hers one by one from her grasp upon her curls; and she lay quite still; with a lovely warm feeling creeping over and through her, because she knew by the gentleness of the touch and the firmness of it that she would be gathered up safely into his arms, and carried away to happiness.

And, just as she had thought he would, he put his arms around her and lifted her like a feather and crushed her up against his heart and got to his feet and lifted his head to the glory of the sky.

But she would not look up; she could not, because she had taken the jewel of her youth and flung it carelessly far from her, so that she lay as a woman in his arms, and a woman who had looked deep in the passing of a few hours into the heart of those things which have to do with love.

The wind whispered in her ear as it carelessly touched her face, and it whispered in a voice out of the past.

And this is what it whispered:

". . . for love will have come to her, maybe for a day, maybe for a second of time, but a love which will mingle her soul with the soul of her desert lover . . . yet it is the love of the soul that endureth for ever, yea, even if the body of the woman passeth into another's keeping."

And Ben Kelham, feeling her shiver and thinking, in the simplicity of his heart, that she was cold and hungry, tucked the satin cloak with sable collar still closer round her, then looked across to the east, where lay a pall of smoke upon the air.

"I am taking you back, Damaris my little love." He spoke slowly, with his eyes on the burning tents, the significance of which had sunk deep into his heart. "Won't you look up? Won't you just say that you will marry me, so that I can tell everyone directly we get back?"

He put her on her feet when she suddenly struggled and pushed against him, and stared aghast when she bowed her face in her hands and sobbed.

"Damaris—dear—what is it? Don't you want to marry me?"

Damaris nodded, her lovely head which glistened like a hall of silk in the blaze of the sun.

"You do? You will?—Then what are you crying for? Oh! Damaris—"

The words came muffled as she shook with sobs.

"Because of the scandal, Ben. Because of what people will say about me—I mean about me when they know I am engaged to—to you—they will—laugh at you behind your back—they will—they will know about—about—"

He pulled her to him quite roughly and pressed her head against his shoulder, which it barely reached.

"Laugh!" he said. "Laugh—at me—or you! I should just like to hear them, darling. There is a way out of all this, sweetheart, somewhere, and I am going to find it, and all that has happened, beloved, rests on my shoulders, and heaven knows they are broad enough to bear it. And if we have hurt others, darling,"—and he looked over his shoulder to the tents,—"it has been through my carelessness, and we shall be shown a way in which to try and make amends. Laugh, dear? Let them laugh, dear heart, when they see how we love each other."

But, for all that, he frowned above her curly head, because he had all the Englishman's horror of scandal in connection with any of his women-folk; but he set his teeth and crushed her up closer, then let her go suddenly and swung her round, pointing across to the west.

"Look, darling; look!"

And the tears streamed down the girl's face as she flung out her arms.

"*Irja Sooltan!*" she called. "*Irja Sooltan!*"

Her voice carried on the still air like the note of a bell over water.

And the stallion, who had broken from his *sayis* as he was being led from the stable in readiness for the sad procession to the river, and who, terrified at the sight of the burning tents, had rushed on in search of his master, stopped dead, with his head up and tail and mane streaming in the wind.

He had not found his master, but he knew the voice

that called.

"*Irja Sooltan!*" it came again. "*Irja! Irja!*"

And he reared and wheeled in the direction from whence it came, then raced to where he saw the girl standing.

He stamped, and whinnied, and nuzzled her hand and her shoulder as she stood in her lover's arms.

"Tell me you will marry me, sweetheart," Ben Kelham was saying, with one hand on the stallion's bridle. "Say it, Damaris."

She shook her head and looked up piteously, with tears in her wonderful eyes, as she made a great sacrifice to her honour.

"I can't, Ben," she whispered. "I—I—Oh! I can't tell you—I haven't—the courage—Oh! Ben, you would never understand—"

He gave a great shout as he leapt to the saddle and took the stallion back a hundred yards, then wheeled him and raced him back along his tracks.

"Understand, beloved?" he cried, as he bent as he rushed past her at full speed and lifted her to the saddle. "There is nothing to understand." And he turned the stallion as he spoke and headed him towards the tents. "We will just go back, dear; we will just pass to say goodbye—together."

And they swept across the desert.

Then he reined in the stallion and sat staring, then whispered, as he bent and kissed the bonny curls:

"The way out, dear; the way out. Someone is waiting for us."

Stubbornly, heavily, across the desert, with occasional pauses for rest and investigation of the track of small footprints, and the horizon, came Wellington.

He was very hot and very thirsty, and it seemed to him that he had been walking for many days through many, many endless deserts, but he intended to criss-cross the Sahara, or any other desert, through all eternity, until he could deliver the book he held between his formidable teeth to his beloved mistress.

And she slid from the saddle, and knelt, and put her arms around him, and took the somewhat moist keepsake from him.

She swung up like a bird into her lover's arms and took the reins whilst he leant right down to lift the dog. But Wellington's great heart was troubled. He looked up at his mistress and said as plainly as could be with reproachful eyes. "Two's company," and turned to walk stubbornly and heavily, back across those many, many deserts to the tents.

Ben Kelham cheered him on as they thundered past him. "We'll wait for you, old fellow," he cried, then looked down on the woman he loved.

Her hands were clasped upon the silken bodice where she had pinned the brooch which had been fashioned in the shape of the Hawk of Egypt.

It was not there.

It had come unfastened as she lay in her grief; she had left it to be buried so deep just a few days later, when the greatest storm which had ever been known to sweep the desert piled the sand, the desert's own cloak, to the height of hills, under which slumbered all those who had sought peace at her breast; under which, guarded throughout all ages by his dogs, peacefully slept her son.

"Ben," she cried, opening wide her eyes in which shone love and tears, "Ben, can you ever—ever forgive me?"

And he bent and kissed her as he replied:

"There is nothing to forgive, beloved of my heart—I love you!"

THE END

Choose from Thousands of 1stWorldLibrary Classics By

A. M. Barnard
Ada Leverson
Adolphus William Ward
Aesop
Agatha Christie
Alexander Aaronsohn
Alexander Kielland
Alexandre Dumas
Alfred Gatty
Alfred Ollivant
Alice Duer Miller
Alice Turner Curtis
Alice Dunbar
Allen Chapman
Alleyne Ireland
Ambrose Bierce
Amelia E. Barr
Amory H. Bradford
Andrew Lang
Andrew McFarland Davis
Andy Adams
Angela Brazil
Anna Alice Chapin
Anna Sewell
Annie Besant
Annie Hamilton Donnell
Annie Payson Call
Annie Roe Carr
Annonaymous
Anton Chekhov
Archibald Lee Fletcher
Arnold Bennett
Arthur C. Benson
Arthur Conan Doyle
Arthur M. Winfield
Arthur Ransome
Arthur Schnitzler
Arthur Train
Atticus
B.H. Baden-Powell
B. M. Bower
B. C. Chatterjee
Baroness Emmuska Orczy
Baroness Orczy
Basil King
Bayard Taylor
Ben Macomber
Bertha Muzzy Bower
Bjornstjerne Bjornson

Booth Tarkington
Boyd Cable
Bram Stoker
C. Collodi
C. E. Orr
C. M. Ingleby
Carolyn Wells
Catherine Parr Traill
Charles A. Eastman
Charles Amory Beach
Charles Dickens
Charles Dudley Warner
Charles Farrar Browne
Charles Ives
Charles Kingsley
Charles Klein
Charles Hanson Towne
Charles Lathrop Pack
Charles Romyn Dake
Charles Whibley
Charles Willing Beale
Charlotte M. Braeme
Charlotte M. Yonge
Charlotte Perkins Stetson
Clair W. Hayes
Clarence Day Jr.
Clarence E. Mulford
Clemence Housman
Confucius
Coningsby Dawson
Cornelis DeWitt Wilcox
Cyril Burleigh
D. H. Lawrence
Daniel Defoe
David Garnett
Dinah Craik
Don Carlos Janes
Donald Keyhoe
Dorothy Kilner
Dougan Clark
Douglas Fairbanks
E. Nesbit
E. P. Roe
E. Phillips Oppenheim
E. S. Brooks
Earl Barnes
Edgar Rice Burroughs
Edith Van Dyne
Edith Wharton

Edward Everett Hale
Edward J. O'Biren
Edward S. Ellis
Edwin L. Arnold
Eleanor Atkins
Eleanor Hallowell Abbott
Eliot Gregory
Elizabeth Gaskell
Elizabeth McCracken
Elizabeth Von Arnim
Ellem Key
Emerson Hough
Emilie F. Carlen
Emily Bronte
Emily Dickinson
Enid Bagnold
Enilor Macartney Lane
Erasmus W. Jones
Ernie Howard Pie
Ethel May Dell
Ethel Turner
Ethel Watts Mumford
Eugene Sue
Eugenie Foa
Eugene Wood
Eustace Hale Ball
Evelyn Everett-green
Everard Cotes
F. H. Cheley
F. J. Cross
F. Marion Crawford
Fannie E. Newberry
Federick Austin Ogg
Ferdinand Ossendowski
Fergus Hume
Florence A. Kilpatrick
Fremont B. Deering
Francis Bacon
Francis Darwin
Frances Hodgson Burnett
Frances Parkinson Keyes
Frank Gee Patchin
Frank Harris
Frank Jewett Mather
Frank L. Packard
Frank V. Webster
Frederic Stewart Isham
Frederick Trevor Hill
Frederick Winslow Taylor

Friedrich Kerst
Friedrich Nietzsche
Fyodor Dostoyevsky
G.A. Henty
G.K. Chesterton
Gabrielle E. Jackson
Garrett P. Serviss
Gaston Leroux
George A. Warren
George Ade
Geroge Bernard Shaw
George Cary Eggleston
George Durston
George Ebers
George Eliot
George Gissing
George MacDonald
George Meredith
George Orwell
George Sylvester Viereck
George Tucker
George W. Cable
George Wharton James
Gertrude Atherton
Gordon Casserly
Grace E. King
Grace Gallatin
Grace Greenwood
Grant Allen
Guillermo A. Sherwell
Gulielma Zollinger
Gustav Flaubert
H. A. Cody
H. B. Irving
H.C. Bailey
H. G. Wells
H. H. Munro
H. Irving Hancock
H. R. Naylor
H. Rider Haggard
H. W. C. Davis
Haldeman Julius
Hall Caine
Hamilton Wright Mabie
Hans Christian Andersen
Harold Avery
Harold McGrath
Harriet Beecher Stowe
Harry Castlemon
Harry Coghill
Harry Houidini

Hayden Carruth
Helent Hunt Jackson
Helen Nicolay
Hendrik Conscience
Hendy David Thoreau
Henri Barbusse
Henrik Ibsen
Henry Adams
Henry Ford
Henry Frost
Henry James
Henry Jones Ford
Henry Seton Merriman
Henry W Longfellow
Herbert A. Giles
Herbert Carter
Herbert N. Casson
Herman Hesse
Hildegard G. Frey
Homer
Honore De Balzac
Horace B. Day
Horace Walpole
Horatio Alger Jr.
Howard Pyle
Howard R. Garis
Hugh Lofting
Hugh Walpole
Humphry Ward
Ian Maclaren
Inez Haynes Gillmore
Irving Bacheller
Isabel Cecilia Williams
Isabel Hornibrook
Israel Abrahams
Ivan Turgenev
J.G.Austin
J. Henri Fabre
J. M. Barrie
J. M. Walsh
J. Macdonald Oxley
J. R. Miller
J. S. Fletcher
J. S. Knowles
J. Storer Clouston
J. W. Duffield
Jack London
Jacob Abbott
James Allen
James Andrews
James Baldwin

James Branch Cabell
James DeMille
James Joyce
James Lane Allen
James Lane Allen
James Oliver Curwood
James Oppenheim
James Otis
James R. Driscoll
Jane Abbott
Jane Austen
Jane L. Stewart
Janet Aldridge
Jens Peter Jacobsen
Jerome K. Jerome
Jessie Graham Flower
John Buchan
John Burroughs
John Cournos
John F. Kennedy
John Gay
John Glasworthy
John Habberton
John Joy Bell
John Kendrick Bangs
John Milton
John Philip Sousa
John Taintor Foote
Jonas Lauritz Idemil Lie
Jonathan Swift
Joseph A. Altsheler
Joseph Carey
Joseph Conrad
Joseph E. Badger Jr
Joseph Hergesheimer
Joseph Jacobs
Jules Vernes
Julian Hawthrone
Julie A Lippmann
Justin Huntly McCarthy
Kakuzo Okakura
Karle Wilson Baker
Kate Chopin
Kenneth Grahame
Kenneth McGaffey
Kate Langley Bosher
Kate Langley Bosher
Katherine Cecil Thurston
Katherine Stokes
L. A. Abbot
L. T. Meade

L. Frank Baum
Latta Griswold
Laura Dent Crane
Laura Lee Hope
Laurence Housman
Lawrence Beasley
Leo Tolstoy
Leonid Andreyev
Lewis Carroll
Lewis Sperry Chafer
Lilian Bell
Lloyd Osbourne
Louis Hughes
Louis Joseph Vance
Louis Tracy
Louisa May Alcott
Lucy Fitch Perkins
Lucy Maud Montgomery
Luther Benson
Lydia Miller Middleton
Lyndon Orr
M. Corvus
M. H. Adams
Margaret E. Sangster
Margret Howth
Margaret Vandercook
Margaret W. Hungerford
Margret Penrose
Maria Edgeworth
Maria Thompson Daviess
Mariano Azuela
Marion Polk Angellotti
Mark Overton
Mark Twain
Mary Austin
Mary Catherine Crowley
Mary Cole
Mary Hastings Bradley
Mary Roberts Rinehart
Mary Rowlandson
M. Wollstonecraft Shelley
Maud Lindsay
Max Beerbohm
Myra Kelly
Nathaniel Hawthrone
Nicolo Machiavelli
O. F. Walton
Oscar Wilde

Owen Johnson
P.G. Wodehouse
Paul and Mabel Thorne
Paul G. Tomlinson
Paul Severing
Percy Brebner
Percy Keese Fitzhugh
Peter B. Kyne
Plato
Quincy Allen
R. Derby Holmes
R. L. Stevenson
R. S. Ball
Rabindranath Tagore
Rahul Alvares
Ralph Bonehill
Ralph Henry Barbour
Ralph Victor
Ralph Waldo Emmerson
Rene Descartes
Ray Cummings
Rex Beach
Rex E. Beach
Richard Harding Davis
Richard Jefferies
Richard Le Gallienne
Robert Barr
Robert Frost
Robert Gordon Anderson
Robert L. Drake
Robert Lansing
Robert Lynd
Robert Michael Ballantyne
Robert W. Chambers
Rosa Nouchette Carey
Rudyard Kipling
Saint Augustine
Samuel B. Allison
Samuel Hopkins Adams
Sarah Bernhardt
Sarah C. Hallowell
Selma Lagerlof
Sherwood Anderson
Sigmund Freud
Standish O'Grady
Stanley Weyman
Stella Benson
Stella M. Francis

Stephen Crane
Stewart Edward White
Stijn Streuvels
Swami Abhedananda
Swami Parmananda
T. S. Ackland
T. S. Arthur
The Princess Der Ling
Thomas A. Janvier
Thomas A Kempis
Thomas Anderton
Thomas Bailey Aldrich
Thomas Bulfinch
Thomas De Quincey
Thomas Dixon
Thomas H. Huxley
Thomas Hardy
Thomas More
Thornton W. Burgess
U. S. Grant
Upton Sinclair
Valentine Williams
Various Authors
Vaughan Kester
Victor Appleton
Victor G. Durham
Victoria Cross
Virginia Woolf
Wadsworth Camp
Walter Camp
Walter Scott
Washington Irving
Wilbur Lawton
Wilkie Collins
Willa Cather
Willard F. Baker
William Dean Howells
William le Queux
W. Makepeace Thackeray
William W. Walter
William Shakespeare
Winston Churchill
Yei Theodora Ozaki
Yogi Ramacharaka
Young E. Allison
Zane Grey